The Sexiest Woman in the World

by

Glenn A. Bruce

Cover Art by *Tina Lynn Stout*

The Wild Rose Press, Inc.
PO Box 708
Adams Basin, NY 14410-0708
Visit us at www.thewildrosepress.com

Publishing History
First Edition, 2025
Trade Paperback ISBN 978-1-5092-6267-0
Digital ISBN 978-1-5092-6268-7

Published in the United States of America

Dedication

To all the beautifully "average" women who really are
the sexiest in the world!

Chapter One

Rebecah Jayne Darnell had just turned thirty-five, which by her own estimate, represented the beginning of middle-age. RJ to her dad and Becky to everyone else, she figured that "condition" would last twenty years before she was "over the hill and un-marriable," a nuptial experience she'd already had the misfortune of suffering twice. Both divorces had been unpleasant, mostly because her husbands "turned into total dicks." Which only got worse once she called them out on it and filed papers.

Fortunately, thanks to good lawyers, she got to keep her small but classic early twentieth century rehabbed house both times, and though both men asked for alimony, her woman judges suggested the slackers find employment rather than "leech off the good graces" of the woman they'd beleaguered for nine and six years, respectively.

Becky told her concerned friends she would be fine because she was "free, white, and twenty-one," to which one of her two best black friends Myrna replied, "Lucky you." But none of the three were serious because they knew the truth. Becky Darnell was one of a kind in a sea of *dissimilars* and would find a way to go on without a man, white or not.

"It's the Midwest, hon," her other favorite black friend Briana said, meaning Becky was safe, but not necessarily due to her skin color or dark blonde hair. Both knew what really made Becky safe in the Midwest was her blandness. Nothing unusual about her would ever draw attention.

She fit in.

Becky Darnell was middle-of-the-road in every respect including her open Midwest kindness, something at which she personally excelled. Becky loved everyone and everyone loved her, mainly because of her very best quality—accepting everyone and denouncing no one. Ergo, not being a challenge to anyone.

By all local practical standards, Becky Darnell represented the "pinnacle of average," as another of her friends, Darla "Moneymaker" Devaughn often kidded. Darla earned her nickname by winning five dollars in the state lottery six weeks in a row, once. She got away with chiding her BFF Becky because brunette Darla considered herself "stupidly normal" as well, if in second place. "Becky takes the vanilla cake."

Darla said of herself, "I have my dark side. I hate Neapolitan ice cream and Crocs. Becky does, too. But she can eat it while wearing them. I'd rather die. Becky's a *saint*."

Becky, as the object of their taunts, accepted all the ribbing in style because she believed in her background, in everything her loving parents and extended family had taught her—especially those parts about Midwest Nice as a way of life.

Becky had been born in Fort Wayne, and never lived more than fifty miles in any direction of it. She worked at the same place since graduating community college, Littleman Agricultural Implements, a company known for their top-of-the-line manure spreaders. They had so much success with them in the 1930s they discontinued making other machinery to "focus on cow shit," as Herman Littleman said at the time. He died a multi-millionaire and handed Littleman Implements down to his heirs.

Becky started, as all new-hires did, in what was magnanimously referred to as the Research Area—that being where the spreaders were tested in their natural habitat. That being piles of various kinds of manure. New hires left their overalls to be washed in the company laundry at the close of every workday, for "odor edification."

Back when, Becky served her mandatory month "out in the field" then began her ten-year ascent into production, finally earning her way up to line foreman. She eschewed "foreperson" because she said, "It sounds like a feminist failure," and thought the alternate "forewoman" even worse.

"It's just a title. It's not who I am inside, and that's all that matters. I have ovaries." It was all that mattered to her devoted cadre of female pals as well who knew Becky to be a hard worker, a fair manager, and most of all a decent human being.

When it came to looks, Becky assessed her own as, "Too Indiana for my own good." She meant *plain*. Not everyone agreed. Darla said Becky was "pretty in her own understated way." Some thought this translated as homely, but Darla didn't think that, nor did anyone else. Becky, they all thought, was "naturally pretty" and told her that. She didn't object.

Becky said, "That means without makeup, I don't scare cattle. But I don't attract bulls, either." Typical of her lack of self-aggrandizement. However, that wasn't the case either, at least not when it came to *human* males.

Becky couldn't go to her favorite bar in Fort Wayne on a Saturday night without getting asked out by at least three men. "Some of whom are actually single," she assessed. She could tell because they invited her to their apartments instead of a motel.

Though Fort Wayne was larger and had more bars with larger dancefloors and clientele, Becky lived closer to Auburn and generally preferred the local ambiance—its "lack of anonymous divorced horndogs," as she put it. Plus, Auburn was mostly where her friends gathered, specifically the bowling alley with its grill and bar.

"The three Bs," Becky claimed as her touchstones. "Not including me."

She didn't consider herself to be an important component of "Bowling, burgers, and beer." But what Friday night was complete without all four? "Not a one," she said, and made sure she went every weekend unless she was direly ill.

The other nights, Becky stayed home listening to whatever was on the radio while embarking on DIY projects. Since her house was over a hundred years old, it required constant attention—replacing a banister, repainting a porch, rewiring a light fixture. She could do them all. Her father had been a handyman and taught her well. After he retired, she visited him and her mom every month to help with their projects as well.

She drove down and back in her older sporty compact, a car she had coveted then bought as a present to herself after her first divorce. It still symbolized freedom to her, and she loved pushing it up over a hundred on a straight two-lane from time to time. To show the car love, she changed the oil herself, every four thousand miles, and always filled up with mid-grade gas even though it technically didn't need the extra octane.

Her lone hobby centered on collecting weird dolls and small collectible art pieces. She favored Victorian dolls with an eye missing and paintings of trees for some reason she couldn't explain other than they reminded her of a road she had once seen or possibly imagined in her mind or a dream. Maybe in France. She wasn't sure. Whatever, it stuck, and she had amassed a total of nearly seventy small tree paintings.

"Trees, right?" she said when someone asked. "How boring is that?" To Becky, it simply served to confirm her averageness.

"Not so the dolls," Darla jibed every time she held up a one-eyed vintage visage. "Creepy as fuck."

"I know. That's why I love them. No one else will." Also why she kept one by every window in the house with a nightlight underneath, peering out at any potential intruder. Asked if it worked to keep them out, she always said, "So far." A beacon of positivity.

Auburn, Indiana wasn't known for much other than the old Auburn plant that had built the prestige Auburn cars of the Thirties, as well as Cords and the ultimate, finest automobile ever manufactured anywhere, the properly vaunted Duesenberg. That the town also produced the "World's Finest Manure Spreader" was not wasted on Becky, much less Littleman's employees.

Since all Duesenberg chassis were manufactured in 1928—bodied by coachbuilders in other places and times—Becky and the Littleman workers always said they were born a hundred years too late to have been Doozies themselves, that particular accolade being born due to the incomparable quality of the motorcar.

5

But she acquiesced to their company banner, "The Doozie of Manure Spreaders!" And they joked, "It's better than being at the bottom of the pile." The *racy* joke back in 1960s' Midwest circles had doggedly hung on, and Becky chuckled along with everyone else anytime she heard it over a half-century later. It suited her Midwest sensibilities—politeness and tact over sour reminders of cliches or outdated material.

So overall, Becky was happy with her lot in life. She had gainful employment in a stable company, worked in a clean factory, had decent medical and retirement benefits, went to the gym four nights a week, had a lean body to show for it, and didn't scare tame animals in their pens or wild men off the streets at night. She thought how, with a little makeup and the right clothing choices, she "cleaned up pretty good," so why complain. Whining wasn't in her daily affirmation practices.

All of this meant Becky Darnell saw herself as being "in a good place, now," post-divorces. She fairly assessed that she had few real challenges in life, hadn't begun to show any devastating signs of aging, enjoyed general stability far above most people on the planet, and wanted for little more than she already had—the very definition of average in or near Auburn, Indiana in the very middle of the Midwest. She assumed that would never change.

Chapter Two

The sole remaining Littleman, Clarina, a granddaughter, had been the company's dispatcher for as long as Becky and anyone else could remember. At ninety-five, Clarina occasionally sent out a repair van rather than a delivery truck, but she refused to retire, and her errors were easily corrected when someone else caught it, usually the driver.

Then, that problem solved itself. Clarina died. Everyone at the factory attended the funeral.

The current CEO, COO, and Managing Director, Harold Harmon—a Littleman relative twice removed by marriages, and himself no spring chicken—called Becky into his office. "I'm moving you off the line," he said and proudly offered the news. "You're our new dispatcher."

"Oh," Becky said, because she didn't want to be their new dispatcher. It meant being alone in an office all day long, sitting on her ass, doing nothing but talk on the phone.

Her boss said, "It comes with a pay increase."

"Oh!" That sounded more promising.

"Let's see," he said, perusing some papers on his desk. "I believe it works out to…twenty dollars a week!"

"Oh." Becky had to wonder which decade Harold Harmon might be stuck in. She asked, "Isn't there someone else?"

"No one with as many years and as much experience

as you, Rebecah," he said. "We need someone who knows our business inside and out. We're expanding into India soon, and we have to keep things here at home ship-shape!"

"Oh."

"Or is it Pakistan?"

****

Becky dragged back to her factory line and into the office of their production manager, Floyd Bitterman, fittingly named due to his chronic foul mood and endless griping about his job and pay.

"Floyd," she said, barely keeping herself from whining. "Do I really have to leave the line? I do a good job. Otherwise, you wouldn't have kept me at it for all these years."

"Ya gotta go, ya gotta go," he said in his inimitable dour style. Floyd was well known for his empty philosophies on living.

Becky let herself whine. "But I *like* it here, Floyd. I don't want to have to sit in an office all day long, five days a week."

"Could be worse," he said. "Could be six."

Becky reminded him, "We don't work weekends, Floyd."

"We could."

"But we don't."

"I sit in this airconditioned hellhole five days a week and haven't keeled over yet."

To counter her boss's spectacularly glowing recommendation, Becky said, "I'm not afraid of dying in there, Floyd. Maybe from boredom. But I'll miss all my friends on the line."

"Maybe they'll stop yacking all the time and do

some work," he lamented.

Becky reminded him, "We haven't missed a target or deadline in six years."

"Business has been slow," he said.

"The newsletter said last year was our best ever."

"The world needs manure spreaders."

"Right," Becky said. "And I'm good at making sure they get 'em."

He said, "Well now, you can be sure they get 'em."

Becky was lost. "What?"

"Sending them out, ordering the drivers around, making friends all over." He laughed ironically because he knew the potential rigors and complaints associated with dispatch.

She said, "Won't you put in a word for me? Tell Mr. Harmon you need me down here and you can't afford to get rid of me. Something like that."

Floyd said, "I already gave Briana your job."

Becky was floored. "But I just found out about it twenty minutes ago."

"Lazy goose misses the liver."

Becky stared. "Floyd."

"It's too late. Time moves on. Can't stop it." He stood. "Speaking of which, it's lunch. I got a date with the Missus. It's bedroom Wednesday." He raised his eyebrows.

"Okay, I could have done without that image," Becky said.

Floyd shooed her out. "Go on. I gotta lock up. Don't want anyone getting in here and fudging their time cards."

"We wouldn't do that. Nobody on this line would do that," Becky said.

"Can't be too careful these days," he said—and locked the door.

Becky watched her boss walk to the side door and exit as Darla and Briana came up and joined her. Darla asked, "Did he tell you about Bedroom Wednesday?"

"Unfortunately."

"I don't know how his wife puts up with him," Briana said.

Becky defended him. "He's all talk. A secret softie."

"With a hardon for every one of us in his *gulag*."

Becky couldn't argue—partly because she wasn't sure what Briana meant—so she said, "So, you got my job."

"Guess I did," Briana said. "He sent me a text ten minutes ago."

Becky said, "You want my new one? You can have it."

"Hell no, girl," Briana said. "Sit inside a tiny little office talking to truckers all day? No thank you. I'd have to move to Fort Wayne and find something else."

"I've already thought of that," Becky said, though she knew she wouldn't.

Darla said, "Lunch?"

Becky said, "No thanks. I think I'll go sit in my car and pout. Maybe cry a little."

"Aw," Darla said, putting her arm around her best friend. "It won't be that bad. You'll get used to it."

Becky said, "I won't get used to my ass getting wide as a D-486 shit-spreader."

"You? Never happen," Darla said.

Briana added, "You'll start going to the gym every night and working out twice as long. It's in your bones."

Becky knew they were right because she'd already

thought it. She wished them a happy lunch then went out to her car to eat her turkey sandwich and pout. At least she didn't cry.

****

Becky spent most of Thursday learning the ropes of her new job. Since her predecessor was dead, she had to rely on logs and loose advice from drivers and clients. By the close of business, she had a handle on the basics and, overall, it wasn't as bad as she'd imagined. She liked talking to so many different people for a change, all of them Midwest friendly and supportive, and she decided maybe it wasn't so bad after all.

Friday came and went quickly due to a flurry of orders and deliveries, some of them to Canada and Mexico—three to Pakistan—and a few calls for maintenance and repairs. She ate lunch at her desk and by the time the clock hands clicked over to five o'clock, Becky was spent. She almost didn't go to the gym. But after a medium-hard workout to avert her spreading ass problem, she felt much better and went home to eat chips and watch a documentary on monkeys that fashioned tools from rocks and twigs.

"No crescent wrenches yet, huh? Well." She turned it off.

As she had already blocked out Saturday to replace aging wooden steps leading up to her back porch and kitchen, she spent the day running back and forth to the lumber store for planks and nails, porch paint, and electrolyte-rich sports drink. By four-forty, she was done and happy with her work. Which, she noted, neither of her two husbands could have done without a gun to their heads; and then it would have been inferior to her work.

After a light dinner of poached salmon, steamed

kale, baked yam, and half a pint of dairy-free caramel-coffee gelato, she showered, dressed, and headed into town for a somewhat rare Saturday beer, bowling, and a late burger to even things out. Two games, half a Bleu Burger, and three pitchers later, she and her friends took their phones out to share gossip. Embarrassing celebrity posts often topped the list.

The ladies howled at reports of showbiz sightings gone wrong, including one male movie star who exited the bathroom of a fellow celebrity's Malibu mansion and left it "reeking like a zoo cage," according to an entertainment stringer who reported verification by "two independent sources who prefer to go unnamed."

Myrna said, "Guess they got the poop on him, huh?" Which brought groans and giggles.

Becky speculated, "Probably all the caviar and rich cheese."

Briana agreed. "Oh my. Stuff flies right through me."

While the three discussed food items that didn't agree with them, Darla scrolled through fashion ads and purported trends for the coming season. At one point, she stopped and said, "Hey, check this out. L'Odeur, *Face* Magazine, and Snug Foundations—you know, the 'we're not a girdle company' girdle company—they're sponsoring a Sexiest Woman in the World contest." She looked up. "We should enter!"

Becky said, "Because there's no one sexier than three babes from a manure spreader company."

"We're hot," Briana said. "No doubt about it."

Myrna said, "I was looking in the mirror this morning, you know, naked, and I thought to myself, someone out there needs to be appreciating this. Soon!

Before I dry up entirely."

Darla opined, "I went out without makeup and scared an entire family of Canadian geese off my street."

"They're rough. You'd definitely win something," Becky said.

Myrna suggested, "A booby prize. Since you have the biggest rack in the valley."

Briana said, "These girls are sought after high and low." She modeled her profile.

"Mainly low," Myrna said. "And getting lower by the hour."

After the howls and hoots settled, Darla said, "Seriously. We should all enter as a goof. See how fast they reject us with letters of shock and alarm. Unfettered dismay."

Becky said, "I think I'll pass. If I did win, my dad would have a heart attack. He wouldn't have any idea in the world what to tell his church people."

Darla said, "I think your mom would think it was fine."

"But she wouldn't tell my dad."

Myrna thought, "If you did win, those rotten exes of yours would have to eat a lot of crow."

"Might make the humiliation of entering worth it," Becky opined.

Briana pointed out, "But if they found out you lost…"

"I'd never hear the end of it. And I haven't spoken to either in years."

Darla put her phone down. "We're entering and that's it. *I* have spoken."

The three other women eyed her warily. "Why?"

"For the laughs," Darla said. "We could use a few.

Especially Becky after her 'promotion.' "

"*De*motion is more like it," Becky said darkly on being reminded.

"See?" Darla said. "We could all use a good chuckle." She picked up her phone, scrolled down to the entry form, then showed the others where it was.

They all ignored the rules, but Briana noted, "It says you have to submit a picture. I'm gonna use someone *famously* black."

"Perfect!" Darla said. "Maybe I'll use someone famously *dead*. See if they catch it."

Briana reconsidered, "Love it! I'll have to find a recent shot of Josephine Baker."

Myrna laughed and said, "I'm gonna be basic me. If they're nasty about it, I'll sic my brothers on them. They're the ones who set the portable on fire in seventh grade when that nasty white man called me a 'darkie' in class."

Becky said, "That was them? I never knew that."

"You still don't," Myrna said.

"Got it." Becky scrolled through old photos on her phone with some disappointment. "I don't have any shots worth a crap on here. I look like the old maid farmer's wife after he got gored by the bull and she took over slopping the pigs."

Darla leaned over to scroll with her. "That one's not bad."

"I look like a serial killer's sister."

"How about this one?"

"Different serial killer. And not his sister."

"It's the glasses," Myrna offered.

Briana said, "You look nice tonight. Give me your phone."

"In *here*?" Becky said, not sure a bowling alley background was the best choice.

"Makes you look all-American," Myrna agreed.

Becky checked behind her. "At least don't get the bar and shoe rental in it."

"Okay, turn around. We'll use the far wall. Maybe it'll blur out if I get close enough."

"Don't make me look like a bubble-face."

"We'll do a few. Give you a choice. Smile nice."

Becky knew how to do that. She'd had plenty of practice at weddings and other social events she hadn't wanted to attend. Darla once marveled, "You look so natural and happy to be here," and Becky told her, "I'm not." But she had to admit she'd mastered the art of appearing pleasantly content.

She put on her familiar smile and Briana tapped the button. Everyone agreed it came out great and they all filled out their online entry forms. Briana settled on a photo of a popular pop star well-known to everyone, but Myrna and Darla used real shots of themselves, though Darla's was from junior high. "Now, we wait to see."

"See what?" Becky conjectured. "Who loses the worst?"

"Worst winner gets three-Bs free as soon as we hear, complements of the others."

Becky said, "We should get it for a *month*. This is so embarrassing."

Myrna said, "A month it is!" And so the great anti-contest began.

****

Unknown to anyone, including the pageant sponsors, in the basement of a plain house in New Jersey, a young hacker, paid to change the contest algorithm, was busy doing just that.

Chapter Three

Six weeks came and went. Becky settled into her dispatch position with mixed feelings. Being in a quiet office proved to be a nice change from the noisy assembly line, not to mention her back appreciated her not being on her feet all day long. She missed her friends, male and female, only getting to see and socialize with them on breaks. But overall, the work was light and people seemed happy to hear from her.

During a mid-morning break, Becky shared insights with her old pals who said they were happy for her but also missed her upbeat presence on the floor. Briana had found replacing Becky turned out to be more work than she'd imagined. *Plus*. Even though she'd heard nothing specific, she believed some of the white men, especially the older ones, perhaps didn't respect her as much as they had Becky.

"Oh, they didn't respect me, either," Becky said. "I may be white like them, but I don't have a penis like them." She felt that anatomical difference in their interactions nearly on a daily basis. "At least once a week."

Myrna said, "Add in black and you see what Briana is up against."

"I suppose it's true," Becky admitted—with a caveat. "I'd advise you stay away from the Bubbas as much as you can. Try to interface with Ned and Toby.

Let them pass along anything important."

Ned Miller was white; Toby Roman was black, two young men in their early thirties. The former, being a third generation Littleman employee, got along with everyone, mainly because he was white; whereas Tony got along well with the handful of black men and women on the line and seemed to be tolerated by the whites.

Briana said, "That's what I'm doing."

"It isn't working?"

"Mostly. But the undercurrents."

Myrna added, "Let's just say, if they had a cross-burning day, we know who'd bring the matches."

Becky half-laughed and said, "They're not that bad." Both Myrna and Briana raised their eyebrows. Becky said, "Right."

She knew north-central Indiana was no different than anywhere else in America—marginally nicer on the surface, but race had torn more than one town apart. Fortunately, the people she knew had managed to get along without strife. Still, she—

"Would the sexiest woman in the world please come to the front office." The main executive secretary's familiar voice on the PA system broke Becky's ponderings.

Laughter broke out in the breakroom and out on the floor. One of the burliest men shouted, "They must mean me!" and strutted in a *feminine* way to howls from the other workers. He pretended to fluff his hair gaily to some whistles.

Only Darla seemed to remember what the call might be. She said, "Wait a minute. Could it—"

"Rebecah Darnell, please come to the front office."

Darla's jaw dropped. "No!"

Myrna said, "Oh my Lord. Becky!"

Briana said, "Can it be, girl?"

Becky thought a moment then said, "All right. Which one of you put Charlene up to this?"

Myrna said she didn't, and the other ladies agreed by shaking no. "Not us."

"Rebecah Darnell, sexiest woman in the wide world of manure spreading, to the office right away, please."

Darla said, "Oh. My. *God*! You won! You did! You won!"

"Nooooo," Becky said. "It's some kind of prank. Probably a rejection letter they're gonna make me read over the loudspeaker."

"I bet not," Darla said, and Briana urged, "You better go." Myrna *opined*, "If you're the sexiest woman in the world, we're *all* in trouble."

"Tell me about it," Becky said, laughing along.

Darla said, "Go on! You don't want to get on Charlene's bad side."

"Okay, okay. I'm going!" Becky said and started for the front of the building. "But I am not reading a damn rejection letter over the PA."

Everyone applauded and whistled and jeered, even Floyd, as Becky waved and bowed, certain she was the butt of a practical joke. She could be a good sport.

Then something occurred to her and she turned to Darla. "You set this whole thing up from the *get-go*, didn't you? Admit it."

"No!" Darla said, convincingly. "It was online. You saw it."

Becky said, "Well, I don't know how you did it, but I'm getting you back. You can count on it."

Briana and Myrna shooed her on. "Go see, go see!"

Becky said, "Okay!" again and dragged up for the office.

When she walked into the front office, Becky found Harold Harmon, CEO, standing by Charlene, his executive secretary—a woman of sixty who appeared staid but had a wicked sense of humor. She said, "Congratulations. This came over the fax machine a few minutes ago."

Becky said, "We still have a fax machine?" Charlene nodded and Becky said, "And it still works?" Charlene nodded again with a broad smile.

"This isn't real. It's a joke, right? Darla and the girls put you up to this?"

"Not at all," Charlene said, and looked to her boss. "Isn't that right, Mr. Harmon."

Harold Harmon, who had no sense of humor, said, "I'm afraid it is."

Becky said, "It's a joke or it isn't?"

"Is *not*," Harmon said with specificity.

Becky eyed the paper. "Let me see it."

"Oh. Sorry," Charlene said, and handed over the page from the aged Epson.

Becky looked it over. It appeared real with the same sponsors' logos spread across the top and text in the form of a personal letter.

Dear Ms. Rebecah Darnell,

You have been selected along with 1,000 other women from across the nation from a pool of over 10,000 entrants to participate in our first annual Sexiest Woman in the World contest and pageant.

Please confirm your further interest and availability immediately to ensure your spot on our limited roster. Should you be unable to attend, please notify us without hesitation so that you can be replaced by another entrant outside the first 1,000.

Preliminary first-round judging will be held in Cleveland, OH on...

There was a more but Becky's eyes fell out of focus. She had to ask one more time, "Is this even real?"

Charlotte said, "You entered it. You tell us."

Becky stammered, "I...well, Darla...we..."

She looked over the fax again and decided on, "Holy crap."

****

Though Becky had barely settled into the new job, Charlotte arranged for her boss's grandniece, Sharon Harmon, to come in and train as a temp replacement. "In case you win and move to gay Paree!" Charlotte said with entirely too much glee.

Becky said, "Not...no...um...no."

"Well, one never knows, does one?" Charlotte said with arched eyebrows.

"But—"

"Train her. Harold wants it."

Ah.

Since the regional competition in Cleveland was a month away, Becky had plenty of time to train Sharon the boss's grandniece, who apparently had no appreciation for the opportunity or interest in the job. The first call on her own resulted in three service trucks arriving at the Fort Wayne Airport FedEx office to pick up a single box of sheet metal screws.

"Ooops," she said when the drivers called in to bitch. She handed the phone to Becky.

"Sorry, guys," Becky said. "Still training Harold's niece, here." She looked over to find Sharon admiring her new nail appliques.

Fortunately, the men understood and went for bar-b-cue. She told them to, "Bring me back a receipt. I'll make sure Connie covers it." Connie Brighton being the Littleman comptroller.

After a month and a few other "newbie mistakes" as Becky graciously referred to them, Sharon seemed modestly capable of taking the reins and Becky readied for her weekend *trial strut* in Cleveland, though she had no idea why she should bother as she had absolutely no hope of winning anything but a consolation tube of lip balm at best.

Over those thirty days, Becky stood in front of her bedroom mirror analyzing her plain appearance every night. She never considered herself ugly or homely, but nothing above average. She tried different looks with makeup, always seeing it as too much no matter how little she used, and ended up wiping it off.

I'm no good at this, she decided and turned to wardrobe. She modeled her everyday clothes—floor coveralls and drab office attire of mom jeans and a collared polo shirt to Bowling and Beer outfits—and came to the same conclusion.

"Boring."

She tried dresses, including her one "nice" dress for more formal affairs, and decided, *too funereal*. So, she chose the nicest *normal* dress she had and set it aside.

She also evaluated herself in lingerie and fully naked, happily determining that at least she was holding up well, aside from a few extra *pizza pounds* which she could easily shed. Extra workouts in the gym with evening walks and morning strolls on the weekend got her looking, in her estimation, as good physically as she had in years. Maybe it was the impetus of the contest—or the onus.

Always one to see the positive, she appreciated the change and bought two new bathing suits—a one piece and a modest bikini—in case the judges wanted to see her in something skimpier. She also ordered new clingy lingerie to wear under her chosen dress. She considered buying new shoes but decided it was simply a luxury she couldn't afford and likely wouldn't need once she *failed miserably* and came home. So, she polished her one pair of black heels and her tan pumps.

All the preparation seemed pointless when she took one last look in the mirror, "dolled up," as she put it, and gave her final opinion. "Lipstick on a pig."

Becky was ready to quit—to stay home, eat "redemption rolls," and watch the latest *Housewives of* "wherever the hell." It didn't matter. She didn't even like the show. Anything would be better than driving three hours to Cleveland to be humiliated.

Darla wasn't having it. "No way, Jose! You are going, Missy. And you are going to stand on that stage and proudly represent the women of Littleman Implements!"

She made Becky laugh, but didn't persuade her. "It's a lost cause, D. There is no way in hell I'm going to place in the top ten, much less win anything."

"It doesn't matter," Darla said. "You're gonna go there and have fun and we're gonna go there and have fun with you. Myrna already booked the rooms and Briana filled up her tank. We'll be out there cheering you on and that's all there is to it."

Even though Becky felt sure she didn't want to go, if her three besties were going, how bad could it be?

23

"Disgracefully humiliating," she told herself, but packed her bags.

Friday after work, rather than go to the bowling alley or their favorite bistro, Lancaster's Pub & Ale, Briana picked up Myrna, then Becky, then Darla who said, "We've got some surprises for you."

Becky said, "Oh, dear God."

Briana said, "We're stacking the deck," but wouldn't say how.

Three hours later, after checking into their budget hotel a few minutes before nine p.m., the four friends went for a cocktail. Becky pressed for more info, but all they would say is they were going to make her "stand out for the win!"

****

Ten hours later, the "contest tag-team" went down together for the complimentary breakfast of "wettened powdered eggs and store brand wheat toast." Becky had granola. All four had three cups of coffee to get their day going.

Back in their two adjoining rooms, Becky's pals revealed their surprises. They'd gone on their own shopping spree and bought what they thought would help Becky secure a win in the regionals. Their ensemble included a snazzy wig, a low-cut hi-rise "gown," with costume jewelry and "hooker heels." They even added an "Aging pop star mole."

It took two hours to apply. However, when Becky saw it—they had not allowed her to peek until they were done—she panicked. "No. No, no, no, no, *no*. I look like a cartoon ostrich *vamp* turned real-life streetwalker."

Her pals disagreed, saying she looked "fabulous," "hot," and "testosterone inducing." A good thing, they assured her, as Myrna clarified, "I heard the judges are all men."

"But what if you heard wrong?" Becky countered. "If there are women, they'll think I'm there to steal their husbands—or their husband's *wallets*."

"But—"

"No!"

Becky pulled off the wig and brought out her industrial-strength cold cream to remove the heavy makeup. She tossed the mole in the toilet.

She then did a quick hot curl, applied reasonable makeup, if a little heavier than for daytime use—or say, for a hot night at Lancaster's—and smoothed out her "average girl" dress. Briana seemed less than impressed. "At least you brought nice underwear."

Myrna agreed. "If all else fails, you can take off the dress."

"I'll be fine," Becky said. "The point here is not to win. It's to not look foolish."

****

If not appearing foolish was Becky's goal, most of the other women in the regional competition did not share her belief. Most looked like their concept of other famous celebrities with their own spin on it. She saw six famous and dead movie actresses, three R&B singers, and one…it was hard to say. Someone…short. Most of the younger women looked like they were attempting to emulate social media influencers and were likely streaming themselves as they strutted and pranced.

Darla wondered, "Why didn't we think of that? Could have been worth some endorsements."

"For what?" Becky wondered. "Other farm implements?"

"Hey, don't laugh. Herman Littleman died a multi-millionaire. With *one* machine."

"Died," Becky said. "Operative word."

When it was time for the contest to begin—they were not calling it a pageant—Becky was summoned backstage to a holding area as her three best buds took their seats in the smallish convention center ballroom.

Backstage, Becky noted many of the contestants were much older up close than they appeared at a distance. Being generous of spirit, she felt proud for them, but at the same time doubted they could compete in any way with the majority of young hotties. And there were many.

But "hotness" doesn't always translate to a roomful of Midwest men and women who did not, by outward appearances, look like they were eager to redefine "Sexiest in the World" in more *coastal* terms.

Of the nine judges, only three represented the sponsoring companies. The rest appeared to be locals, perhaps chosen from the Town council, which led Becky to think she might at least get two or three votes. She held little hope beyond that.

Two of the younger girls who seemed to have modeled their looks on rappers' music videos passed by with the comments, "Did you leave the kids at home, Mom?" and "Hope they don't get in trouble while you're here being so *sexy*."

Becky laughed with them and wished them, "Good luck out there. You're bound to do better than I will." Her smile annihilated them both. They walked away grumbling.

As Becky's Number 98 drawn from a hat came closer, she was able to stand in the wings and watch the other contestants work their acts on stage—and they did appear to be acts worked on at home, practiced in front of husbands or boyfriends—maybe livestreams on a porn website.

One of the older women said being sexy to her meant, "Getting my man hot and heavy while cooking him dinner—then skipping dinner for a 'four-course meal' in the bedroom." She winked at the judges. Becky cringed.

A younger woman in a black leather teddy said that, for her, being sexy meant, "He don't look at no one but me. Just this big ol' fine butt." She pirouetted *daintily*.

A third buxom woman simply bent forward until she practically fell out of her dress and said, "Actions speak louder than words, if you get my drift."

Finally, *Dr. Ruth* said, "I have no idea. My grandchildren sent in a picture of Farrah Fawcett or someone and here I am." At least she and Becky found it funny.

Finally, an announcer said, "And from 'somewhere near Auburn, Indiana' is Rebecah Darnell—Becky to her friends who, I understand, encouraged her to enter and are here in the audience."

Darla, Myrna, and Briana stood up and whooped and howled and whistled as Becky walked onstage. She looked across the crowd but no one else seemed interested, which suited her just fine. She was ready to go home, and it wasn't even eight thirty yet.

She got through the standard "Tell us about yourself" paragraphs, which included self-deprecating soft jokes about her life, her "meddling" friends, and her work at a plant that manufactured manure spreaders. She got some chuckles and relaxed more.

One of the company sponsors asked her which cosmetics she preferred, and she said, "Yours, of course." Then she added, "Which ones are yours, again?" getting more laughter, even from the company rep.

Another company woman asked which lingerie she preferred. Becky said, "Whatever lasts longer than a month and doesn't come out of the dryer looking like a cat running from a house fire got ahold of it." More laughs.

Finally came the big question. "Rebecah, what do you think can make a woman feel like the sexiest woman in the world?"

"What an interesting way to ask that," Becky said, honestly. "I thought you were going to make me tell the world how to do it."

The older woman said, "No. It's your opinion I'm interested in."

"Okay," Becky said. "Then I'd say honesty. Whether it's in the kitchen or the bedroom. If I make dinner, as one of the earlier ladies said, and it's awful, I don't expect my…partner…to say it's wonderful. Tell me it sucks and then offer to cook tomorrow night. That's sexy." Some chuckles and nods followed.

Becky said, "In the bedroom, it's all about communication. Playing a part you imagine is sexy, or what you think your partner will think is sexy, is plain dumb. If I try something I've read in a magazine or seen on, well you know, a video…"

People laughed and whistled.

She said, "I mean, I might think it's okay or interesting, but what if my partner thinks it's ridiculous or somehow even emasculating? What good would that

28

do? But if I ask him first—if I say, 'Honey, I was thinking about trying this or that,' and he says it sounds like fun…go for it. If it doesn't work, it doesn't matter. No one's feelings are hurt and you both go on to be sexy another day."

Some applause went around the room, then the third company rep asked, "What about how you present yourself? As you know, this contest is about more than conversations in the kitchen or the bedroom. It's about what we all can agree is sexy to the eyes. So, my question is, what do you think is most visually sexy when it comes to a woman? What makes her the 'sexiest in the world'?"

This brought a round of applause which unsettled Becky. Her level of comfort had been increasing up to that point. Now, she felt decidedly *un*comfortable. She knew what the company woman was trying to get her to say, even if she didn't agree with it. But, if the point was honesty, as she'd been advised by the pre-screeners and had said herself, then how could she say what she truly felt and not offend or get thrown off the stage?

She nodded, taking a moment, then said, "First off, I don't think we *can* all agree on what is most sexy to the eyes. To some it's more cleavage, toned legs, pretty skin, nice hair, a great smile—or some combination of those things. To me, it's what's *behind* the package that makes the package.

"How we adorn those qualities depends on what our own best attributes are. If I'm small-chested but have great legs, well, I'm not going to wear some plunging neckline that would have made Jayne Mansfield blush, I'm gonna wear some nice shorts or a short skirt, or…" Becky grinned. "If my best quality is slightly above those legs…*short*-shorts."

Men in the audience hooted and howled. A few whistled. The more matronly woman on the panel looked as if she was trying to ignore them, but the company reps smiled. The makeup woman said, "What about enhancing your look with makeup?"

"Sure," Becky said. "I wear some, even to work—and the bowling alley."

People burst out in laughter, but Becky said, "No, really. My friends and I go bowling every Friday night, all year long, to end our workweek. We call it Three-B Night—bowling, beer, and burgers. It's a small town and a hub for meeting people. So, there are always available men there who are interested in more than fixing a seven-ten split."

Laughter, whoops, and applause returned. She let it die then said, "So, I want to look my best—maybe not my 'sexiest' per se, but, depending on my mood and my…needs at the moment, sexy *enough*.

"So, I guess it's relative to where you're going to be and who's gonna be there and what your goal for the event is. If it's to win an award for best manure spreader handle-maker of the year…meh. Not so much. But if it's to impress your fellow male bowlers, a little more. If it's a grand night out at an awards ceremony, I'd have to check with the internet to see what I should put on my face, because I don't have a clue."

Full applause, laughter, and cheers filled the room.

The main woman judge said, "Okay, then. Thank you, Ms. Darn—"

"If I may, ma'am?"

"Yes?

"I wasn't quite done."

The woman checked her timer and said, "You time

is almost up, but—"

"I won't take a minute," Becky said. "I have one more point to make."

"Okay, then," the woman allowed.

Becky said, "I was going to say 'sexy is in the eye of the beholder,' right? What's sexy to one person is not to the next. We've seen it in all these wonderful women here, tonight. Some wear it well, some wear it loudly, but they're all trying to project to you guys what they think, what they *perceive* as sexy—not some universal ideal of a sexy woman, because, heck, that doesn't exist.

"For you people who represent products that aim to help us be sexier, they're all great. They all appeal to someone. If not me, then Doris. If not Doris, then Emmanuelle. If not her then someone else. It's all relative. Sexy is in *here*."

She pointed at her head.

"What these see," she said, pointing at her eyes, "is what our brains tell us to see, not what's actually there. So, I go back to what I said at the beginning. Communication is the sexiest thing of all. If you tell me what you think is sexy and I can be that, we're good to go. But if I can't, or if what I think is sexy and I project, well, if you don't like it, no amount of makeup or jewelry or expensive lingerie is going to change anything. Sorry."

She gave the sponsors a wry look then turned to the audience. "So, all you guys out there—and gals, too. Talk to each other. That's sexy as *hell*."

On that note, the entire audience burst into cheering applause. Most everyone rose to their feet.

Becky said, over the roar, "Anyway, thanks for having me, Cleveland! It's been a blast!" She waved to more applause and cheers and left the stage feeling pretty good and relieved to be done with it. She could go back to Auburn having not sucked.

****

Becky's good mood lasted four minutes. Backstage, one of the floozier women said, "What the hell was *that*? You some kinda preacher?"

Her friend said, "Just show 'em your tits and wiggle your ass. Every man on that panel will vote for you."

Becky had to admit that particular entrant had the tits *and* ass for such an act. But the Midwest in her caused her to say, "Thanks. I'll remember that." She prepared to accept her loss feeling she'd done her best, been honest, and somehow didn't feel like an idiot or a loser.

A few minutes later, one of contest organizers came back to tell the ladies, "We were going to take a dinner break then come back and announce the finalists. But since we went so far over…" She glared at Becky. "We're going to take a ten-minute bathroom break to give the panel time to choose ten semifinalists, then we're back."

One of the women complained, "I'm hungry. Do we still get supper?" She glared at Becky.

"You'll all get a voucher good at the restaurant."

"Which one? It better be good," another woman said—and glared at Becky.

The organizer said, "I'm not sure, but it won't be King Burgers."

Another woman jeered, "McDougals." She glared at Becky.

The organizer said, "No," glared at Becky again, and left.

Becky noted most of the women staring at her and

said, "Sorry, everyone. I just said what I thought."

"That's not the point of these things," one of trashier women said. "You don't get it."

"I guess I don't," Becky said. "I'm sorry. Really, I am."

Her genuineness must have worked because everyone turned away.

Ten minutes later, to the second, the organizer woman returned. "Okay, ladies. Everyone onstage. We're going to make the announcement."

Most of the women did a last-minute primp-check in the wall of mirrors then started to walk out—some tromping in their six-inch platform heels.

Since the stage was not large, the hundred contestants crammed together in a line, four deep. Becky's manners and embarrassment put her in the back row, of course. But after the usual banter to get the audience amped up, she heard her name called, the last of the "ten central national semifinalists."

Even from the back of the line, Becky heard the distinct yells of her three friends. And when she made her way to the front past several massively disappointed and angry woman contestants, Becky saw Darla, Briana, and Myrna right up front, leaning on the stage apron, yelling and whistling joyously.

"You did it!"

"You won!"

"I told you!"

Becky couldn't believe it, not even when the main judge brought a small trophy and certificate to her with the encouragement. "I don't know how that'll play in California, but you sure got it done here in Ohio, Ms. Darnell. Congratulations."

Becky accepted her goodies and the compliment with the nine others—and cried, like any beauty pageant winner worth her Midwest oats. Everyone else continued to glare. It should have been a warning signal.

Chapter Four

The Sunday ride back into Indiana proved less exuberant than the girls expected. Myrna drove while the other three slept—Becky from exhaustion, Briana and Darla from too much alcohol during winning night celebrations. Moans were heard; gas was expelled. Windows were opened.

Back home, Becky felt the letdown. Though she hadn't even wanted to go, she had to admit it had been fun, even exciting. She hadn't been on a stage since *Jane Eyre* in junior high, by all indications a traumatic rather than ecstatic brief time in the limelight.

Before she knew it, bedtime arrived. Though a few odd friends had called to congratulate her, nothing about going or coming home seemed worth mentioning. She set her clock, turned off the light, and laid there reliving the events of the past three days and nights, ending with a sleepy smile at her unanticipated accomplishment.

Monday morning brought a different and unexpected reception at the spreader plant. Several second-tier friends had strung up a banner reading, "Welcome Home Sexy Becky!" with balloons bedecking the breakroom. They cheered like they would when the Auburn Boattails won at home.

It seemed to Becky like everyone at Littleman came up to congratulate her. She gave an exaggerated low bow complete with big hand flourish only to find Floyd standing in front of her when she stood up. He said, "You're back. That was quick."

"Just long enough to win," she said, a mix of mirth, irony, sass, and defense.

He said, "Well, don't let it go to your head. You still work in a manure spreader factory."

"And I love it here. You know I do."

"You won't if you get a taste of California." Apparently he'd read about the next phase of the contest being held in Los Angeles.

Becky countered, "You don't have to worry about me, Floyd. I'm a Midwest gal through and through. I'll be back quicker than you can say Rodeo Drive."

He grunted and headed back to his office. She called out "Thanks, Floyd," because she knew it was the best he had in him, and accepted felicitations from the next in line.

Then it was back to her own cubicle and nine voicemails, though CEO Harold Harmon did stop by to offer his two cents. "Don't know what all the fuss was about or what you were up to down there in Ohio, but I hear it was noteworthy. Carry on."

His grandniece Sharon came in twenty minutes later—late—and said, "Okay, I'm here. You can go back."

"Go back where?" Becky asked.

"To the line," Sharon said, making it sound akin to acquiring Black Death. "I'm in here, now. Did you leave anything in the desk?" She opened it to make sure.

Becky had mixed feelings. Should she be happy to be back on the line, doing what she preferred, or pissed off the boss's grandniece took over her latest job with no fanfare and fewer skills. And why hadn't Harold mentioned it? Or *Floyd*. He had to have known.

Becky's concerns washed away when she walked back onto the floor to a final round of cheers. Feeling better immediately, she mocked a "parade wave" to further cheers. Then Floyd reappeared, grumpy as ever, and everyone went back to work.

Everything was back to normal—thankfully.

****

Two weeks passed without a word from contest organizers. Becky was beginning to think it had been cancelled or maybe, "They woke up and realized they made a terrible mistake." Maybe they recounted the votes.

She had already resigned herself to such an outcome when a voice came over the floor loudspeaker. "Rebecah Darnell to the main office, please. You have a call."

"What now?" Becky moaned, sure that either her mother couldn't find *Wheel of Fortune* on her TV again or the contest had definitely decided they had erred.

When Becky walked into the main office, Harold's secretary Charlene said, "You can take it here on my desk." She appeared to be smirking. "If it's your mother about her television set again, would you please ask her to call you at home in the future."

Becky said, "She doesn't watch TV at night. Her shows are all on in the day." Charlene's face didn't change, so Becky picked up the phone. "Hi, Mom. What's up?"

A woman's voice on the other end said, "Is this Rebecah Darnell?"

"Yes."

"I have contest organizer Saul Peters for you. Please hold."

Becky told Charlene, "It's the contest."

Charlene raised her eyebrows like a schoolmarm but didn't move away an inch.

A man came on. "Becky, this is Saul Peters, Sexiest Woman President." He then joked, "I'm not a sexy woman, myself. It just comes out that way." He laughed.

Becky tried to laugh.

He said, "So, you're one of our ten east coast mid-central western regional winners as I hear it. Did quite a slam-bang job out there in Columbus from what they say."

"Cleveland. And I don't know about that," Becky said. "I suppose—"

"Excellent, excellent!" he said as if not listening. "Impressive!"

"Okay," Becky said, warily.

He said, "We have you booked on a connecting flight through Chicago out of Fort Wayne. Does that sound right?"

"Wait. Am I going to LA?"

"Are you going to LA!" he said with entirely too much verve. "Yes! LaLa Land! Palm trees, beaches, movie stars, and more beautiful people than you can shake a purple surfboard at! Are you excited?"

"I guess, yeah," Becky said with very little excitement.

"You don't *sound* excited."

"Oh, I am. It just hasn't sunk in all the way, yet."

"I understand, I understand!" he nearly shouted. "It will when you step off the plane and see all that glamor everywhere. It'll knock your socks right off!"

"Oh," she said. "Are you out there? In LA?"

"No, ma'am! I should be so lucky!" he said. "I'm

down here in Augusta, Georgia. We call it—"

"Disgusta," Becky said, having heard the joke a thousand times.

"No," he said, sounding almost despondent. "Masters City. Amen Corner. Golf? Green Jackets? The *Masters*?"

"Oh. Sorry. I don't…" she said. "Play."

"Have to take it up once you win and get famous!" he roared, back on task. "We'll roll out the red carpet, give you the key to the city, and parade you through town in the convertible of your choosing. The Sexiest Woman Alive! I'd recommend the Rolls."

"I thought it was sexiest in the *world*."

"Same thing," Saul said, quickly. "Anyway, we'll be sending all the info you'll need in an email and a text, FedEx, UPS, and postal, to be sure you get it all. If you have any questions, feel free to call us back any time. We're here to help!"

"Okay, thanks," Becky said. "Is that…it for now?"

"That's it for now!" Saul bellowed.

"Okay then. Thanks."

"Youuuuuuu're welcome!"

"Okay."

"Hanging up, now!"

"Okay."

She didn't hear a click-off, so she said, "Bye," and hung up.

Charlene asked, "Why do they call you at work?"

"I have no idea," Becky said. "Sorry."

Charlene said, "So, you're going to Cali, huh? I always wanted to go to Cali. San Fran. Sac. The works."

"Well, if I get to any of those places, I'll tell you all about it."

"Would you send me a postcard?"

"Sure."

"You have the address?"

Becky knew where she worked but said, "I think I can remember."

Charlene thought that was funny enough to laugh out and say, "I certainly hope so. We don't expect you to forget us when you're famous!"

"I won't," Becky said. And thought, *Be famous.*

****

Darla, Myrna, and Briana were elated, but Becky felt something more akin to annoyance at how everyone was making such a big deal out of her minor win. The notion she might change, might get a big head, absolutely stumped her. She was one of ten from a tenth of the USA. What was the big deal? *One in a thousand chance.*

Or less.

Becky had never been egotistical in her life as far as she could remember. Sure, she assumed everyone had some ego in them, but *change*? Because of a dumb sexy woman contest? She found it absurd. She could barely find enough excitement to check her email for the ticketing info.

But she did and was surprised to find the contest was being held at the Chateau LaMonde in Beverly Hills, and they were putting her up in the hotel. Not only that, "A car will meet you at the airport and deliver you to your suite."

"A suite and a limo?" Becky said aloud. "Okay, that's kind of cool."

She hadn't expected star treatment—or that the contest would stretch out over a full week; but according to the email, she would arrive on Sunday evening to begin her "contest responsibilities the first thing Monday morning." The list included interviews with contest officials, wardrobe professionals, cosmeticians, speech therapists, and something called "poise specialists."

"Sounds like *My Fair Lady*," she muttered. "Hope I don't slip and say 'arse' at the wrong time, *'enry!*"

The meetings and training sessions would extend through the week it said, leading up to a run-through on Thursday night, two dress rehearsals on Friday, and the actual contest Saturday afternoon, "Thru to midnight."

It all seemed official—and daunting. Suddenly, Becky Darnell from *Auburn I-N* had her doubts. She'd figured the LA part would be like the Cleveland part: quick and over with; back home before she knew it. Instead, she'd be out there seven days.

She'd have to ask Floyd for the whole week off.

"That's okay," she reassured herself. She had two weeks of vacation left for the year. It would mean taking one early, but hopefully Floyd wouldn't *be a dick* about it.

"What does he care?" she asked, and answered her own question. "He cares if he looks weak." She'd have to work on her presentation. "Too bad I don't have a *poise coach* here."

She read on to find she'd have a roommate at the hotel. "Oh. Not cool."

After having seen the regional contestants, Becky could only imagine what any other regional winner in the Sexiest Woman in the World contest flown to LA and limo'd to their suite at the Chateau LaMonde Hotel in Los Angeles roommate might be like.

"For a whole week. Oh my." Bad visions of dorm

life danced in her head.

The email ran longer than she had anticipated as rules for travel were laid out in detail, along with instructions for interacting with the public, the hotel staff, the contest staff, and especially the press. In the middle of the page, in red caps, it read:

DO NOT ENGAGE WITH ANY MEMBERS OF THE PRESS WITHOUT A CONTEST DOCENT PRESENT! NO EXCEPTIONS!

She said, "Docent?" then laughed and misquoted one of her favorite movie lines with the proper faux Castilian accent. "I do not think that word means what you think it means." Then she acceded, "But okay. I won't talk to the press." And finally, "As if anyone's going to be interested in me."

Becky could already see how the whole thing would go. She'd arrive in the limo, be led to her room where she'd meet a total floozie starlet wannabe, have breakfast the next day, get put in some ridiculous outfit, then be shoved out onstage to get laughed at by every mogul and other beautiful person in the glamourous state.

"Cali," she bemoaned. "See-ment swimmin' pools, big ol' famous movie stars."

The list of rules ran onto three pages, which she decided to read later—maybe on the plane ride home after she lost. That idea made her feel better and she set off for bed, rehearsing her Floyd speech until she finally dozed off sometime after two a.m.

****

Floyd did not disappoint. "A whole week? You think you're special already?"

"I have two weeks coming, Floyd."

"Not until September."

"That's not that far off."

"I don't know," he said, shaking his head.

"Come on, Floyd. Don't be a jerk." She barely avoided calling him a dick.

"Rules are rules, Missy."

Becky's brow tightened. "Missy? Really?"

She turned to shout over the low roar of the manufacturing machinery. "Hey, guys. Guess what our Father Figure Floyd just called me?"

Floyd's eyes went wide. "Okay! No," he said quickly.

She turned back.

"But only the five days. You'll have to wait for your other…" He seemed to be calculating.

Becky helped him out. "Five days."

"And not until they're due. Not a day sooner."

"That's fine, Floyd. I won't need them. Just the five, starting a week from Monday."

"Well, okay," he said, saving face. "If it's only those."

"It's only those."

"Well, okay. As long as it is."

"It is.

"Well, okay." He stood there, silent.

She asked, "Should I get back to work, now?"

"Yeah, get back on the line. And I want to see some improved numbers this week."

"Got it," Becky said, turning away. "And thanks for being a standup guy, Floyd."

"No problem," he said without irony and retreated to his tiny office with the dirty Berber industrial carpet.

Becky went back to the production line to man her handle-making machine, taking it back from a new hire, a pale young girl of nineteen in training. Becky told her, "You're doing a great job. Keep it up."

In typical Midwest mode, the young woman said, "Oh gee, thanks, Ms. Darnell."

"Becky, please."

"Okay, Becky. What should I do now?"

"You can watch me until break in…" She looked up at the clock and realized break time was still over an hour off. Disappointed at her lack of time control, she said, "You know what, watch me do this next piece then you can go train with Myrna on the press."

"Is she the black one?" the girl said.

Becky fought the urge to smack the girl and said, "One of our African American employees, yes." Somehow, that sounded worse.

"With the pretty hair?" the new girl said.

That alleviated some of Becky's ire. "Yes. Myrna. She knows her shit."

The girl said, "Well, it's good to know your shit."

"It is," Becky said, and thought, *And your limitations*.

She didn't see the new girl lasting more than a year.

Chapter Five

Myrna and Briana had family commitments, so Darla drove Becky to the Fort Wayne airport to see her off on a Sunday two-twenty p.m. flight. Contest organizers had instructed Becky to bring a single carry-on with one change of clothes; the contest would provide everything she'd need when it came to wardrobe, makeup, and other personal items.

"What if I want to go sightseeing?" Becky asked Darla. She'd always wanted to see, "Every tourist attraction listed anywhere!" The Hollywood Walk of Fame, Universal Studios, and Rodeo Drive. "The beach!"

"Maybe they're gonna lock you up and throw away the key," Darla joked.

"I wouldn't be surprised," Becky said. "Every time I hear from them it's 'Do this' and 'Don't do that' and 'Remember, you're a representative of whoever-the-fuck is running this damn thing in the shadows.' "

"The wizards behind the curtain."

"Don't look! You'll melt!"

Darla patted her best friend. "You're getting yourself worked up over nothing. This is gonna be great for you. You get to see California and do all those cool things, plus be in a *sexy* beauty contest. I'd trade places with you in a blind sec."

"Please do," Becky said. "You can go and say

you're me."

"I think they'd notice the hair color."

"I doubt it. I don't think they care one whit about me. They see me as the homely one they get to make fun of, so the winners look better."

"Becks, come on, man. Be positive."

"I don't think I can."

"So, you're gonna lose," Darla conceded. "So what? You get a free trip to Cali. You always said you wanted to go, and now you have a chance. So, screw 'em. Go on their dime, do what you want, see what you've always wanted to see, lose the contest, eat some fabulous food, and come home relaxed and ready to build the best manure spreaders money can buy."

Becky had to laugh at that option. "Well, since you put it *that* way."

****

Becky's flight to Chicago landed on time, but the connecting flight to LA was delayed six hours. So, despite that leg being nonstop, she didn't arrive at LAX until eleven-oh-one p.m. PST—one-oh-one in the morning her time—and, having managed only a fitful nap on the plane, she got off bleary-eyed. She dragged her single carry-on back through the concourse and down to baggage claim as instructed where a man in jeans and a red polo shirt held a sign with her name on it.

She approached him and said, "I'm Rebecah Darnell. Are you taking me to the hotel?"

"Yes, I am," the man said cheerfully. "My name's Ricky."

"Hi, Ricky. You can call me Becky. Is the limo outside?"

"Limo?" he said.

As it turned out, Ricky was a driver sent by the contest to pick Becky up in a nine-year-old compact. A small one even for an econo-box. He told her, "I want to buy a new car, but they're so expensive, and I don't make enough right now, so jump in and I'll try not to scare you on the way."

Becky hoped his smile was an indicator of a jokester and not a sociopath. But Ricky turned out to be charming and down to earth, talking about his wife and three children, his in-laws in Riverside and Oaxaca, his other job as a school custodian, and of course LA traffic, which proved heavy even in the middle of the night.

"Is it always like this?" Becky asked with some horror.

"On the 405," he confirmed.

A half-mile on, it opened up and traffic flowed the rest of the way to Santa Monica Boulevard which was almost empty by comparison. Ten minutes later, Ricky pulled under the porte-cochère of the hotel a few minutes after midnight.

Before Ricky could get around to open Becky's door for her, she had opened it for herself—and come face-to-face with a late-fifties white contest rep. "Rebecah Darnell?" he said, tersely, comparing her in-person image with one on his phone.

"Yes?"

"You're late."

"I'm late?"

"Yes. Late."

Becky wasn't sure how to respond, but the Midwesterner in her choice civility. "I'm sorry," she said. But the practical side of her Midwesterner persona contravened. "I was on time for both my flights. The one out of Chicago was delayed six hours." And she threw in her newly acquired local knowledge. "Traffic on the 405 was backed up two miles."

It worked. The gruff older man said, "Fucking 405. This way."

But when he saw that Becky had two bags with her, he stopped. "Why do you have two?" in a nasty tone. "Didn't you read the email?"

Becky, taken aback by his tone, said, "Are you always like this?"

"Like what?"

"Rude."

"Why would you say that? I'm not rude. I've never been rude a day in my life. I merely asked if you'd bothered to read the email that clearly stated—"

"One carry-on," Becky said.

"Right," he said, seeming bewildered.

"This is a tote," Becky told him. "In it, I have my necessities for travel. Motion sickness patches, pills for cramping, lip balm. You know, tampons and the like." For effect, she added, "Feminine spray," though she had nothing like that in her *tote*. "Is that a problem?"

He winced and regrouped. "This way." He started ahead without her but stopped when an Asian bellman holding the tall doors open looked back past him. The grouch asked her, "Are you coming or what?"

Becky wanted to say, *Or what. But try rubbing me the right way and it might make a difference.* Instead, she said, "I'm tipping my driver."

"Forget it," the man said. "You don't need to."

Becky said, "I disagree. He was quite polite." Another little Midwest nicety-dig. She tipped Ricky who thanked her.

He also glared at the contest man and said, "Watch out for that one."

"Thank you, I'll be fine," Becky said with confidence. After all, she'd dealt with drunken idiots at the bowling alley for two decades. A low-level minion hiding behind a veneer of grouchy authority wasn't much of a challenge.

As he had apparently already checked her in, he told the two ladies at the front desk, "This is Darnell. We're going up."

One of the ladies said, "We need her to sign the register." She and her compatriot appeared to be Filipinas, professionals.

"I already signed," he said, dismissively.

"You're not the guest," the lady said with a pleasant, practiced smile.

"We're paying for it," the guy said gruffly.

The woman looked at Becky, held up a pen, and said, "Ma'am? Please?"

"Certainly," Becky said with her usual pleasantness and came over.

The desk woman pointed at an electronic screen. "You can use the stylus or your finger. It says you agree to be responsible for any damage you incur and will report anyone staying overnight in your room who isn't a guest."

The contest guy said, "Guests aren't allowed. Contest rules."

The desk woman barely acknowledged him with a barely patient smile and turned back to Becky who said, "I understand," and signed.

"Thank you, ma'am. Enjoy your stay at the Chateau LaMonde Hotel, an Ultima Brandings property."

"Thank you," Becky said, as she was wont to do whenever possible.

On their way up in the elevator, Becky said, "I've never seen an Asian person in person."

"They're everywhere," the man said as if he loathed them.

"It's lovely," Becky said. "We don't have a lot of diversity where I live."

"Lucky you," the man said.

"That's…" Becky started to reply then felt at a loss. She settled on, "Rude." She felt the urge to mention that two of her three best friends were black, but decided on contemptuous silence. He returned it.

Once on their floor, the man led Becky to her room and opened the door. As they stepped inside, the lights came on. "They do that on their own?" Becky said. "Neato."

"Neato?" the man said sourly and snorted with sarcasm.

"Midwest," Becky said.

"I wouldn't know," he said. "New York."

"Obviously," she said.

He stopped. "You better work on that attitude if you wanna win this contest."

"*My* attitude?" Becky returned the sarcastic snort.

"Your contest." He said and moved to the wall-mounted table to pick up a sheet of paper. "Here's the rules. Read 'em this time and follow 'em all or you'll be disqualified. No exceptions." He rattled the page in the air then slapped it back on the counter.

"Okay, boss," Becky said, channeling her inner convict.

"No calls on the hotel phone. Use yours. But don't

convey anything about the contest."

"*Convey?*" Becky said with a sour squint.

"Blab."

"That sounds a bit stringent." Becky ignored the high school reference.

"Rules are rules," he said. "No talking to anyone outside this room or outside the contest site about anything having anything to do with anything about the contest."

Becky didn't think that sounded unreasonable overall, if redundant, so she said, "Okay."

"Especially the goddamn press. Avoid them like the fucking plague-carrying rats they are. Vermin."

"Rats *are* vermin."

"Yeah." The angry scowl in his voice was palpable.

"So, I'm guessing you don't like them, personally," Becky said, tongue in cheek. "That you *know* them personally, so you've made an informed decision as to their character as a group."

"Lying maggots," he said. "Make up anything to sell their papers. Do not engage."

Becky wondered who still read actual "papers," and doubted that he did. She silently doubted that he could read at all, but kept that to herself.

"I trust the MSM as far as I can spit into a stiff wind."

Becky said, "We have a lot of wind in the Midwest, and I've found that to be a good rule to live by."

"Not reading the fake news?"

"Not spitting into the wind. Anything else?"

"You're a representative of a prestigious contest," he said, not sounding like he agreed with that assessment. "So, act accordingly."

"And that includes what, exactly?"

"Exactly don't leave this room unless accompanied by a contest official."

"I can't go out of my *room*?" Becky felt claustrophobic already.

"Only to official contest events. But don't worry, you got a full schedule ahead. By the time they finish with you every day, you won't wanna go anywhere but to bed. Trust me."

Becky emphatically did *not* trust the man. As he headed for the door, she asked, "Do you have a name?"

"Have a nice night." He left, leaving Becky to doubt that he wanted her to have a pleasant anything and wonder if he really was associated with the stupid contest.

She sighed, looked around at the room that had two queen beds and an ample bathroom—all things considered, very nice for a hotel in her limited experience. She set her carry-on on a stand to unpack and went to the window to check out her view.

Since she'd never been to California, she hoped for a great view of mountains and palm trees, or mansions with palm trees, or maybe a glimpse of the beach with palm trees. What she saw was a strip mall of storefronts that included a taco joint, a shoe repair shop, and a botox clinic. No palm trees.

Chapter Six

Becky heard an unfamiliar noise and popped awake in a chair by the hotel window where she'd drifted off. Looking toward the sound as the lights came on bright and hard, she squinted, unable to see who was there.

Then she heard a familiar voice say, "Don't make any outside calls on the hotel phone, don't talk to anyone from the press, and don't leave this room unless someone comes to get you."

Becky closed her eyes and thought, *Here we go again. I already—*

"I know the routine, pal," a woman said with an equal edge.

Becky narrowly opened her eyes to find a twenty-something who resembled a young starlet she'd recently seen in an old sci-fi movie late at night but couldn't remember her name—a feisty female star trooper who took on the men with strong, female big-dick B-movie panache. Whoever this girl was, she wasn't taking any guff from her escort.

"What's your name?"

"My what?"

"Your. Name."

"Why?"

"That's all you've got for me? 'Why'?"

"Yeah. Why?"

"Because I'm going to report you to the bustier

boosters for being a complete dickwad, that's why. Any problem with that?"

The lout stared.

She said, "Fine. I'm sure if I describe you, they'll know who I mean. 'You know, the fat fuck with the shitty attitude.' " Her eyes widened.

His eyes narrowed. "Do whatever you want. I'm on salary."

"Not for long, asshole."

He stared, glaring, then nodded at the wall counter. "Rules are over there. Read 'em and do what you want. I'll wave bye-bye when they kick you out on your ass."

"Never happen in a million years," she said confidently, as a bellman brought in six suitcases on a luggage cart and began stacking them off to one side.

Becky watched it all with some amazement, until the lout said to her, "Your roommate. Have a blast."

The young woman said, "Aren't you gonna tip the bellboy for me?"

"Fat chance," he said and left.

She took out a ten and handed it to the bellman, "Here you go, sweetie. Thanks for the lift."

"No problem, ma'am," the young guy said. He took the tip, bowed, and left.

The woman turned to Becky. "Hey, honey. What's your name?"

"Becky."

"How do ya do, Becky. I'm Genie Vintier. You new to this?"

"How could you tell?"

"No luggage, sleeping in a chair in your street clothes, no smart remarks for Mr. Unsociable Fuckwad there, and I don't know, those wide Midwest cow eyes."

"Is it that obvious?"

Genie said, "Don't worry, doll. I'll look out for you. Guide you through the festering morass. Which bed you want? I usually like the one closest to the bathroom so I can get up and drain my cocktails during the night."

Becky said, "The rules say we can't drink."

Genie laughed. "They say we can't have sex, either. Next thing they'll be claiming Eminent Domain over our ovaries."

Amused and in agreement, Becky said, "So, you've done this before."

"This is my twenty-seventh."

"Sexiest Woman contest?"

"First one'a these. But they're all the same. They act like they own you for a week then won't take your calls two days after the show when you call about your bed bug welts."

Becky said, "Twenty-seven pageants, wow. That's…"

"Twenty-six too many."

"How old are you?"

"Twenty-three," Genie said. "I started early. My mom was one of those helicopter stage moms who made me up like those horrifying little adult-infants you see on the news. And we know what happened to *her*. I was slightly more lucky. Though, considering what did happen, maybe not."

"What happened?"

"Groped when I was nine, raped when I was fourteen. Other than that, all peaches and cream."

Becky was rightly appalled. "That's *awful*. Did they, uh, were they—"

"Arrested? No. No one believed me, and they lied

like prayer rugs."

Becky shook her head and said again, "That's…awful." It's all that fell into her bludgeoned sense of right and wrong.

"It is what is," Genie said. "If I ever run into any of them in a pageant again, I'm gonna seduce them and cut off their balls with pinking shears. So, it'll all work out."

She sat on the bed nearest the bathroom and picked up the phone. "Give me a minute, I need to call my brother and let him know I made it here safe. He worries."

"Does he live here in LA?"

"Hong Kong," she said.

Becky spat a laugh. "Hong Kong? And you're going to call him on the hotel phone?"

"Sure. Why not?"

"The rule sheet says—"

"Right," Genie said. "Well, let me tell you *my* rule, since they're exploiting us for profit. I only have one: Ignore all the other rules. Call home. Bill it to the contest. Get a cab, go out to dinner. Bill it to the contest. Have fun. Don't inform the contest. And most importantly: Don't take any of it seriously. It all ends too quickly, then you're back to being Little Miss Nobody Farmgirl, USA, who no one wants until the next contest, and probably not even then if you don't win, place, or show."

Becky considered all that, appreciated Genie's candor, and said, "Okay." But then her Midwest conscience kicked in. "But I don't think I can do all that."

"You will in time. Once you see how they treat you, you'll be *looking* for ways to break their stupid rules. I'd suggest giving the head judges head. That's why they're called that. One blowjob and you've got their vote."

Becky wasn't sure she believed anything Genie said, but she was sure of one thing: She liked her. A *lot*.

Genie called the operator, gave her the Hong Kong phone number, told her to bill the contest, and gave an organizer's name that authorized it.

"Really?"

"Nah. I got her name off the list," Genie said.

"Couldn't you...get in trouble?"

"Trouble's my middle name," Genie said, sounding proud. "I make leprechauns look like novices. But don't worry, I won't get you in trouble. Or if I do, I'll get you out of it." She smiled *cutely* and winked.

Becky offered a thin smile in return, because she didn't want to get into any trouble and didn't want to need Genie Vintier to get her out of it. But she also was already not having the time of her life, so she'd wait and see.

She didn't have to wait long. As soon as Genie had assured her brother that she was safe and sound and they shared some family updates, Genie hung up, looked over, and said, "Good. You're dressed. Let's go!"

****

Though Becky was close to petrified about sneaking out, and *most importantly*, breaking the rules, Genie assured her they'd escape unscathed. "If they catch us, I'll threaten to expose the prison-like nature of our captivity to *Entertainment Tonight* and they'll run back to their Clinique caves with their over-coiffed tails between their legs."

Becky asked, "Are you a writer?"

"English minor."

"You should write about this."

"Someday, I shall. Cover me."

"What?"

"Watch the hallway. I'm gonna check the door at the end for an alarm."

She slipped out and padded down the hall. Becky nervously kept watch. Genie called back in a loud whisper, "We're good. It's normal. Come on."

Becky let their room door close and skittered down the hall with her room card-key in hand. Genie noted it. "It's amazing they even let us have those. I worked a pageant in Ohio where they kept them so that if we ever slipped out of our rooms we couldn't get back in."

"That's terrible," Becky said.

"I put tape on the latch," Genie said and moved into the stairwell. "Have you ever been to LA?"

"No."

"Well, hold onto your reins. We're going for a wild ride."

Chapter Seven

Becky's LA night ride started with a tame taxi trip to one of Genie's favorites, the Forum Café. She always made it her first stop to see if any new celebrity photos had been added to the walls. Once inside, she walked along those vaunted walls and said, "They redid it then un-redid it, but it's mostly the same. Old school. Charles Bronson, Lee Marvin. Veronica Lake!"

"Who's she?"

"*Sullivan's Travels*?"

Becky shrugged, but saw plenty of headshots she recognized—James Dean, John Wayne, Frank Sinatra, and the rest. "Looks like they all came here, huh?"

"Along with Bugsy Siegel and Mickey Cohen. I love a place with real history. Especially a weird one. What're you drinking?"

"Beer, I guess."

"Oh, come on. Have a cocktail. You're in Hollywood!"

"Okay. How about a gin gimlet."

"Didn't know they made 'em, but okay." She signaled for the bartender.

Becky figured they were in the Forum for the duration, that Genie would settle into a booth and order cocktails until she was blasted then have Becky call a cab. But after one drink, Genie said, "All right. Mild to wild! We're off!"

"Where're we going?"

"You'll see."

A few minutes later, when they stepped out of their ride, Becky looked up and said, "All nude?"

"Yeah, baby," Genie said.

Becky felt confused. "Are you...gay?'

"No," Genie said. "But you wanna find the horniest men in LA? They're in there."

"I don't know."

"You'll be fine. It's fun. I promise."

"What's it cost?"

"Nothing for ladies."

And in they went.

Becky had never seen so many naked women in one place since high school gym showers. Even then, none of them were *this* naked. "You can see...everything," she noted.

"Don't look if it bothers you. Check out the horny dudes."

"Are we...are you...planning to pick them up?"

"Oh, hell no," Genie said. "I love watching their frustration."

Once she heard that, Becky relaxed and enjoyed seeing the tortured look on the male patron's faces. And she gained a new appreciation for nude performers. They did things she'd never tried or even imagined, and they did it all *onstage*. After a few minutes, Becky couldn't decide which was more entertaining, the dancers or the hopeful *slatherers*.

After thirty minutes, Genie said, "Enough of that." She stood. Becky followed her out where a cab waited for aroused drunken men. Genie told the driver to take them to her favorite wine bar, which happened to be on the way back to the hotel.

The atmosphere couldn't have been more different, at the other end of the Night on the Town scale—calm, peaceful, serene. "This is nice," Becky said.

"I love this place. It's my favorite wine bar in the world. I'll order for us if you don't mind."

"Go ahead. I don't know much about wine."

"Perfect," Genie said and ordered two glasses of her favorite white. They sipped the lovely nectar while having a nice chat about back home.

For Genie, it was Florida. "Suburb of New York," she claimed. "And Havana." Born in Tampa to an Air Force father who somehow managed to be transferred solely to bases *in* Florida, Genie got to experience the entire state.

"What's it like?" Becky asked.

"Somewhere between a giant shithole and a tropical paradise. How's Fort Wayne?"

"Dull but nice."

"I can see that," Genie allowed with an agreeable nod.

When the glasses were empty, she said, "All right. We better get back before the pageant sex Nazis do a bed check and threaten to throw us out on our asses."

"Would they do that?"

"Probably not, but they do like to make noise."

So, into another ride-hailing vehicle she and Genie went and rode the short distance to the hotel. Genie said, "I'm beat. It's been a long day."

Becky saw the nice pool area and said, "You go on up. I think I'm gonna hang out here for a few and enjoy the California night air."

"Don't let the contest Gestapo catch you. They

might send you to a camp in Idaho."

"I'll keep an eye out."

Genie yawned, looking genuinely exhausted, waved, and went around for the back entrance.

Becky breathed in the cool night air and, for the first time since leaving Indiana, felt a bit of peace. Her late-night hours out with Genie had proved more taxing than relaxing. Now, she wanted to be alone in the quiet night.

Noting the slick, blue pool water, Becky realized her feet were sore from all the travel and cavorting. So, she took off her shoes and sat on the edge to dangle her dogs in the cool water. It felt dreamy and brought another deep sigh of relief.

"Sore feet?" a man said.

Becky hadn't realized she'd shut her eyes to savor the sensation. They popped open. She turned, looked, and saw a good-looking tallish man about her age who didn't have the LA look she'd seen everywhere in her night travels. He looked *normal*.

"Yeah," she answered. "Long day."

"Art," he said.

"No," she said, and started to say strip club, but decided on, "Seeing the sights with a new friend."

He said, "I'm sorry. I should have clarified. My *name* is Art. Art Lane."

"Oh." Becky laughed. "Sorry back atcha. Becky Darnell from the great state of Indiana."

"May I join you?" he asked politely.

"Your feet hurt, too?"

"No, but it looks inviting."

He took off his running shoes and socks and sat near her to dangle his bare feet in the water. "Feels nice. You're right."

"Mmm," she agreed.

"Your new friend is…"

"A girl," Becky said. "A young lady."

"So, you're…"

"Huh?" She looked over then got it. "Oh. No. I'm straight. She's uh…"

Becky had a brief internal battle over how much to admit about her reason to be in LA, then thought *Fuck it*. She already felt like a fish out of water with no idea how she even got there in the first place.

"She's my roommate. We're here for a…beauty pageant kind of thing."

"Sexiest Woman in the World?"

"You look surprised."

"Not the answer I expected."

"Yeah, I don't really fit that bill." She felt mildly repudiated.

"I didn't mean it that way," Art said. "I meant the posters in the lobby. They're rather…"

"Lurid? Obscene? Pathetic?"

"Provocative."

"Which would seem to be their intention," Becky said. "*Which* underscores why I can't figure out for the life of me what I'm doing here."

"You don't think you're provocative?"

"Hardly."

"Those are some pretty racy looking models they chose for the hype."

Becky pictured the *hot babes* in scanty lingerie. "And me in my ten-year-old underwear." Then, thinking maybe she'd said something inappropriate, Becky added, "TMI, right?"

He shrugged. "Sounds like you're a regular human

63

being."

"Thank you," Becky said honestly. "I think I am."

"So, how'd that all come to be? You being here for this…whatever it is."

Becky told him. She talked about the manure spreader plant and her many great friends, detailing each one, her cranky boss Floyd and snooty CEO Harold Harmon—his older secretary who turned out to be far less prim than Becky had first thought.

She told him about entering the contest on a lark with her buddies and how surprised they all were when she got picked for the Cleveland regionals and how they were stunned when she won a slot for the main show in LA.

She talked about Genie Vintier and how she thought Genie had a real chance to win, how she was kind of a rebel, and how they snuck out for laughs—the Forum Café and the strip club—and how Becky felt a tad overwhelmed by it all. How she worried about being busted by contest *weirdos*.

Art chuckled. "Sex Nazis can be unsettling."

Becky cringed. "I shouldn't have told you all that. We were warned not to talk to anyone about anything having to do with the contest." She rolled her eyes. "Like it matters to you."

"It's interesting," Art said.

"You should see it from my perspective," Becky told him. "Needlessly stressful is more like it. But here I am for a week and I guess we'll see what other nightmares they have in store for us."

When a lapse came in the conversation, Becky stood. "I guess I better go up and get to bed. We've got wardrobe and makeup fittings tomorrow, training on how to walk and present ourselves on Tuesday, and God knows what else the rest of the week. I stopped reading at 'posture directives.' "

"Sounds demanding," Art said, standing with her.

"Sounds demeaning and pointless," Becky said. "But hey, I got a free vacation to somewhere I've never been before, so I guess I'll make the best of it and be happy."

"Sounds like a plan," Art said.

Becky said, "Maybe I'll see you around. Or are you just here for the night?"

"Oh, I'm not staying here," Art said. "I can't afford the Chateau LaMonde. I live in the Valley. I drove down to see what was going on."

"At four in the morning?"

"I didn't figure anyone would be around to throw me out." He offered a nice grin.

It made sense to Becky, more or less, so she stuck out her hand. "Nice to meet you, Art Lane. Maybe I'll see you again if you come poking around some other night."

He shook her hand and said, "Nice to meet you, Becky Darnell. And good luck in the contest."

"I'll need it." She smiled, and walked back for her room with a last smiling glance over her shoulder. Art returned it and watched her go.

Chapter Eight

Rather than an alarm to wake up contestants, contest organizers sent aides out to do the dishonor. Having a key, not respecting privacy, a loud woman opened Becky and Genie's door and shouted, "Up, up, up, girls! Time to get a move on! Lots to do!"

"Fuck off!" Genie said and threw a pillow.

"I'll make a note of your response," the uptight woman said. "You have two hours to shower, dress, and eat a small breakfast before your interviews. Notice I said 'small.' To make sure no one cheats, we'll be sending it up in the next half hour. Wardrobe for the initial interview session will be sent up after, and we expect you do your own makeup for today. Someone will come up to make sure it's appropriate and acceptable."

"I said fuck off!" Genie said again and threw her other pillow. "We know how this circus works! Go away before I call the bitch police!"

The woman scowled and left.

Becky sat up in her bed and groaned, "What was all that about? I thought I was dreaming."

Genie mumbled, "Unfortunately it was real. Welcome to the nightmare."

"We have to do interviews? Already?"

"Standing press gaggle," Genie said as she forced herself up. "They want to show us off and tease the

66

contest."

"What do we say?"

"They'll tell you what to say. And if you say it wrong, they'll tell you that, too."

She stood and stretched, Becky only then registering that Genie was stark naked. Genie said, "The whole thing's orchestrated to appear real."

"It's not real?" Becky yawned, trying her hardest to wake up.

"Not a bit," Genie said. "Why would you think that?"

"Um, because…"

"Honey, it's the 'Sexiest Woman in the World' contest. What could be faker than that?"

"I guess it depends on who's deciding."

"Exactly," Genie said. "And who will be deciding this?"

"Judges?"

"Who all have skin in the game. All they care about is one of us fits their idea of sexy and they can put that face and body on everything they sell. Like Deep Throat told Woodstein, 'Follow the money.' " She put her hair up. "We're well-paid pawns in their devious plans to take over the world with useless products they want to sell to insecure wives and girlfriends for their horny clueless husbands."

"You're getting paid?" Becky asked, surprised.

"My agent nailed me a side hustle with a local realtor. They're putting me in their ads as a 'hot' contestant."

"How much do you make?"

"After my agent's cut? A few grand for the week."

"Wow. I had no idea."

"You're new," Genie reminded her. "I'll piss it away by the end of the month," Genie admitted. "I'm'a grab a shower. Don't fall back asleep. It'll put bags under your eyes."

"I think I'm already sporting PBS totes."

Genie laughed. "Good one." And she went in the bathroom. She left the door open.

Becky watched her go, minimally noting the open door, and muttered, "If that ass doesn't win, there's no God." She felt certain hers wouldn't even be in contention, despite it being one of her proudest assets.

****

After her shower, Genie *paraded* around the room naked—that being Becky's view—gathering makeup and clothes, trying on a few dresses provided by the organizers then tossing them aside. "Seriously?" she said of the most garish items. "We're not whores. Well, technically I suppose we are. But seriously. No."

By the time Genie got around to helping Becky pick out something to wear, Becky had gotten used to her roommate's unabashed preference to go clothing-free and decided it was no worse than panty parties with her buds back home when they all said, "Fuck it!" to convention and men and other *impure thoughts* and tried on new underwear.

By the time Genie was done, she had laid out every ensemble around the room, on the beds, chairs, dresser, even the sink and toilet. "Trash," she assessed. "But what can we expect? It's some male idiot's idea of sexy, not ours." She pointed at her exposed flesh. "*This* is sexy. The rest is cheap window dressing. But it is our lot in life. So…"

She had Becky stand in one place and held up

possible outfits, none of which were anything Becky would be caught dead in back home. But she too accepted the premise of the contest and what the judges wanted to see. Which Genie categorized generally as, "Tits and ass. They'd have us showing off our ass*holes* if they thought they could get away with it."

Between the two of them, a dress got selected. Becky put it on and looked at herself in the mirror. "You're right. I look like a movie hooker with none of the charm."

Genie laughed and slipped on her own revealing outfit. "I'm not wearing underwear. You?"

"Oh... Yeah. I think so."

"It's more fun without," Genie assessed. "Give them more than they bargained for if we bend over. It'd be fun to see that old biddy from Clinesse faint dead away."

This time, Becky laughed. "She does seem kind of uptight."

" 'Kind of'?"

Genie looked in the mirror again and decided, "No." She stripped off the dress and stood in the front of the room, looking around at her winnowing choices.

Someone knocked on the door. Becky said, "I'll get it," since Genie was—

"I got it," Genie said and opened the door buck naked to the older woman she'd referenced. "Well, if it isn't Ms. Extra Foundation. Whoever chose these outfits for us must work for a knockoff Ferdinand's of Hollywood. So I was thinking of wearing this. It's about as sexy as I get. What do you think?" She modeled her nakedness.

The older woman closed her eyes as if trying not to faint—or slide into an alternate parallel universe—then opened them and tried not to look. "Please adorn yourself with the *accoutrements* we've provided." She used the French pronunciation of course.

Genie said, "I'll do my best, but don't expect anything but infantile drooling from the grinchy old horndogs." She turned away.

Becky noted how the matron's eyes fell to Genie's perfect derriere, then she said, "We'll expect you for the orientation lecture in—"

"We'll be there, honey," Genie said and went in the bathroom, this time closing the door. Becky wondered if it was meant for a statement or because she had to poop.

The woman looked to Becky, seemingly for help. Becky said, "I'll make sure she's dressed appropriately."

"Thank you," the woman said, then looked confused. "Are you with her team?"

"Her team?"

"Wardrobe, hair, makeup?"

"No, ma'am. I'm in the contest."

"As?"

"As a *contestant*."

The woman appeared even more baffled. So, Becky said, "I haven't got my makeup on, yet. Or my Knockoff Ferdinand's dress."

"Oh."

Becky felt offense in her bones. "Would you like to see me naked, too?" She pretended to start stripping.

"That won't be necessary," the sponsor woman said quickly. "Thirty minutes."

"Got it," Becky said with fake enthusiasm. "We'll be there in all our sexed-up glory."

The woman stood there long enough for Genie to return. "You're still here. Is there something else?"

The woman looked away, turned away, and walked away. Genie closed the door and assessed, "Bitch."

Becky wondered, "Is she one of the judges?"

"Who cares? The thing's probably rigged, anyway."

"You think?"

"Most of them are in my experience. At least at this level. This kind."

"And what kind is this?"

"The kind that goes for sleaze and image over content."

Becky surmised, "So, I truly don't stand a chance."

"Probably not," Genie said. "Me either. They won't like my attitude, but I couldn't care less. I've got four more this year with bigger purses. So, whatever."

"You aren't going to even try?"

"Oh, I'll try. I'll give it my damnedest. But I don't expect to win."

Becky opined, "Sometimes an attitude like that can help you win."

"Not one'a these, sweetie," Genie said. "This is pure porn-pulchritude. You'll see." She picked up a dress. "I'm going with the red see-thru monstrosity. I guess I'll wear something pushy-uppy under it. Have you decided yet?"

Becky said, "I'm thinking this one is the least awful." She held up a black faux-leather dress with provocative cut-outs and slings that accentuated off her smallish but fabulous boobs.

Genie said, "Yeah. That should appeal to the BDSM crowd. My guess? Half of everyone here. Are you good with doing your own makeup?"

"Sure," Becky said and stared at her dress choice, wondering.

****

When Becky saw Genie all put together in the sponsor-provided wardrobe, she said, "It looks a whole lot better on you than me."

When Genie saw Becky's makeup she said, "I thought you said you could do makeup."

"I thought I could. It's worked for twenty years."

"In Indiana farm country. Let me touch you up a bit," Genie said. "This isn't Sunday sermon time. This is a fancy poodle walk and we're the poodles. Coif, baby!"

In less than ten minutes, Genie rearranged Becky's hair and added what looked to Becky like a few extra pounds of makeup, but somehow it didn't look awful or even overdone. She looked in the mirror and nodded appreciation. "Wow."

"Not bad, huh?" Genie said. "The advantages of being an old pro."

"At twenty-three," Becky pointed out.

"And twenty-seven pageants."

"It shows. Thanks."

"You're welcome," Genie said. "Now comes the worst three hours of the week. *L'orientation*. Since it's your first, I'll hold your hand."

"Is it really going to be that bad?"

****

For Becky, the three-hour "orientation" was worse than bad. It was tediously, interminably redundant. She gave her opinion to Genie. "Like getting your teeth cleaned for ten hours."

"What did I tell you?"

"Did they have to repeat absolutely everything thirty times?"

"So they believe. Like we're illiterates and won't get

the message."

"What was it again?" Becky kidded.

"Don't say anything to anyone that isn't flattering to everyone, or they'll send you home in a squad car."

"Right."

In truth, the only reason for the three-hour indoctrination session was to drill home the singular message because of a one p.m. press conference with all the ladies and sponsors on the big stage. The contestants were to stand as a group, wearing sashes provided at the orientation. Becky's read "Ms. Fort Wayne."

"I don't actually live in Fort Wayne," she told the ribbon distributor.

"Doesn't matter," the woman said. "It's so people don't think you're from China."

"China?"

"Russia. Ethiopia. The South Pole. Doesn't matter. You're homegrown."

"Aren't we all?"

"Different homes, different dysfunctional families, all one-hundred-percent USA."

"Okay."

Fashionably late, at one-fifteen, the contestants were led onto the wide stage in their "sexy" outfits and identifier sashes to stand as a group with the sponsors off to one side, The organizers stood close by in the wings to, as one of them put it, "Avert any disasters." Apparently, they planned to rush out onto the stage if anything happened they didn't like.

"Feel safer?" Genie joked.

"Completely," Becky joked back. Then she asked for real, "What kind of disaster are they expecting?" She took a sip of water to calm her nerves.

Genie said, "Reporter asks if you prefer oral or anal more."

Becky almost choked on her water.

"You'll see," Genie said. "Some of these reporters are nice, some are assholes, some are provocateurs trying to get a rise or some clickbait. Ignore them if they hit you up with anything stupid. Say, 'Could you repeat the question, please?' and act all demure. Bat your eyelashes to stall. One of the do-gooders will come to your rescue."

"Are you sure?"

"They seriously don't want bad press."

Becky considered, "But this is about being 'sexy.' So…"

"Sexy. Not sexual."

"Aren't they really the same? At least connected."

"Not outside of real life."

"And this is…"

"Nowhere near real life."

As Becky witnessed the opening gambits by both sponsors and the press, she had to agree. The bizarre tenor of the event was like nothing she had ever experienced before as an almost manic air filled the room.

Reporters shouted at contestants to be first to ask a question, organizers hollered back for them to take turns, and sponsors grinned at the attention—until one of the organizers asked the assembled, "Are you all from the *Post*? Calm down."

A man with a goatee shouted, "Martin Brimm, *New York Post*. Whose idea of sexy are these outfits and who provided them, the girls or the sponsors?"

An organizer lied, "Some of both. Next question."

Martin Brimm said, "I was asking the ladies and the

sponsors. Who—"

"Next question!"

The reporters shouted at once. Becky wondered if they had been conditioned during an earlier presidency to shout over the roaring helicopter.

The same organizer patted her hands to get everyone to quieten down, then said, "Ladies and gentlemen, please. These ladies are here because they did well in regional qualifiers. They're here to enjoy themselves and be representatives of the alluring side of womanhood, not to be badgered. So, please limit your questions to feelgood issues and avoid anything that might tend to take away from the fun and spontaneity, the *excitement* that is socially-accepted sexiness, today. Not tawdry *eroticism*."

Her plea elicited a round of groans from the assembled press and mutual finger-in-mouth gags from Becky and Genie in the second row. But the request seemed to work. The next few questions centered around the event itself.

"Can you tell us about the order of events of the week, access to any of the training sessions, or interviews with specific contestants?"

The organizer said, "No, no, and no."

Another rumble of disapproval rose from the reporters. But the woman organizer chirped, "Kidding! We have a packet for each of you that details all the stages of preparation for the ladies and the contest itself, including times and spaces for some interviews with candidates. Excuse me, contestants. Our sponsors will be available throughout the week."

"What about the girls?" someone shouted from the rear.

"Like I said, we will arrange several gaggles throughout the week. Those times are listed in the packet along with a link to our website and contact information to request a pass for those sit-downs."

Becky leaned over to Genie. "Sounds like they don't want us talking to anyone unless they arrange it."

"Pretty standard," Genie said. "They don't want any of us leaking anything about the way things are run, or how they choose who to do what, our rooms, our meals, our shoe sizes. You know, basically anything to do with anything actually relevant."

Next, the woman organizer announced that a few interviews had already been scheduled for the day in side rooms. "If you check your packet, you'll see if you and/or your organization have been selected for these Day One chats with contestants we have prechosen to represent their regions or special interests or abilities." As the reporters opened their packets, she stipulated, "Those interviews will begin at three p.m. sharp. If you are unable to attend, please let us know or suggest an alternate we can vet in time."

Before anyone could hurl another question at the stage, she said, "And let's have a big hand for our one hundred sexy contestants, only one of whom will wear the Sexiest Woman in the World crown and sash on Saturday night!" She raised her hands to applaud, and everyone followed suit.

Immediately thereafter, the curtain closed, and the same woman said to the group, "Ladies, if I may have your attention, please. We've curated a list regarding which of you is to face this first round of questions from the newspeople. As the week progresses, you will all have a chance at a one-on-one to get your name out there.

Please use it wisely. Remember the rules, remember your place in this special event, and do your best to make us all look sexy and terrific!"

Genie summed it up. "Oh, brother." She made another gag face. "And we're off and running. Welcome to the horse track."

****

To Becky's great surprise, she heard her name called for the first round of interviews. When she saw the other ladies chosen in her group, she noted they did not represent the cream of the crop. "Oh," she said, getting it. "Least first. Get us out of the way early on so the real contenders can have the better interviews closer to the end."

Genie grinned. "You're getting the hang of this."

"Thanks." Becky grimaced.

Genie said, "But here's the thing. Walk in there and go blockbusters. Be real, be honest, be yourself. Don't try to be anyone's idea of sexy but your own."

"So, I can wear PJs?"

"No. But you never know how these things will turn out. You get some raging feminist who hates everything traditionally sexy, and well, I'd advise not answering. Say they'll have to check with the contest organizers. But if you get a reporter who thinks you're hot, all bets are off. They write a flattering piece, these contest assholes read it and realize maybe they were wrong, and you move up the ladder."

"And if I don't pull it off?"

"Meh. You're still here for the week, and the pressure's off. You can chill and not worry about the outcome. It's happened to me more than once and I can tell you, it's not the worst thing. You still get all the perks and meals and trips out and whatnot, but you don't have to keep honing yourself for the win. You can relax. There's a lot to be said for not having to compete too hard in these damn things, I promise you."

Becky thought everything Genie said sounded reasonable, even remedying. So, she took her advice and went into the interview room expecting nothing—especially not that one of the reporters would be someone she'd already met.

Chapter Nine

Becky immediately spotted Art Lane from the night before—standing with the press scrum, pad and pen in hand—and remembered every *verboten* bit of pageant dirt she'd shared with him. She broke out in a sweat and felt like she couldn't swallow. Her throat got so tight she couldn't have gotten a drop of water down it.

She closed her eyes and hoped for some kind of divine intervention while feeling dark anger at how he'd tricked her those eleven hours earlier. But as it happened, the first person her personal organizer-handler called on seemed to be some kind of new-feminist.

"Ms.…Fort Wayne, is it?"

Becky responded, "I don't actually live in Fort Wayne," and got a glare from her wrangler. So, she amended, "Nearby. So, they used Fort Wayne for my sash."

"And you're not ashamed to be wearing that sash?"

"Why would I?" Becky answered honestly. "It's a great little town. Me and my friends go there all the time."

"And what do you do there?"

"The usual," Becky said, not sure where this was going.

"Enter demeaning contests like this one?"

Becky found a chuckle inside her. "No. Usually a movie or dinner out. We like clam strips."

Art Lane barely stifled a laugh. Even Becky's handler chuckled.

The feminist reporter persevered. "So, you condone this hyper-feminization of women's looks, pitting women against each other to celebrate wholesale denigration in service to the male gaze?"

Becky said, honestly, "I don't really understand the question." And she recalled Genie's advice. "But I'm sure the contest has prepared a statement addressing your concerns. You should ask them."

"I already have and—"

"That's enough, Ms. Sterline," Becky's handler said, cutting in. "You'll have many more opportunities to complain before the week is out."

Becky wanted to laugh but kept it to a smile reflecting both an appreciation for the answer-directing and the rescue.

"Mr. Lane," the organizer said. "You're up."

Becky's body tensed from hair to toenails, sure that anything he brought up about their previous conversation would end in her being immediately disqualified and sent home on her own dime.

He said, "Ms...." He looked at his notes. "Darnell, is it? Rebecah?"

"Becky's fine," she said, cautiously.

"Okay, Becky," he said with a smile. "Can you tell us a little about your home town 'outside Fort Wayne' and how you came to enter this offbeat fun little contest?"

Becky was so startled by his neutral question she sat still in silence. Her wrangler said, "Rebecah. You may answer, please."

"Sure." Becky described her smalltown home—the

manure spreader factory, the bowling alley, and her three best friends who all entered as a joke—noting how Art Lane made notes on everything even though he'd already heard it all.

Keeping with the camouflage, he asked two follow-ups, standard stuff about how she'd found herself in contention, how it felt, and how the contest organizers were treating her.

To the last question, Becky said, after a glance at her eyebrow-raised wrangler, "I thought I'd have a better view from my hotel window, instead of the strip mall across the street." A few reporters chuckled. She said, "But who can complain about staying at the *Chateau LaMonde*? It's like a dream come true."

"Is the contest a dream come true?" Art asked.

Becky thought a moment and decided on honesty. "It's more of a total surprise. I'm an average Midwest gal with a regular job and a normal life. I don't consider myself the 'sexiest' woman anywhere, much less in the *world*. But I must've said the right things in Cleveland, because here I am. Who knew?"

"You're glad to be here?" he asked.

"So far," she said—and threw him a cautionary glance she hoped conveyed her gratitude for him not ratting her out and hopes that he would continue to honor her unspoken request.

He smiled and told the contest person, "That'll do it for me. Thanks. And thank you, Ms. Darnell."

"Becky, please."

"Becky."

****

Becky's wrangler sat with her for a few more interviews in the tiny room then called an end to it.

"That's all for today," she said. "But we'll be providing plenty of other opportunities during the week. Thank you all for coming. I trust your articles will be accurate and supportive of our efforts to celebrate womanhood."

The ERA-inspired woman snarled, "Ha," and left in a hurry, no doubt chomping at the bit to lambast those efforts in print.

Becky watched Art Lane leave with the rest of the reporters then her handler told her, "You may go, now. Remember, no talking to the press outside these arranged settings."

Fortunately, she walked away, not waiting for Becky to agree. Because one minute later, as Becky was headed for the next "required" meeting on her list, set for twenty minutes later, she found Art Lane waiting for her. "Walk?" he asked nicely.

Becky eyed him a moment. "If you won't ask me anything about the contest."

"Did I do all right in there?" he asked as a double-entendre of sorts.

Becky smiled. "You did. And thanks. I was expecting much worse."

"You're welcome." He indicated for her to walk ahead. She did and chose the first door they came to which led them outside into the side pool area where she was pleased to find no one lingering. So, she stopped to face him.

"You lied to me," she said.

"I did?"

"You didn't tell me you're a reporter."

"I wouldn't call it a lie."

"Error by omission."

"I suppose," he said. "I apologize for that as well."

82

"You could have gotten me thrown out and sent home."

"But I didn't."

Becky had to admit, "No, you didn't. And thank you for that."

"You already thanked me, and I appreciate your gratitude," he said. "But it wasn't difficult."

"What wasn't?"

"Not ratting you out."

"I wouldn't...what? Why...not?"

"I like you." He shrugged and gave her a genuine smile. "I came here expecting everyone to be carbon copies of someone else's idea of what constitutes 'sexy.' Some mix of a twenty-something celebrity influencer and porn star—which, by the way, describes most of the ladies here. But I found you.

"You stood out because you didn't fit the same old, tired narrative. You seemed fresh and spoke honestly— didn't need to put on any airs to get your answers across, didn't add any breathless, 'sexy' comments, just spoke your truth. Quite frankly, it struck me as sexier than any of these other trope-kittens with their lacquered appliqués."

Becky remained suspicious. "Is that another ploy to get my trust so you can fool me some more and get me to talk out of school?"

"Not at all," he said.

"Good, because I'm not going to."

"Okay."

She had to wonder, "So, when you saw me out here last night, you didn't know who I was—that I was with the contest?"

"Not until you told me."

Becky grimaced. "I don't know what the hell I was thinking. Jeez."

"Chatting to a stranger in a strange town," he said, making it sound innocent.

But Becky pointed out, "Who didn't tell me he was a *reporter*."

"Again, sorry. I hope I made it up to you in there."

After an awkward moment, Becky said, "I guess I better be getting back."

She turned away and he touched her arm. "Hold on."

She looked down at his hand on her arm. He said, "I have something else to tell you—to even the scales." He removed his hand.

"What would that be?" Becky said tersely, not sure she wanted to hear it.

He seemed conflicted. "Well, two things, actually. One, you might not want to hear and the other…well, you might not want to hear that, either. But it's true and it might impact how you feel about me and this whole contest thing."

"That's not a comforting lead-in,"

"No, I suppose not. But hear me out. I was impressed with you last night—this morning—and, well, I wrote a piece, quoting everything you told me."

Becky felt her jaw fall open. "You *what*? But you said—"

"You wouldn't want to hear it, I know. That's why I told you."

"Then why—"

"Because I do like you."

Becky threw her arms out in frustration. "What the hell is wrong with you? Why would you say those two things in the same conversation?"

"Because I didn't use your name in the article," he said. "I was going to. You know, out of the rules of *righteous reportage*."

He made it sound silly, but she still felt the need to say, "Is that even a thing?"

"Our code, such as it is." He shrugged. "But I decided not to, because…"

"You *liked* me?" she made it sound ridiculous.

"Yes," he said, abashed. "Because of what you said and how you said it."

"I told you the truth."

"Exactly. You didn't lie about your background or your *unmitigated joy* at being here. But you also didn't throw blame around like an over-eager wannabe or a whining bitter former loser. Some white-privilege first-world-problem convoluted runaround. You were being…you. And I found you charming."

Becky wasn't sure how to respond, but she said, "Enough not to use my real name."

"Not any name."

"My background? Indiana? Fort Wayne? Cleveland?"

"Nothing that could identify you in any way," he averred. "It took me until eight this morning to word it properly to assure that, but I managed. I referred only to a contestant who asked for anonymity."

"I didn't ask for that."

"Exactly why I decided to give it to you. You were open and honest."

"I didn't know you were a sneaky reporter."

"I wasn't," Art claimed. "Not in the moment. I was just talking to you."

"But you *are* a reporter."

"I am. And, if I'm honest, I was probably digging for dirt. Can't help it, I suppose. But your honesty and forthrightness caught me off guard and impressed me. I decided I couldn't give your name or any details about you because I didn't want you to suffer any consequences of my deeply built-in dishonesty."

"At least you're honest about being dishonest."

"Doesn't happen often."

"But you like me."

"And…" Art said, sounding hesitant to continue.

"Yeah?"

"I was…well, I was hoping to maybe ask you out."

"Out? Like on a date?"

"Out, yes. On a date."

Becky let the concept settle in a moment then said, "You said there were two things."

"I did."

"And?"

Art looked around as if making sure they were alone and no one was listening, then he turned back. "This is the squaring-up part." He seemed hesitant to proceed.

"Go ahead," she encouraged. "I already blabbed to you. You might as well go for it. Confess away."

"It's not about me," Art said. "It's about something I know—or think I know."

"You're not telling me anything," Becky pointed out. "Quit dancing around it."

Art seemed to steel himself up then said, "I think the contest might be rigged."

"Rigged? How?" Becky said—thinking of what Genie said earlier—then felt the need to check around for eavesdroppers herself.

"I got an anonymous tip, through my publisher.

Someone, maybe one of the sponsors, has somehow set something in motion that can alter the voting, the public voting at the end."

"There's public voting?" Becky hadn't heard about that.

"They're keeping it a secret, sort of. It's the cul de sac, as a friend of mine used to say. Later in the week, they're going to have a big splash announcement about how the final results will be decided by an online vote. People can download a free app—probably with a hundred ads from the sponsors for their beauty crap—then on Saturday night, they can vote."

"Anyone?"

"Anyone with the app."

"And they will determine who wins?"

"That's what our source claims."

"So, the whole voting thing is a sham."

"Or they manipulate the algorithm. Our source didn't say."

"But you don't know who the source is."

"No."

"So, it could be a lie."

"Could be. But it doesn't feel like it."

Becky thought and sighed. "So, I never had a chance in hell."

"Probably not," Art projected.

Becky said, "They've already decided who they think is the sexiest woman in the contest and they're going to pretend the public has chosen her."

"That's how it sounds."

"Great." Becky was even more depressed than she'd been.

"Could be you," Art suggested.

Becky laughed. "Right." Then she recovered. "Well, shit. Like Genie said, I might as well enjoy the vacation before I go back to the spreader plant."

"There are worse things."

"White privilege first-world me."

"I…" Art started, then stopped. "Yeah, no."

Becky nodded, letting the new information percolate. Then she realized, "You didn't need to tell me all this."

"No."

"So, you figure we're even, now."

"I'm hoping you see it that way."

Becky looked him over. He appeared to be telling the truth. And it looked like he felt bad about not revealing who he was, why he'd questioned her, and that he felt bad about it all. Plus, she had to admit, knowing about the contest being possibly fixed…

"You haven't told anyone else about this rigging thing?" she asked.

"The only ones who know are my publisher, me, and now you."

"If it's even true."

"And it may not be."

"But it might."

"It might."

Becky took a breath. Then she asked, "Do you have a card?"

****

Back in her room, Becky sat under a heavy veil of guilt and worry. Had she done the wrong thing in talking to Art, privately? *Again.* Should she have instead reprimanded him for not telling her who he was initially? Should she have *screamed* at him and run away in tears like Audrey Hepburn in a dated musical tearjerker?

The idea made her laugh. Becky Darnell was not the screaming, running away type. Plus, doing so might have inspired Art to take revenge and publish her name. Of course, if he'd done that, she could in turn mention his real reason for being at the contest to reveal evidence of a fix. If any of it turned out to be true, all hell could break loose.

Becky closed her eyes and felt darkness surround her. Nothing about any of her thoughts brought her a sense of peace or closure. Art Lane had shaken the hornets' nest and she'd gone along. At *best* they were at a stalemate. Neither could afford to out the other. So, maybe he was right: Keep quiet and go through the motions.

But what about going on a date? A voice inside her howled, *No!* It could only add to her stress levels. And, though she found him appealing, despite his earlier misrepresentation, finagling a secret date didn't have the ring of a great plan.

Plus, she'd probably never see him again after the contest. He lived in LA, she lived in Indiana, and never the twain would likely meet at any later date. She certainly had no plans to vacate her home state to live in Southern California, despite the palm trees. Plus, it would mean selling her house, packing, and—

"Oh my God. What is wrong with me?"

Becky's brain had leapt from the contest to a date to moving to another state a thousand miles away simply because a man had asked her on a date she had no intention of going on. *I'm a mess.*

It seemed like forever since she'd had any man interested in her who held equal interest beyond a romp after a night of ales at Lancaster's Pub. She stared at Art's plain, dark grey business card which displayed his name, website address, email, and phone number. Nothing about his occupation.

"Smart," she said to herself. She wouldn't allow herself to put it away as a wholesale dismissal of his interest in her—and hers in him. This whole damn contest thing kept getting more and more complicated.

She longed to be back on the factory line making spreader handles, looking forward to beer, bowling, and burgers on the weekend instead of parading on stage with a bunch of oversexed women, feeling as out of place as a muddy sow on Rodeo Drive.

The image made her laugh just as Genie burst in with her usual high energy. "Whatcha laughin' at, hon?"

"Oh, nothing," Becky demurred. "This stupid contest."

"It is what it is," Genie said. "What's that?"

Becky looked down having already forgotten she held Art Lane's business card. "This? Oh, uh, some guy who hit on me."

Genie said, "If I took a card from all of those, I could start a paper recycling business."

Becky said, "Yeah, well, this is my only one."

Genie must've thought Becky sounded forlorn because she came over and sat close to her on the bed. "Come on, now. It's not so bad. You're cute and smart, a great person, and you're gonna do fine in life."

"Just not here," Becky said, tucking the card away.

Genie said, "*Here* is not the end of the world, babe. Just the end of sanity."

She patted Becky's leg and stood, stripping as she walked for the bath. "I need a shower to wash off all the grime from talking to all those horny, creepy reporters. I swear, they're the worst I've ever seen. Not one of them cares a whit about me as a person. It's all, 'What do wear to bed, darlin'. Chanel Number Five like Marilyn?' And 'What's your favorite *position*? Running back or end guard.' So damn un-clever."

"Those aren't even the same sport."

"Right?" Genie said, already naked. "I need to find another occupation."

She turned on the shower, checked the water temperature, and stepped in. Becky watched her, thinking her roommate had the most amazing body she'd ever seen in person and said to herself, "I don't know what else you'd do, Genie, but God knows, you were born to this."

She pulled out the card, looked at it again, then set it aside on the nightstand. "I, on the other hand," she mused quietly, "have no frickin' idea what the hell I'm even doing here. Maybe the damn thing *is* rigged."

The idea made her chuckle again, but she knew her doubts would only grow as the week progressed. She couldn't have been righter.

Chapter Ten

To keep from going completely insane, Becky called one of her good buddies back home every night to give an update—and whine. Myrna said, "What're you bitchin' about, girl? I'd've given my right leg to get a free week in Cali."

Briana agreed. "The weather here's been shit. Rain every day. My driveway is nothing but mud."

Darla summed it up in one call with, "My life sucks ass. Enjoy it while you got it."

"You're right," Becky acceded. "But these people… I've never met this many shallow, hollow, empty people in my life."

"Those all sound like the same thing."

"Because they are and these people think they're all that," Becky said, harkening doom. "If they're not going on and on about the 'perfect lip liner,' then it's the 'perfect lip filler' and how botox *changed their life*."

Darla allowed as how, "It didn't change mine, much. Just made me look like I wasn't paying attention to anyone. When Omar died, his wife thought I didn't care."

Becky gave an *Mmm* then said, "But seriously, all of the ridiculous fake-look stuff is *nothing* compared to the gossip. I swear, they make us talking in the breakroom sound like we're Pablo Neruda waxing poetic about Floyd's love handles. They're vicious."

Darla said, "Well, I hope they're not talking about you like that. I might have to fly out there and punch someone in the nose."

"Oh, you know they are. I'm the black sheep. You should see these women. I've never been around anyone like it, and I'm surrounded every day by a hundred of them. Not to mention everyone else even remotely associated with this thing is every bit as bad as they are. No, make that *worse*. The hangers-on are weirder by a mile. And the reps from the makeup companies and lingerie companies and wig makers? Oh my God. You've never seen a phonier bunch of human sheep in your life. It's frightening."

"Don't worry about them, Becks," Darla advised. "You're grounded in reality and always will be. That shit's not going to your head in a million years."

"I fucking hope not," Becky agreed. "I feel like a stalk of ragweed in a field of overdone, plastic corsages."

"So, enjoy your uniqueness in a field of phony."

"I'm trying, but it's not easy," Becky admitted. "Every hour of every day we're barraged with ads and commercials and people telling us how to dress and act and wear our hair differently. How to put on base with a trowel, and enough red lipstick to paint a fire station. I've seen more push-up bras in two days than I've seen in my lifetime in magazines and TV and cheesy lingerie departments all put together."

Darla said, "It should at least be good for a laugh."

"It would be if they weren't trying so hard to make me feel like some kind of sad little tomboy."

"Well, you've always liked fishing, and I always said you could climb up and over a rail fence better than most boys I ever knew."

"Thanks," Becky said darkly.

"Oh, come on, Beck. It's just a stupid contest. You're not gonna win. You know that. You've said it a thousand times. So—"

"Try to have fun, I know," Becky said, despondent. "But you don't understand the pressure we're under. It's all day, every day. I'm not used to this kind of…supervision. I wouldn't be surprised if they're piping in 'beauty' messages while we're asleep. Stuff like, 'How to be a cockteaser in tights and a tutu.' "

"That's a funny image," Darla said.

"Seriously, D. They have a constant string of plastic surgeons hitting us up for boob jobs and butt lifts, chin-enhancing, lip-exploding, tummy-tightening, and I don't know what-all."

"I could use some of those," Darla said.

"You're fine," Becky said.

"You haven't seen me naked in a decade."

"Thankfully."

"What?"

"No, not that way," Becky said. "My roommate is Ms. Nudist USA."

"Really?"

"Never wears a stitch of clothing in our room. I've never known anyone who parades around completely naked every minute of every day."

"Does she really *parade*?"

"Not literally, but—"

"You don't need to see it all the time."

"No! It's depressing. She has the body of a teenager."

"How old is she?"

"Twenty-three."

"Well! You're thirty-six. What do you expect? You can't compete with that."

"Thirty-*five*. And thanks, again."

"Oh come, now," Darla said. "You're perfect. You always have been. You've got the best body of any of us—of anyone at the plant. Even the young things. I've actually heard them hoping they look like you at your age and complaining how they already look more like Attila the Hun than Cleopatra."

"I'm no Cleopatra, Darla."

"Not my point and you know it."

Becky sighed. "I'm sorry, D. It's this whole contest thing. I have no business being out here and it's making me *crazy*. I need to come home."

"No! Now, stop it!" Darla said sharply. "I'm tired of hearing that. It's not like you. You're beautiful inside and out and you're lucky as hell to be there. So, damn it, stop the complaining. You're breeding a scab, girl."

Becky sighed again. "I'm sorry. I know. It's…" She had nothing more to add. She was just whining with no cause, which wasn't her nature. "You're right as always. I don't know what's gotten into me, but…it's relentless. All these people basically telling all these women, who by the way are already sexy as hell, telling them they need to be *more* sexy. I mean, how? None of it, not anything they're selling, makes anyone sexier in my opinion. My stupid little Midwest opinion. But Jesus, they never let up." Becky took a pause then said, "It gets in your head, D. And I've only been here three days. By the end of the week, I might be begging one of these doctors to blow up my boobs, puff my lips, and explode my ass! It's fucking brainwashing."

"Which," Darla said, "will have no effect on

95

Rebecah Darnell, because she is above it all. She's a real and wonderful human being who is, from this moment on, going to ignore every negative thing about her *week-long paid vacation*, and have the time of her life—or she's gonna stop having her friends answer their phones."

Becky nodded to herself. "I get it." She took a deep breath to energize her positive outlook and said, "No more complaining. I promise."

"That's my girl," Darla said, the letup audible in her tone. Then she asked, "What about man flesh? Have you met anyone at least *kind* of interesting?"

Becky looked at Art Lane's card on her nightstand. "As a matter of fact…" She gave a quick verbal rendering of her thoughts on Art Lane, which she cut short when Genie barged in and stripped per her usual grand entrances. Becky then made small talk, which Darla detected as cover. They said goodnight, and for the first time in three days, Becky went to sleep with a relaxed smile on her face.

The smile went away however first thing in the morning when their man handler—they had their own version of it—swung the door open to have it caught with a bang by the chain, which Genie kept hooked despite his warnings against it.

She asked him, "What? You want to be able to barge in here and catch us in our underwear? Naked? Locked in a passionate embrace?" She looked at Becky who shook her head no, but understood the gibe.

He said, "I don't want you hiding contraband while I'm stuck out in the hall."

"Too bad," Genie said. "You wanna see my pussy, you gotta pay to do it."

He spluttered, "I don't…I…you…"

"Perfect," Genie said, satisfied with her counter-attack.

Nonetheless, he shoved the door open every morning. Every morning the chain caught with a loud bang, which he apparently engaged with pleasure, and the ladies took their sweet time going over, but not opening it.

"What now?" became Genie's go-to, which Becky adopted as well.

He read off his announcements for the day, gave his instructions—which Genie always told him she planned to ignore—and he went away, hopefully pouting mad. They never saw him anywhere else on the property at any other time of the day.

"Perfect," as Genie again labeled the situation. Becky wondered if he even really worked for the contest.

****

The rest of the weekdays proved routinely dull, tiring, and obnoxious to Becky, but mostly repetitious. They did walk-throughs every day at least twice—on Friday, four times, with the last two being dress rehearsals.

Of her final wardrobe selection, Becky said, "Really?"

Her male dresser said, "It's what they chose for you."

"Who designed it? Oscar de la Busta Hyman?"

"Good one," the dresser said. "I'll see what I can do."

At least he seemed somewhat caring and normal.

"Gay," Genie pronounced.

"At least he's more on our side than the tonguedraggers and rouge-queens."

Genie said, "I meant it as a superlative. Lunch?"

"Sure."

Two days prior, on Wednesday, the hundred contestants all received poise lessons. Genie called them "poison" lessons, but Becky got a kick out of being told how to walk, talk, eat, and even sing. "Never loudly, never nasally, never rap."

To which one of the black girls said, "You gonna tell me what I can listen to, what I can sing to, what I can enjoy on my own terms? I suggest you crawl back into your little white cracker box, listen to some bluegrass, and allow me the same courtesy on mine."

"You have no free time," the white lady said. "We own you for the week."

"*Own*?" the beautiful and tall black woman said. "You sure you don't want to rethink your word choice?"

"Not for a second," the contest woman said. "Every one of you in this contest, including every girl on the standby list who is jumping at the bit to take your place should you be asked to leave—every one of you belongs to the contest for all six days. On Sunday, you can go home with your complimentary swag bag and never have to answer to another one of us ever again. But until the winner is announced Saturday night, and you're sent offstage to celebrate your loss, we own you. If you don't like it, go home and give someone who's hungrier a shot."

Becky watched the tense interaction with interest and some fear, half-expecting a fist fight to break out. Instead, the black girl—who, Becky noted, was surrounded by five other gorgeous black contestants—said, "We'll see about all that." Her friends laughed and they walked away as a unit.

The woman called after them, "We're not done with your poise lessons!"

The girl called back, "That's okay. We're done with you."

The angry lady proceeded to take out her misplaced anger on the remaining women, for some reason singling out Becky as being "farm fed," and making her do extra "laps" of stage walking. But it didn't last long.

Less than twenty minutes later, one of the main organizers walked into the rehearsal studio with three other men and women and two large men in "Security" polos. He walked straight up to the uptight "slave lady," as Becky and Genie would later call her, and said simply, "You're dismissed. Gather your things. We'll wait."

The rent-a-cops stood, as most do, with their thumbs in their belts, bulging forearms and biceps at the ready.

The slave lady said, "You're kidding. I've been doing this for twenty-seven years."

No one said anything, but eyes remained wide open.

She said, "I'll be writing a letter of protest demanding full pay."

No one said anything. Continued to stare.

She said, "You won't get away with this."

The organizer said, "We're not getting away with anything. We're *doing away* with an undesired element."

"I'll take that as a direct insult!" the slave lady said.

"Take it any way you like it," the organizer said. "If you're not out that door in two minutes, these gentlemen will escort you out. They have permission to use any means necessary to remove you from the premises."

The poise teacher, who had shown no poise whatsoever in the face of unwanted pressure, started to talk back some more when the doors opened and all twenty-nine black contestants walked in, stopped as a group, and watched—smiling.

The angry woman grabbed her bag and stormed out past them with security close behind. When the doors closed, a female organizer said, "Ladies, I apologize for the intrusion. Please continue your studies." One woman remained, the replacement, and the others left.

Becky said, "I'm glad that's over. I was half-expecting a knife fight."

Genie said, "Nah. I left my blade in the room."

The first black girl who had the confrontation to begin with said, "Thanks, but she wasn't worth fileting. Too bony." Chuckles erupted from the other women in the room and their training continued.

****

As it turned out, according to the contest brochure, the Sexiest Woman contest more closely represented racial breakdowns than society itself. Where the 2020 Census revealed America to be sixty percent non-Hispanic white, the contest ran closer to half and half—fifty-three percent.

Contest literature celebrated the fact, of course, noting entrants and reginal winners comprised the other forty-six percent with "Black, Asian, Pacific Islander, Hispanic, and Native Indigenous cultures being represented across the board."

Becky thought it "pretty cool" and Genie agreed, but that was as far as Becky's appreciation for contest press results went. For though she had done as many interviews as Genie, she could find none of hers in any paper, on any site, on any podcast, or on any radio station. On the other hand, Genie's were everywhere.

Every time Becky sought out coverage of the contest, she found Genie, never herself. She thought she'd had good interviews, enjoyed her chats with the reporters, and given honest answers.

"Maybe that's your problem," Genie suggested. "You're being too truthy."

"Why? What do you tell them?"

"Whatever they want to hear," Genie said with a shrug.

"And what's that?" Becky wondered, because she had no idea.

"Oh, you know, like how excited I am to be here in this contest."

"I say that."

"It's the best contest ever and how it would be so great to win."

"I say that—more or less."

"How all the girls are great and all, but I know I'm special and I'm gonna win."

"I never say that," Becky admitted with a downturn.

"See? There's your problem. These reporters? They like *winners*. They like confidence. They like braggarts. *Swagger*."

"That's not me."

"And that's why no one's running your interviews."

Becky knew one person who was—Art Lane. But according to clicks, almost no one was reading them. They read his other interviews with sexier contestants, but not Becky's. Engagement time displayed on the link indicated hers averaged thirty seconds. "I don't know," she said. "I guess I'm not built for this."

"Nobody is, hon," Genie said. "It's an acquired skill."

"Lying?"

"That, too. But mainly stretching the truth to fit what you think they're wanting to write. You give them that and they'll print it. You don't fulfill their little writery female fantasies and you're relegated to the dustbin of irrelevance."

"Great," Becky said, feeling worse.

"Cheer up, kid. It's all bullshit. They know it, we know it, everyone knows it but the public. They suck up the bullshit like it's caviar and raspberry jam on golden toast."

"That sounds—"

"Disgusting, right?" Genie said. "Because it is. But it's also fact."

Becky was loath to admit it, but figured her roommate was right. "So, why do you do it, if you're so cynical, if you know what it is you're doing?"

"Um, *money*?" Genie said as if the answer could not be more obvious.

"You make a living on these contests?"

"And the endorsements, and the ads—the hobby shop openings. I even went to a Radio Shack going out of business 'event.' How sad is that? But they paid me a grand to stand around and look *hot*." Genie ran her hands up and down her naked body like an appliance model. "I mean, how hard is it when God gave you this?"

Becky didn't hear braggadocio because she now knew Genie well enough to understand her dark take on the world. And sure enough, Genie followed it up with, "It's disgusting how everyone puts so much on looks. I mean, I read *War and Peace* like everyone else. But all they care about is my perfect tits and ass. So, if it pays the bills, why not let 'em ogle for an hour outside a Radio

Shack closing its doors?"

"As long as they fork over the cash."

"There you go," Genie said and flopped on her bed.

Becky's depression deepened. "I don't think I'm cut out for that."

"You don't have to be," Genie said cheerfully. "Just do your thing. Because I gotta tell you, there are people out there, men and women, kids, who will look at you and see their mothers and sisters and best friends. Only, you're cuter. So, it works on a whole different level I'll never have."

"You're cute," Becky said, honestly.

"But cute in my line of work doesn't cut it," Genie said. "I go for the jugular. I have to get all gussied up in shit I would never wear on the street or at home."

"You don't wear anything at home," Becky pointed out.

"True, but you know what I mean," Genie said. "I put on this trashy makeup and these stupid outfits, and prance around and act like I'm having the time of my life, and I don't have to work in a factory."

Becky hung her head.

Genie perked right up. "I'm sorry, bae. I didn't mean it that way."

"I know," Becky said. "But—"

"But nothing. I was wrong to say it. You love your work and your friends, and I will never have that. I will be doing this crap until they don't want me anymore. Then I'll go live in a cabin in the mountains and stop looking in mirrors. And it'll be the best years of my life."

"But in the meantime, you don't have to clock into an office and sit in a cubicle surrounded by obnoxious, boring dullards forty hours a week, fifty weeks a year.

You get to travel all around the country—"

"The world."

"The *world*. And have fun and meet people and eat different kinds of food and see different places and live life while I make sure Edna and Gerta Horville—they're twins—while I make sure they affix the spreader handles securely before they add the manure feed control lever." The memory made her even more depressed.

"Since you put it that way."

"Yeah. You're lucky as hell."

Genie rolled over onto an elbow. "I thought you loved your work and your people."

"Sure," Becky said. "I say that, but…"

"It's not all peaches and cream."

"No."

"But what is, doll? This? This phony, plastic, painted-on paean to what marketers think is beautiful or sexy or whatever the next contest uses as a cover for selling more shit women don't need? Come on. At least your world is real."

"It ain't all that, Genie. It's like I'm already living in your cabin, but I can't stop looking in the mirror thinking I'm getting older every year and nothing's changing, except my face."

"At least your boobs are still perky," Genie offered. "And that cute little butt."

"I know," Becky said. "But it won't always be. And then what? I'll have been living in *my* cabin in the woods and I never got to really live, to see the world like you have. To go places and do things and eat weird food and meet interesting people."

"Have sex on the Eiffel Tower," Genie said.

"And have…" Becky stopped. "You did?"

"Eh, finger and a handjob," Genie said.

"Still," Becky said. "I've never even *seen* the Eifel Tower except in pictures. I've never been to France. Never been to Europe. Hell, I've never been to *Florida*."

"You're not missing much."

"But I am, Genie! If I don't…I mean, if I could live *half* the life you're living, it'd be ten times the life I'm living now."

"Like you said: It ain't all that."

"But it's a hundred-thousand times more than what I've got. I mean seriously, who have you ever met who works in a manure spreader plant?"

"You got me there."

"See? And in the middle of nowhere-Indiana. Our biggest claim to fame is a car made in the twenties. The *nineteen*-twenties! A hundred years ago. Talk about a 'doozy' of a reference. Geez. And now, what do we have? A museum. A tribute to something great *a hundred years ago* with absolutely no relevance to today except that only the mega-wealthy can afford to have one.

"Meanwhile, we're struggling to get by on factory-line pay—no union, by the way—and we get thrilled when we earn an extra day of vacation time every two years! I brownbag a peanut butter sandwich every day I don't take pressed turkey. I sit at home by myself every night of the week except Friday when my friends and I have our big night out for 'Bowling and Burgers.' Bowling and Burgers, Genie. Our peak!"

Genie said, "I thought you said you drank beer."

"Wow, yes. Whatever the cheapest special is that night. Whoop-dee-do."

"At least you can drink beer. I can't afford the calories. If I let one extra pound sneak onto this tiny frame, I'm wrapped in a blanket in the sauna for a week."

"You're exaggerating," Becky said, dourly.

"Barely," Genie said. "This circuit isn't all peaches and cream either, honey, let me tell you. You've seen how I eat."

"It's how I've been eating, too."

"But you get to go home and eat normal in four days. I have to eat lettuce and protein bars for, well, until I do move into my cabin in the woods. It's no bed of roses, Becky."

"But you keep doing it."

"Because I can't do anything else."

"That's not true," Becky said. "You do it because you love it."

"I don't love it."

"You *do*. Or you wouldn't keep doing it."

"Only because of the alternative," Genie said, obviously being careful not to insult her roommate again.

Becky reminded, "You said you're going to be a writer, someday."

Genie snorted. "You know what writers make? Nothing."

"But you'd love doing it."

"Not if I was doing it in the backseat of my car because I had nowhere to live."

"Okay, so you do this for whatever reason," Becky said. "But you keep at it because you're *good* at it. You're smart, you're beautiful. You could be doing something else, but you do this because—"

"Because it's the only thing I know how to do," Genie said. "Seriously. I've been doing it since I was three years old. I don't know anything else. And I'm not that smart."

"I didn't read *War and Peace*. I've never even seen a copy of it. I don't even know what it's *about*."

"Russia, Napolean, the tsar. It's long."

"But you read it," Becky said. "And I did know it's long and hard to read and only smart people read it and before you say you're not smart I'm not basing it on your reading list. I'm basing it on knowing you and talking to you and listening to you and seeing how you talk to people and carry yourself and how you deal with the crazy contest world and...you're smart. Trust me. I've been around stupid people. You're smart."

Genie seemed humbled. "Thank you, I...No one...yeah...No. I don't ever hear that."

"Because you play their game better than they do. They're intimidated," Becky said kindly. "And I need to learn that from you. How to do it."

"Why?"

"Because I don't want to go home in four days back to my spreader line, back to my boring sandwiches and routines, back to Bowling and Burgers and beers and the same damn thing every week. I want to get through this and do the best I can. I want to learn something and grow as a person."

"Here? From *this*?" Genie said sardonically. "Good luck."

"Everything in life is a learning experience if you let it be," Becky said with some confidence. "And everything in life is a challenge in some way. My dad always said if we see the challenge and meet it head on, we come out the other side stronger and wiser."

Genie nodded slightly as if at least partially in agreement.

Becky said, "So, I'm gonna buck up and give this

damn thing all I've got. And I'm gonna get everything I can out of it. I know I'm not gonna win, but I'm gonna pretend I can, and I'm gonna act like a damn winner if it kills me."

"It might," Genie said darkly.

"No, it won't," Becky said. "I'm made of tougher stuff."

Genie sat up and grinned. "Well, you know what, Rebecah Darnell? With an attitude like that, you just might win. Wouldn't that be awesome?"

At that moment, Becky felt two conflicting emotions. Her burst of confidence gave her the juice to want to win, which she thought might indeed be awesome. But her sense of being late to the party and unworthy of such acclaim made her fear the pit of despair she might be digging for herself if she didn't win—which was far more likely.

She said, "My luck, I'll come in a hundred-and-*first*. Worse than last."

"No way, babe," Genie said, standing up and coming over. "After that speech? You're gonna be a contender. We're gonna see to it. And by damn, if there's any way you can win this, you will. How's that for an attitude?"

"Its…pretty cool, actually."

"That's the spirit!" Genie threw her arms around her roommate.

"I've never been hugged by a hot naked woman before."

"Don't get any ideas," Genie said, letting go to saunter for the bathroom. "Speaking of. What's the latest on your secret admirer?"

"My…who?" Becky said, caught off guard and

unsteady.

"We've all noticed, honey," Genie said. "The cute reporter dude, Lane something?"

"Art Lane," Becky said, almost silently.

"Him," Genie confirmed as she grabbed her toothbrush.

Becky felt extremely uncomfortable. "I don't...he hasn't...we haven't..."

"And you better not," Genie said. "Not until the contest is over. But then? That boy wants in your granny panties. Big time bad."

Becky let the unflattering lingerie reference slide and asked, "You think?"

"He can barely contain himself," Genie said, and squirted white toothpaste onto her bristles then raised her eyebrows.

The symbolism wasn't wasted on Becky. She didn't have a tart oral hygiene comeback, but the tingle she felt made her uncomfortable and hopeful at the same time. *Just like this stupid contest.*

Which she now was determined to win.

Chapter Eleven

Saturday morning saw the final dress rehearsal for the night's "final showdown," as Becky started calling it. "Have your *shootin' arns* loaded-n-ready!" Genie kidded.

Becky tried to hold onto the positive attitude she'd professed in her last long convo with her *truly* sexy roommate, but seeing all hundred women in their carefully-crafted outfits threw Becky for a loop. She'd never been in a room with so many beautiful, buxom, long-legged, voluptuous, oversexed women. She felt like the town cur at Westminster.

"Oh my God," she said quietly to Genie. "Look at these women. They're amazing."

Genie had a different take. "It's amazing they aren't down working Figeroa."

"What's that?"

"Hooker central."

Becky had to admit Genie surpassed every woman on stage. She somehow wore it better than anyone else, probably because she had that certain something neither men nor women could pinpoint, but they knew it when they saw it. And Becky had seen Genie naked—many times. But clothed, decked out, she exuded true sexiness.

"I don't know," Becky told her. "You sure do clean up good."

Genie laughed and encouraged, "You did pretty

well, yourself."

"Thanks to your help."

"My pleasure."

On seeing the gussied-up women, some of whom did look more like hookers than Ms. Americas, Becky realized she had absolutely zero chance of winning and said so. Genie told her, "Honey, you never know. I keep telling you. These things are all crooked as hell. They probably picked the winner long before we even flew out here."

"You think?"

"I know," Genie said. "I've seen it before. You go through all the protocols, all the meetings, all the wardrobe fittings and hair and makeup lessons, then go out there and the one person you thought had no chance in Hell wins it all. I'm over it."

"Well," Becky acceded, "I still hope it's you. It sure won't be me. You deserve it."

"Thanks, hon," Genie said. "But seriously, any one of these women could take the prize. One of them probably already has but doesn't know it yet."

Becky remembered something. "But I thought the final decision was going to be based on online voting."

"And you can't rig that?" Genie said cynically.

"I guess so," Becky conceded, remembering Art's implication.

Genie said, "Look, bae, I'm not saying it's rigged for sure. I'm saying I've seen it before, and if it is, there's nothing you or I can do about it. It is what it is. We all got a week in LA at this great hotel. Great food—if short on calories—great weather. Great new friends."

"Awww," Becky said and put her head on taller Genie's shoulder for a second.

"Seriously, how bad is this? I've seen worse. Much worse. I did one contest down in Alabama where I swear a plucked duck could've won—and did, come to think of it. Homely? Eee. This? At least most of these ladies have their own teeth."

An older woman, one of the organizers, appeared and said in a loud, piercing voice, "Ladies. Ladies! Your attention, please. We are going to do our final walk-through now. If you miss your marks, you will be fined a hundred dollars per infraction. So, be on your toes. Tonight is for all the marbles and needs to go perfectly. We're being watched by hundreds of millions all over the world. In a nutshell: Don't screw this up or you'll regret it the rest of your lives."

Becky said, "I feel threatened."

Genie picked up on her sarcasm. "Yeah, I seriously doubt there'll be more than a few thousand idiots watching this drivel."

"Good to know. I can limit the damage to my friends back home."

Genie said, "Nobody will maul you on the street."

Becky kidded, "Damn. I was kinda hoping for the publicity."

"Never give up hope," Genie advised, also with sarcasm.

"Oh, I gave up all hope around noon on Wednesday."

"That's my girl!" Genie said. "Now, let's show 'em how this shit's done."

****

The dress rehearsal went smoothly, and no one received a fine as far as Becky could tell, despite several women missing their marks a few times. All Becky knew for sure was she was happy to be out of the waist-pinching, boob-shoving, ass-clinching "sexy" outfit the pageant had chosen for her.

Since officials had advised a short nap before final preparations—getting back into the ridiculous outfit and having pageant employees "adjust" their makeup—Becky laid down and closed her eyes…

****

Becky is backstage at what she thinks is the pageant finals, but when an official physically shoves her through the curtains onstage, she realizes she's in a fashion show, possibly in Paris, and the clothes are bizarre. Crazy hats, weird leggings, impossibly tall shoes. Feathers everywhere, animal skins, a beaver dam.

A volcano made of mashed rutabagas.

But since this is a "Sexiest Skank on the Planet" catwalk, the other overly tall, expressionless international models wear outfits with clear panels over their breasts and butts, as well as crotches. Some wear BDSM gear, ball gags and strange harnesses, and some have giant dildos on their heads. None seem aware or concerned.

All but Becky, who is horrified to find she is walking naked next to Genie who's wearing a broad smile and says, "This is more like it! I feel like I'm at home in my living room!" She struts ahead, waving at the hollering fans both male and female. Becky covers her breasts and crotch, bringing boos.

Finally, she stops midway down the catwalk and decries, "This is horrible! I hate this! I'm not sexy like this! I'm ugly and horrible! I have sex in the dark!"

Macabre faces straight out of a Fellini nightmare laugh maniacally. Some look like evil clowns, some like circus freaks from the Thirties, some like Becky's neighbors Bob and Betty Tillamook.

She tries to cover herself, but when she looks down, she sees her hands are tiny, like a baby's. She screams, "That's it! I'm going home!" and runs—not for the curtains, but out through the audience who paw her and grab her and laugh at her and shout profanities as she runs past for the doors and...

Outside onto the pool patio where Art Lane waits, naked. He says, "I've been waiting for you. I've got a big surprise."

He nods down at his huge—

****

Becky jerked awake in her Chateau LaMonde queen bed in a cold sweat. Her eyes were open as wide as they would go and she wondered if she'd been dreaming with them open. "Holy crap," she said low. "Off the charts."

Genie said, "Bad dream? You were muttering something about totem poles and someone named Mandrake."

Becky nodded. "Oh yeah. Dr. Strangelove. I forgot that part."

She sat up, remembering she was, in fact, naked along with Genie, but getting used to it.

Genie said, "Must've been the extra pepperoni in your salad."

"Anchovies," Becky said.

"Ah."

Becky shook her head. "I don't think I can go through with this."

"You have no choice at this point," Genie said plainly. "Unless you want to get billed for your flights and ground transportation and hotel and food and…whatever else they can think to add."

Becky remembered all of it being in the contract and groaned. "I'm doomed."

"Now stop that," Genie said and put down her crossword. "How many times do I have to tell you—"

"I know, I know. But I had no idea how demeaning and traumatic this whole thing would be."

"Welcome to my world. I put myself through this bullshit three or four times a year, however many contests will have me."

"Does it get easier?"

"Are you planning to enter more?"

"Oh, God no."

"Then, no. It doesn't get any easier. Not really. But you learn to tune it out, focus on the paycheck, and hope you meet at least one hot guy to tide you over till the next one."

Becky wondered, "You go through that many men?"

"If at all possible," Genie said. "It keeps me from getting married."

Becky understood, given her own two "failed" marriages.

"You'll be fine, babe," Genie assured once more. "Put on your tolerant face—the one you use in a new bar or your first time at a football game when you're newly single—and walk through it like the Hell it is, but you don't let it touch you inside because you are one tough, steely, strong woman. It's how we survive out there, and how we survive in here. Same deal. Men are pigs and they run the world."

"I'm surprised you haven't switched to the other team."

"I tried it," Genie said with no shame. "Not for me.

You have to keep an open mind on those things, but I was left wanting. Despite men being big dumb babies who have no idea how to act around women, I find them a better choice in the end. So to speak. Until the next contest."

Becky nodded and went in to pee. While sitting there, she thought of *her* contest man Art Lane. How she was so disappointed he lied to her about being a reporter—committing his error by omission in not telling her—and how, if she'd met him at a bar or football game, or Bowling and Burgers, she'd have been delighted. Maybe even thrilled. He was nice looking, had kind eyes and a gentle feel about him—nothing like she imagined in a reporter. She sighed and wiped. It was a relationship not to be.

"I'm gonna grab my shower if it's okay," she said out the open door.

"Go for it, babe," Genie said. "We'll need to start the final stretch preparations in forty-minutes."

"Great," Becky said softly as she checked the water temperature then stepped in to wash as much trepidation away as she thought possible.

****

Right on schedule, their usual male wrangler shoved the door open till it caught the chain and he said, "Open up, ladies. Time to get a move on."

Genie said, "Go screw yourself, Melvin. We can handle it ourselves."

"That's not what they pay me for," he said.

Becky said quietly, "His name is Melvin?"

Genie said, "Saw it on a list."

She went to the door, opened it wide, and stood there totally naked in front of Melvin, who looked down with appreciation. Genie said, "Never saw one before in person, huh? Hope it lived up to your boyhood expectations. Now, look up here."

He did.

"Fuck off!" she said then slammed and locked the door. He didn't bother to knock again.

"You know, I was thinking—"

"Not more *thinking*," Genie reproached.

"Not that kind," Becky said. "I'm ready to kill it—at least as best I can."

"Good for you!"

"I mean, aren't we arrogant? A hundred contestants? Twice the number of states? Aren't they saying that we're the sexiest women in the *world*? Americans?"

"Yes. They. Not we," Genie said. "We're just going along for the ride."

"And the paycheck."

Genie said, "And honestly, this is the most diverse group I've seen. They must've gotten crap in the news or something, because these deals are almost always ninety-percent white girls. Might be an LA thing, but it's pretty cool, really."

Then she asked, "Do you have any black friends back home?"

"Yeah, I told you. Myrna and Briana."

"Right, right," Genie said. "I don't have a single one. I guess being from Oregon sealed the deal."

"Too bad."

"Yeah, it is," Genie said woefully and moved on. "Well, okay. Let's do our makeup. We can check each other before the mascara Nazis do their thing. Are you wearing a wig?"

Becky said, "I didn't even bring one."

Genie said, "I can't decide between the blue or the green one. I imagine there'll be at least a dozen red ones out there and a few purple."

Becky said, "Why don't you wear your own hair. It's beautiful. I wish my hair was so curly and full. I got stuck with this thin spaghetti wire."

"It looks fine, and it suits you," Genie said. She checked herself in a mirror and fluffed her thick hair. "Yeah, you're right. Might actually give me an edge over all the gals with fake tresses. Okay. You convinced me. One for you."

"Glad I could help."

Genie said, "Now, get over here and blow it out for me. I'll do yours after so it'll last longer."

"Deal."

Becky did as requested and spent the next hour getting more and more nervous. But she was determined to follow her own advice, as well as Genie's and everyone else's—Darla, Myrna, and Briana included—to make the best of the situation.

At the end of their preparations—cinched into their form-fitting skirts and tops, balancing on high heels, hair up, makeup on—Melvin returned. This time he knocked.

****

After Becky and Genie passed muster with the contest "appearance consultants," who made minor *improvements*, the roommates received permission to enter the "corral," a holding area in an adjacent room behind the main stage. The room was a hive of excitement, energy, chattering, and some complaints—even if it was far too late for that.

In short order, an organizer came in to give the "On in five, ladies!" warning, which spurred Becky to, surprisingly, finally relax.

"That's weird," she told Genie. "It was like a Xanax just kicked in."

"Yeah. I put one in your coffee."

"You what!"

"Just kidding," Genie said. "See? You were born to this."

"Yeah, twenty years too late," Becky said.

"But here you are."

"Here I am."

In five minutes, she was backstage, behind the curtain, where the hundred contestants received orders to keep quiet. Which meant being able to hear the crowd out front murmuring, ready for the show. It sounded like a lot.

Because Becky had been stationed close to one end, she was able to sneak a peek out through the curtains. The sight of nearly five hundred people eager for an *event* took her back a moment. Then her calm mostly returned.

But what cemented her composure was seeing Art Lane in a side-front-row press area. He looked more nervous than she did—but extra handsome in a tuxedo. Becky had never been out with a man in a real adult tux, just a pimply boy for junior prom.

Art Lane was no boy. She thought how it was too bad they hadn't gone on that date. Once the contest was over and she was trundled home, she'd likely never see him again. Her heart sank a little—until someone slapped her hand away from the curtain and snapped, "Get back in line."

"Sorry." But the woman had already moved on.

Someone took hold of Becky's hand and Genie said,

"This is when I always feel the nerves. Right before it starts. Then it all goes away."

Becky realized she wasn't feeling *any* nerves. She expected it to start any moment, but so far, it eluded her. Didn't even threaten.

Genie squeezed her hand. "Good luck, girlie."

"You too," Becky said sincerely, because she knew Genie meant it as well—even if Genie had to be thinking she had a much better chance of winning.

Someone said, "In three…two…"

Music swelled and a louder, amplified man's voice led in, "Ladies and gentlemen, welcome to the first annual Sexiest Woman in the World competition from the wonderful Chateau LaMonde Hotel in Beverly Hills, California! Without further ado, let's meet the ladies who hope to be the *sexiest of all women on earth*!"

Those were the last words Becky heard.

Chapter Twelve

The onstage moderator had obviously been chosen for her stature rather than her bustline, but her seasoned poise mostly made up for any *deficiencies*. She stood tall and erect, walked easily in ridiculously high heels, didn't appear to be a single gram overweight, and had the most beautifully piercing green eyes Becky had ever seen. The woman projected confidence and oozed sensuality without being trashy in any sense.

Becky watched as the woman, who went by Rita deLusque—probably not her real name, but it suited her—mentioned the contest was being streamed live then worked her way through each of the hundred contestants, asking short introductory questions in what felt intimate but not intimidating. She sounded genuinely interested in the answers and encouraged the audience to support the contestants without pandering to either.

Everything proved an inspiration for Becky, bolstering her confidence with each carefully orchestrated interview. After all the parading and catcalling, Becky knew her real chance of being noticed would be the three-minute Q&A at the end of the *tribunal*. If she *did* have a chance in Hell, it would be one that involved her mouth rather than any other body part, sexy or not.

When someone called her name, along with the erroneous "Ms. Fort Wayne," Becky felt ready to take on whatever might be thrown at her while knowing it wouldn't be any different than any other of the women's challenges. What she didn't account for was her own inability to stay on track and limit her answers to the specific questions.

So, when Rita deLusque asked, "Okay, Rebecah Darnell, what defines 'sexy' to you?" Becky's mind ran off in another direction.

"For me? Well, I'd say sexy is a touch—a gentle, sweet, loving touch. One I feel in my heart as well as my…well, whatever." She grinned and deLusque returned it.

Surprisingly, her short answer received as much audience response as almost any other statement given by anyone before. So, she rode that wave when Rita asked, "Can you expand on that for us, Rebecah."

"Becky, please. I haven't been a 'Rebecah' since first grade."

Rita chuckled along with the audience in a professional, curated way. "Okay, Becky. Go on. Tell us more about what you consider to be sexy."

"Well," Becky said, "I'd say it's when he gently runs a fingertip down one arm and the hair on my other arm stands straight up. Or when he delicately kisses the side of my neck and every hair on my whole body stands up."

Becky thought she heard some female moans, so she went on. "And when he kisses my eyes when they're closed, because that one has to be tender, kind, and loving. I melt, and I'm his."

What sounded like a group moan came from the audience—and from some of the ladies behind her—followed by enthusiastic applause. Becky turned to look at her fellow contestants as a few of them pretended to calm and cool themselves with waving hands. Some women in the audience cheered and whistled.

Becky looked at the seven judges expecting to see a similar reaction. Instead, they seemed to be indicating something else to Rita, something like: *Nope. Not it. Try again.*

So Rita, professional question-asker, turned back to Becky with a smile and said, "That sounds nice, Becky. But you've described a sexy *man,* and this is about being a sexy woman—the sexiest in the world. As a reminder."

Since Rita didn't say it in a demeaning way Becky could discern, she said, "Sorry, Rita. I got myself a little hot under the collar, there, thinking about…well, we won't go there specifically."

Rita actually laughed as the crowd cheered again. Becky checked the judges to see pasted-on smiles with pencils poised in hands. So, she forged ahead.

"Right. So, I would say what makes a woman sexy—the sexiest women—is not about this…" She waved her hand in front of her gaudy outfit. "But this. What's in here." She pointed at the side of her head. "What we think and how we see ourselves. Then, how we project that self-image to our partners."

Rita seemed to appreciate her direction and said, "Can you elaborate for us, Becky?"

"Sure. I believe how we think about ourselves, how we see ourselves in our mind's eye, is what makes us sexy to a partner. It doesn't matter if we're thin or full-bodied or somewhere in between. It doesn't matter if we have blonde hair or black hair or green hair or no hair. It doesn't matter what we wear or how we see ourselves in a mirror. What matters is how much we believe in ourselves."

"In what way?" Rita asked, sounding genuinely interested.

"I guess I mean in terms of confidence, how we project a belief in ourselves, in our own sexiness, to our partners. How we, like I said, how we touch *them*, how we make *their* hair stand up, because they can tell we're real, we're serious, we believe in our relationship, and we want to demonstrate that with every touch and gesture."

"So, you don't think it's about the external."

"That's part of it, sure," Becky said. "But only in the sense we express what we see and feel inside. If I don't believe in myself, if I'm not relaxed and confident in who I am, it won't matter what I wear. If I'm meek and mild and happy with that, putting on a leather mask and wielding a whip won't do anything for anyone." She thought a second, then added, "Unless of course that's who I was all along and didn't know it."

That brought another round of laughter and applause—some whistles. Becky continued, "Those must be the secret spankers out there."

Rita laughed again. "Becky, you're too much."

"Not really. Just…who I am. And look, I'm *not* much. Compared to this group of beautiful hotties up here…" She turned back to acknowledge them honestly. "I'm an average girl from Indiana."

She turned back. "I don't have any illusions about who I am. I don't even really know what I'm doing up here on this stage with them. Under all this makeup they slathered on me and this ridiculous outfit, I'm very average—probably like most of the ladies out there in the audience. We are who we are and we know who we are and we find our sexiness in whatever ways we do, in whatever corner inside us—or any big ol' billboard advertising 'This is who I am, and I'm damn sexy.' Those are good too."

Becky looked out at the audience and said, louder, "That's us, ladies, right? The silent sexy majority."

A soaring round of applause, cheering, and whistles boomed through the auditorium, causing Becky to add, "Maybe not so silent."

"I'd say not," Rita said with a broad grin. "It's certainly a different take on the question and this contest, given the title. But does your view speak to this in a more, let's say, *conventional* manner?"

"Oh sure," Becky said. "I'm not saying the superficial stuff is useless or wrong. I'm saying, in my opinion, it doesn't matter what you put on the outside if the inside doesn't match it, or surpass it. If we don't have the confidence as women to *be* sexy, to express our needs and desires, our kinks even, then no amount of doctoring up, no amount of add-ons, no 'boudoir photos' or whatever will amount to a hill of beans, if we don't feel it—if we don't *mean* it—in here. It's gotta be real, Rita."

She pointed at her heart this time. The crowd went wild cheering and whistling and whooping and hollering. Nearly everyone rose for a standing ovation.

Elated, Becky looked down at the judges, expecting to see pens and pencils furiously marking down winning numbers only to find them huddled and...*arguing*?

Rita deLusque apparently noted them as well because she turned back, returning to her bland, dispassionate professional mien and said, "Well, thank you Rebecah Darnell for your...unusual answers. And good luck in the judging."

The audience, obviously unaware of any disparities, continued to carry on with full-throated support as the judges broke apart to begin writing down their verdicts. Not one raised their eyes Becky's way.

****

When the final tallies were posted, Becky received one thumb up and four down. She told Genie, "There it went."

Genie said, "Did you expect even one?"

"Not really."

"So, all things considered, not bad. And, by the way, the audience response was almost as big as mine and Ms. Hawai'i, and she's *killer*. If this wasn't her first time, I'd go home, because there'd be no point."

Becky agreed the woman from Hawai'i had more going for her than anyone in the contest with the possible exception of Genie. Because, when taken as a whole, the other ninety-seven contestants didn't come close. They all looked like carbon copies of one another, and all gave stock answers they'd either been told to give or thought were the general consensus on "sexy"—advice column pablum.

Sure, the men in the audience howled and whistled as they likely thought *they* were supposed to do, but no ladies stood out like Genie the pro and Ms. Hawai'i the most beautiful and sexy woman Becky had ever seen in her life.

After the contestants had received their final group round of applause and were led backstage to strut or mope, depending on how they rated their chances at winning, Becky found herself feeling a tad angry. She told Genie, "I was just honest."

"These things aren't about honesty, hon," Genie

said. "They're about stereotypes and manipulation. Those sponsors know who they want to win before we ever set foot out there. Like I said, I think at least half of these things are rigged from the get-go. Maybe most. Hell, maybe *all*. You think these horny old dudes don't rig their contests? It's what they do every day in their businesses. They're the self-proclaimed *kings* of rigging. They *brag* about it!"

Becky remembered what Art Lane told her about his tip about *this* contest being rigged, which brought greater despair. "You're probably right," she said. "If you or Hawai'i don't win, I'd be amazed."

"Not really. You never know what's in their minds—the judges and sponsors. They have an idea of what and who they want to feature in their ads and commercials, and it doesn't always fit beauty norms—or anything else. It's all business for them. If you fit the business model that will make them the most money, you're it."

"That doesn't sound promising for you."

"Meh. Another stop on the tour," Genie said. "In two weeks, I'm in Montreal, and three weeks after that, I'm in Miami. Then I go to Europe for two months, then Australia and New Zealand. If I win, I win. If I don't, I don't. Either way, I get to *see the world*!" She made sure to make the last part sound exciting, even if she was being facetious. "I.e., if I don't win and make money, I might not be able to afford the next one in Hong Kong and South Africa and fucking Little Rock."

Becky heard it all and somehow found comfort. "You're bound to win some of them," she encouraged.

"It's why I go," Genie said. "And why I don't try for Miss America or Miss Universe or any of those. I wouldn't stand a chance, and the stress is entirely too much."

"Worse than this?" Becky said, feeling she'd been more stressed doing this contest than anything she'd ever tried in her life.

"Way worse," Genie said.

Becky wondered, "Then what?"

"After I quit? I'd like to teach kindergartners," Genie said. "Get them ready for grade school and all that follows."

"Kindergarten, really?" Becky almost couldn't imagine it.

"I didn't get to go," Genie said. "And I've always felt I missed out."

"Don't you have to go to college?"

"Oh, I have," Genie said. "Or, well, I am. I'm working on it online. I'm about halfway there. Once I get my B.A., which should take another four or five years at the speed I'm going, I can quit this bullshit forever and intern and well, be a friend to the little ones."

"That's awesome," Becky appraised. "I think you'd be great at it. You've been so cool with me, keeping me focused and on the right track with the right mindset. I think you'd make a terrific teacher for the little kids."

"Thank you, dear," Genie said and wrapped her arm around her roommate. "Coming from you, I take that as a huge compliment and vote of support."

"It is."

"I know." Genie gave her pal a peck on the cheek.

"In the meantime, I hope you beat the pants off Ms. Hawai'i."

Genie surprised her by saying, "Ooo. That could be fun. She's *hot*."

Becky laughed—until Rita came over and said to Genie, "I'd be amazed if you don't take the tiara. Great job out there, kiddo. You had the judges scribbling notes as fast as they could write 'em down."

"Thanks," Genie said. "It felt good, but you never know. I wasn't the only one."

Rita said, "Yeah, the Hawaiian girl. She's got a strong chance. But she's still a little rough around the edges. Doesn't have the confidence like some of the others. I think you did much better on the Q&A, and I read your written answers from earlier. You've done this before."

Genie grinned. "You caught me."

"And your competition hasn't," Rita opined. "So…good luck."

She walked away without even acknowledging Becky's presence. "That was weird," she said.

"She isn't supposed to comment on our chances. No inside knowledge."

"I didn't mean that," Becky said. "She acted like I wasn't even here."

"Oh that," Genie said. "She's a pro. That's all it was. You did great out there, raised the roof."

"But she knows I don't stand a snowball's chance in Hell."

Genie got serious. "Did you think you did?"

"That hurts."

"Be honest."

Becky could see Genie had no intention of being mean, so she sighed and said, "No. You're right."

"And when you go back home, you'll have memories and stories to last a lifetime."

"True."

Genie put her arm back around Becky and said, "What do you say we go back to the room, have a cocktail, and—"

"Ladies! Your attention!" a woman's amplified voice called out. "We're awaiting the online voting results, which should be finalized in the next twenty minutes, so don't go anywhere. If you need to use the restroom, that's fine, but don't leave the auditorium. We'll let you know as soon as the results are in. Then we can all take the stage to greet our winner!"

Some ladies applauded, some cheered, some stood still, certain they would not be greeted as anything other than also-rans.

Genie said, "Hit the can? I'll hold your hand."

Becky said, "Won't be able to wipe, then."

"See? That's why I love you." She elicited a grin from Becky and the two headed for the ladies' room.

Becky had been holding her pee so long, she wasn't sure she could even go. But when she wriggled out of her skin-tight outfit and sat in a stall, she let go a moan of acceptance and gained spiritual as well as physical relief.

"Thank God," she said, and kind of wished Genie was there to hold her hand.

****

The wait for online results ended up being closer to an hour. By then, Becky and the ladies had gotten antsy. "What's the holdup?" one of them shouted. Another shouted, "I've got a three a.m. to Tulsa!" Obviously, she had no plans of victory.

That brought some nervous laughs and Becky said, "I'm with her."

Genie withheld comment, but Becky noticed her roommate looked the tensest she'd seen—going to the mirror several times to adjust her dress, check her makeup and hair, and practice her poses from different angles.

Becky, on the other hand, chose a folding chair and sat.

Finally, the same augmented woman's voice said, "Ladies! Attention! The results are in. You will now be led back onto the stage to crown our winner and runners-up."

A wave of energy surged through Becky and the women backstage as almost everyone rushed to the big mirrors for last-second *reconnaissance*. Most seemed overly satisfied. Becky stood and waited—alone, as Genie had apparently abandoned her to psych herself up for the big reveal.

When a male contest wrangler came back seconds later and shouted, "Here we go! Look happy and be sure to all hold hands in a show of unity and support for one another whether you feel it or not."

Becky muttered, "Cynical, much?" and joined the lineup.

As they were herded onstage, music swelled and the audience whooped and cheered and applauded, though it sounded somewhat less enthusiastic. Despite the bright lights, Becky saw why: It appeared that half the audience had left, having likely gotten tired of waiting. "That doesn't bode well," she told a young woman from somewhere who ignored her.

Becky joined hands with the rest of the excited ladies who seemed pumped up on expectation if not Ritalin as Rita deLusque returned to take centerstage. She said all the expected phrases about judging and results, finishing with, "Drumroll, please."

An actual drumroll followed, and Rita said, "Our third runner-up is…Ms. South Beach, from Miami, Florida!"

The contestants screamed support. Miss South Beach looked bummed for a half-second then put on her best happy loser face and stepped forward to receive her banner and a dozen roses.

Next came, "Our second runner-up, Ms. Idaho! Come on up, you sexy thing!" Rita called out, and the postcard version of sexy trotted up to get her due rewards. She cried.

Rita announced, "And our runner-up for Sexiest Woman in the World is…Regina Vintier from New York!"

Becky let go a happy scream while at the same time feeling sorry Genie hadn't won. Ms. Hawai'i had apparently beaten Genie. If she hadn't known about Genie's solid resilience, she might have felt sorrier for her. But she knew Genie would make the best of second place and fly on to other contests, happy to continue on her path to kindergarten teacher—with a nice check in her bank account.

Genie showed no regret whatsoever as she accepted her banner and large bunch of roses. She stood where she was directed and intentionally threw a smile and blew a kiss toward Ms. Hawai'i who couldn't have looked happier, prouder, or more confident in her win.

Rita said, "And our grand prize winner, our Sexiest Woman in the World is…"

She opened her envelope with her fixed huge smile and…flagged. She looked up, then at the judges, who looked like they were attending a funeral. The head judge nodded, shook his head, and looked down.

Rita looked back at the card as the drumroll continued, no doubt taxing the drummer's wrists. Finally, Rita fixed her smile again, held her head up, turned to the waiting ladies where Ms. Hawai'i looked ready to step forward, and Rita said, "Our winner is…Miss Fort Wayne, Rebecah Darnell!" She barely managed to sound happy.

A weird pause swept the auditorium. The ninety-nine other contestants shared quizzical looks, the judges stared at their table, and Becky stood frozen in time, certain she was stuck in another bad dream.

Five seconds earlier, she had turned to look down at Art Lane in his seat off to one side in the press area. Their eyes had locked, and she had smiled because she had a happy thought. As soon as she lost, she could accept his offer of a date, maybe spend Sunday with him being a tourist in LA, or having a nice meal, or maybe even—

Art leapt from his seat and yelled, "Yes!" startling Becky and snapping her out of her reverie. The audience followed suit and jumped to their feet, showing louder joy than they had the entire contest.

Becky looked over to her good friend and roommate Genie who, for the tiniest sliver of time appeared as stunned as anyone else. Then she screamed, "Oh my God. Becky! You did it! Go!" She nodded for centerstage. "Go!"

Becky had no doubt Genie's thrill was genuine, her support honest, and her words truth. But she said, "I did?" still not believing it until the girls on either side of her screamed along and shoved her forward, their own surprise mitigated by the excitement of the moment. "Go on! Get your crown! You won, girl!"

As the whole place continued to erupt in loud

support and exultation—excepting the judges and possibly Rita—Becky took uncertain steps forward. For a second, she thought her knees might give way and she might fall flat on her face in front of everyone.

But her legs held up and she made her way to Rita. Three overly-done teenaged girls in gowns came over, slipped her "Sexiest Woman in the World" sash over her head, added a tiara, and handed her a bouquet of a hundred red and white roses.

Becky started to cry. Her shock and elation so overpowered her that her body jerked in spasms of joy and release the likes of which she had never felt or even imagined. As tears flooded her eyes and ran down her red cheeks, she looked at Genie who stepped over and threw her arms around. "You won, babe! You won!" She shed her own tears.

Becky couldn't find words. She looked down into the audience where Art Lane appeared to be jumping up and down like an eight-year-old boy, hollering and waving and carrying on with what appeared to be pure, uncontrollable bliss.

When Genie let go, Rita said, "Congratulations, Becky. What a surprise, huh?"

Even though it had a cynical spin on it, Becky replied, "Nothing short."

Rita said, "Well, enjoy it while you can. Take your walk." She pointed toward the front of the stage.

Becky had seen enough beauty contests on TV to understand and did the expected strut to the front of the stage where she waved at her adoring fans, including Art who now appeared to be crying along with everyone else.

She mouthed *Thank you!* to him then shouted, "Thank you! I love you!" to the crowd. Then she turned her look down toward the judges to say, *And thank you.* But seeing their dour, even angry faces staring up at her, she withheld comment. Instead, she offered a pinched smile before turning around and walking back to her centerstage spot, wondering the whole way: *Was* it rigged? But if so, why on God's Green Earth would it have been rigged for *her*? Or did America *really like her*—and why?

Nothing came to mind.

Chapter Thirteen

Immediately after the show, Becky, Genie, Ms. South Beach, and Ms. Idaho were corralled for interviews by the press gaggle in a separate room off to one side. As dour organizers led the four from the larger group, Becky noted different reactions ranging from mild surprise to outright shock on to what appeared barely-constrained loathing.

She mentioned this to Genie who sloughed it off as, "Jealously and an inability to be happy about another's success."

"I hope so," Becky said. "Ms. Texas looked like she might kill me."

"If she had a six-gun or a steer horn, she might," Genie kidded. "Those Texans can hardly take a joke because, you know, everything's bigger in Texas, including their egos." Then she added, "Except that ass. Lord have mercy. She must've left hers in El Paso."

In the press room, the winners were presented in order of their success, moving last to first. Ms. South Beach gushed typically innocuous vagaries, but Ms. Idaho was more on-point, saying all the right things, possibly as coached by the sponsors, including plugs for her makeup and hair products, finally adding, "But if anything pushed me over the top, it's Ferris Foundations, 'pushing us to the top!' " She gave her boobs an under-shove.

On hearing the Ferris logo spoken aloud, Genie raised her eyes toward Becky who enjoyed the overt and prideless saleswomanship.

Genie then took her place before the reporters and gave what Becky considered perfect responses to their sometimes-dumb questions like, "What does coming in second in this pageant mean to you, Regina?"

"It means I have to be sexier next time," Genie said with a happy face.

"How do you plan to do that?" the reporter asked as a follow-up.

Genie replied, "I guess I'll have to do something lewd like chew gum with my mouth open. Maybe ride a unicycle or wrestle a bear naked."

Becky laughed out loud—but not as much as the reporter then asking, "No, really," and Genie holding firm with, "No, really."

Genie cruised through the rest of the questions with rote answers no doubt developed from her other twenty-seven outings—everything a tad teasy but nothing truly controversial, and all with Genie's signature wit and intelligence. Which caused Becky to believe Genie certainly could have succeeded in any career path she'd chosen if she wasn't a self-avowed lazybones.

Then it was Becky's turn.

She expected to be nervous and for a moment had some butterflies, but it quickly passed when she took her place at the microphone. She'd gotten that far without a panic attack or fainting, so a few more questions should be a snap.

But the first one caught her entirely off guard. A woman who looked like she could have competed, herself—big hair dyed witch-black, green eyeliner, huge lashes, and ample bosom—asked, "Ms. Darnell, how is it possible you actually won this title, given your rather pedestrian presentation?"

Becky heard herself let go a small snort of surprise and went momentarily speechless—until she heard Genie said, "Give her both barrels, roomie."

Becky looked over to see Genie nodding and winking, giving her the okay to lay into the phony. But she also saw the same contest officials glowering.

So, she turned back and said, "I guess being honest is a virtue after all."

The overly done-up woman said, "But is it sexy?"

"It is for me," Becky said.

"What about the rest of the world, honey?" the overdone woman snarked.

Genie called out, "She won didn't she, *honey*?"

Other reporters in the small room chuckled and a few applauded, including Art Lane. The big-haired lady had no further questions.

Two other reporters offered more pertinent and respectful interrogatories including some background information about Auburn not in the press handouts. Becky happily talked about Darla, Myrna, and Briana—even Floyd.

She went on to describe taking a drive through farm country in different seasons, seeing the leaves in autumn, rime in winter, the "hope of spring," and the "lazy days of summer," recalling Nat King Cole's version of the song. To make it relevant, she added, "A nice skinny dip in a private river bend," which brought reporters around to making sure their phones were recording.

When no organizer called on Art Lane—for a reason not clear—Becky pointed at him and said, "You, sir. Did you have a question."

"I did," Art said and stood.

"Go ahead," she said.

"I'm wondering how great it must feel to come into this contest being seen as an underdog only to defy stereotypes and show the world how wholesome good looks and honesty can win the day over what many refer to as the 'male gaze,' which is often reflected in how women unfortunately see themselves and therefore take a performative position rather than an earthier and, one could conclude, more honest look and take."

"Wow," Becky said. "What a question."

Art smiled and waited.

Becky glanced over to see the organizers' eyes narrow.

She chose her words carefully.

"It's a great question, though, and one I think I answered onstage. I'm just who I am—nothing special. An average, American Midwest girl who grew up on everything middle-of-the-road. And I guess it had an effect.

"I never aspired to what a lot of people consider greatness. I have a regular job where I'm surrounded by normal, sane, mostly-happy people, many of them close friends. I never in a million years thought I'd enter a contest like this or, holy crap, *win*.

"But here I am, and I think it's a testament to real women, real Americans who called in to vote for I guess what you'd call wholesome down-to-earth sexiness over painted-on façades. Not that there's anything wrong with that. There isn't. If that's what floats your boat, have at it. It's just never been me.

"And I have to tell you, I wasn't what anyone who

Glenn A. Bruce

put this great pageant together had in mind, either. They dolled me up like everyone else, made us all look more or less the same except for hair color and boob size, and had us parade for the audience, here and out there in TV land. And that's okay, too. It's fine. It's why people tuned in.

"But in the end, I think it became obvious that America prefers real over phony. I'm not bragging, by the way. Like I said, I don't think I'm anything special. But I have to tell you, my opinion of myself has changed a bit since this thing started. I feel…I don't know, empowered or something. I feel…dare I say it, *sexier* than when I flew into LAX.

"I feel vindicated—and a representative of all those women out there like myself who love sex and being 'sexy,' but don't necessarily define it the same way as TV shows and websites do. We know who we are and what we are and what we look like and how we're happy with all that and don't care what anyone else tells us to be.

"We're us and we're good to go. And isn't that the best thing this wonderful contest and these wonderful organizers and sponsors have made happen, whether they meant to or not. All these terrific ladies have shown that what's sexy is as varied as the seasons—to use an awkward callback. We're different and that's fine. It's the way we were made and, if I may go so far, it's how it's meant to be.

"So, I want to thank the people who brought me here, the people who supported me, the people who voted for me—and even the ones who didn't. Because it shows we *are* diverse. We're different, each and every one of us, and that's great.

"And all these products are great. Use them, don't use them, whatever. But know they serve a purpose—if nothing else, to bring all these fantastic ladies together to represent. I'm proud to have been selected to participate, to share a stage with every one of them. They're all winners in my book, and I'm sure they'll go on to do great things. I'm happy I got to be a part of all this and, well, I still can't believe I won. But thanks!"

After a brief round of polite applause, a woman reporter asked Becky for any final thoughts, to which she replied, "Well, I guess this just proves that being yourself is about the sexiest thing a woman can do."

She turned to smile at the organizers and sponsors to find…they had all left.

****

When Becky thought about her answers later and the sponsors abandoning her, she realized it was no surprise. They wanted to sell perfume and makeup, hair color and lingerie—every after-market item in the sexual identity arena. They didn't want anyone being themselves without costly enhancements. Where's the profit in *that*?

She wondered how they might retaliate.

Before she could fret too much, Art Lane caught up to her as she left the conference room to tell her, "I don't think I've ever heard a more politically correct answer in all my years of reporting."

"It wasn't meant to be. But thanks…I think."

"It was great," Art said. "My guess is it will be the most quoted interview of the contest, and not because you won. Because it was a fantastic bit of pandering."

Becky felt like she'd been punched. "*Pandering*?"

Art said, "That wasn't what you were doing?"

"No!" Becky said. "I was being honest."

"You were making sure you made your point without angering the management," he said. "I saw you looking over at them."

"And they left."

"They did," he confirmed. "About halfway through the last chapter of your speech."

"Chapter? Wow," Becky said. "You really know how not to impress a girl."

"No, no," Art said. "It was very impressive. I'm not sure how the sponsors are going to feel when they see it all in print, but you painted with a broad brush. If they're smart at all, they'll see that and run with it. If they don't, they'll look petty and foolish. You have a strong opinion. They should milk that for everything it's worth. My guess is they will—after they get over the shock of someone having an opinion they didn't tell you to have."

Becky defended, "I just said what I think."

"You did."

"And it's the truth."

"Maybe not every word."

"Why not?"

"You kowtowed to them. Let them off the hook."

Becky's ire increased. "I couldn't get up there and sound ungrateful. I had just won—"

"A lot of money."

"That too," Becky allowed. "But I don't have any idea how much."

"Because you didn't think you'd win and didn't read that part?"

"I guess."

"I read it."

"And?"

"I did the math."

"*And*?"

"And trying to put a dollar amount on all the endorsements and travel perks and speaking events and the rest…"

"*What*?"

"Probably about three-hundred grand by the end of your reign. Maybe four."

"Four…hundred thousand *dollars*?"

"Could be five," Art said. "Depending on how far you want to go with it."

"How 'far'?"

"If you take advantage of everything, every opportunity the title makes possible. Hell, you could probably sell the lingerie you're going to get on eBay for ten or twenty grand, alone. It will, after all, have the cachet of sexual victory."

"Gross," Becky said, sourly. "I've never worn anything like this, even for my second husband, the football player."

Art chuckled then said, "It's the truth. You like the truth as I recall."

"But I'm not sure I like you, anymore."

"I'm sorry," Art said, sincerely. "I'm just…I don't think you understand what's about to happen to you."

"Happen? What do you mean?"

"Your world is about to change."

"What if I don't want it to?"

"They'll sue you."

"Sue me? Why? On what grounds?"

"You signed a contract. I've read it. You pledged your support for one year, with two-to-three additional years if all goes well. From this day on, they own you.

143

Whether you like it or not. The only way you can get out of it is if you break the rules. Which, as I read it, looks like getting busted for prostitution on national TV or assassinating a world leader, which I don't see happening. So, if you do whatever they tell you to do, when they tell you to do it, *how* they tell you to do it, you should be fine."

Becky thought it all through a moment then said, "I guess that's part of it. I never really thought I'd win, so I didn't pay much attention to the small print."

"No one ever does," Art opined. "But the good news is, you're more perfect for the part than I think you realize. Than *they* realize. Personally, I think you're going to be a huge star—not in Hollywood or anything. Though, that certainly is possible. But on the national stage. Or maybe some new *Real Housewives*."

She said, "Real divorced housewives."

"More of those than the other," he pointed out.

Becky blew out a sigh. She didn't often sulk, but it felt appropriate. "I guess I didn't think this through." She'd done it on a lark with her friends with no projection of success—just a free week "on the coast." Now, this.

"Don't feel too bad for yourself. You're about to be famous. And it does pay well. Exceptionally well if you're willing to play along and do whatever they ask. You could end up a millionaire if you play your cards right. That's not a bad thing, is it?"

"I don't know." Becky looked down. "I've never been one or even thought about it."

"Well, I have," Art said. "And with the economy like it is, I can think of a lot worse states of being."

Becky looked up, feeling slightly better.

"You can quit your job at the manure spreader factory and…spread your wings." He grinned.

She said, sardonically, "I don't want to quit my job. I like my job."

"You have a new job," he said. "And I think once you get used to it, you're going to like it a lot more."

Becky hadn't thought that part through either. Not seriously. Quitting her job due to being crowned the Sexiest Woman in the World had never crossed her mind. What was she going to tell Darla and the girls?

Floyd.

Chapter Fourteen

Becky quickly forgave Art Lane for being blunt. He was right. She clearly had not thought any of it through, especially as regarded the consequences of winning the damn contest. She began to see now how, yes, her life was about to change. And first up?

Calling in to work.

"Floyd, it's Becky. Did you see the contest on TV?"

"Yep. That was somethin'," he said in his usual drab way.

"Well, there are some things I didn't realize when I entered it—when we entered, me and the girls."

"Uh-huh."

"Yeah, see, there's a, well, a lot of money involved."

"Uh-huh."

"Like, five times what I thought—or maybe fifty times."

"Okay."

"And there's a commitment of time I hadn't considered."

"Time."

"Like a year."

"Okay," Floyd said. "You're fired."

Before Becky could respond, he hung up.

Their exchange certainly didn't go as expected. She had thought Floyd would be happy for her and say something like, "Sure. I understand. Take some time off.

Your job will be waiting here for you when you're done."

She told Genie, "He fired me."

"So what?" her roommate for one more day said. "You're on someone else's time clock, now. You don't need the spreader gig."

Even though Becky supposed she understood that, the unexpected notion still struck her as odd. She wouldn't be clocking in at the plant anymore? She wouldn't be taking breaks and laughing with her best friends anymore? She wouldn't be arguing with Floyd any longer about the job performance of people he didn't like but she did?

Well, okay then. Maybe this wasn't so bad. At worst, a mixed blessing.

Becky figured she could still fly home from time to time to hang with Briana, Myrna, and Darla—who, "By the way," she told Genie, "couldn't be happier for me."

"That could change," Genie offered. "But fuck your boss. You don't need him anymore. He sounds like an asshole."

Becky demurred. "He's not so bad. It's more the way he was raised. The times. He's got this cranky shield up all the time. It doesn't bother me because he's always fair in the end. He likes to ruffle his feathers, or ours, so everyone can see his displeasure. Then he does the right thing usually."

"And when he doesn't?"

"Then we adapt."

"Woman's burden," Genie lamented darkly.

"I suppose."

"But that's about to change," Genie said. "From this day on, you're the queen. They need you. Don't forget it. If you're not happy doing something they tell you to do, speak up. Say so. Say *no*. They can't make any of this work without you, so don't hesitate to let them know you're not happy. They may not like it at the time, but you can point out it's better you're in a good mood when you do their bidding—when you put that practiced smile you're about to plaster on your face and make them look good.

"That's all it's about, this whole thing. Making them look good. The regionals, the contest, the results. The *endgame*. You represent their interests. So, it's in their best interests to keep you happy. Don't ever forget. You're in control whether they act like it or tell you otherwise. This is *your* show from this minute on. From last night. It's your game. You're the boss."

"Wow," Becky said, not having thought about any of what transpired in those terms—or anything like it. She'd always been a team player, in life and at the factory. It's what cost her two marriages, thinking she was on a team when in fact her husbands were playing alone. They only had her along for convenience. She figured it out too late in both instances.

"So now, don't wait. Plan your divorce from Day One."

"How? I don't get it."

"If they mess with you, threaten to call them out," Genie advised. "They're always up to something, some kind of no-good behavior. Keep a log, a journal, and write down every weird, unkind, or illegal thing they do to use against them later if you need to."

"Illegal?" Becky said, having no notion of what that might look like.

"You'll be amazed," Genie promised. "So, write it

all down. Keep it locked away so they can't read it or see it or steal it. Put it in a lockbox if you have to. And don't get lazy. Don't skip over anything. If it seems odd or a little off, write it down. Because you're probably sensing trouble brewing. If it doesn't come to be, then fine. But I guarantee you, some shenanigans are being planned even as we speak. So, be on high alert and don't hold back if you need to save yourself."

Becky felt assaulted. "You're making winning sound like losing."

"Oh, it can be," Genie said. "It can turn on a dime. One minute, everything's going great, and the next you feel like you're drowning. And it's not your fault. These people have no scruples, hon. All they care about is making money. That's it. And they will use and abuse you right up to your limit. *Beyond* it if you don't stand up for yourself. If you smell trouble, your nose probably isn't lying. Write it down then tell someone you're not comfortable with doing whatever it is.

"And if any of these corporate clowns get handsy at all, record it on your phone if you can. Use it. Prove it. Shut them down. You don't have to take their shit. They touch your tits, you take 'em down. And by the way, it won't only be the men. There are some pushy women out there who think they can get away with it because they're female. Not many, but a few. So, don't take it if you don't want to. Because you don't *have* to."

"It all sounds so dark and daunting."

"It doesn't have to be. I'm just letting you know it *might* be, and you don't have to take it," Genie said. "Look, right now, where you're sitting, you're thinking one of two things—it's only a year, or it's a whole year and how am I going to make it that long. Both are true.

149

"While it's happening, you're going to wonder if it'll ever end. Then at the end, when you're crowning the *next* 'Sexiest' queen, you'll wonder where it all went, how it flew by so fast. So, try to stay as grounded and centered as you can, take each day on its own for its own value, good or bad, and try to get a good night's sleep. Because the next day is going to be exactly the same or extraordinarily different. You never know. I've been doing this a long time and I still get surprised by some of the bullshit they try to pull or shove down my throat."

Becky felt better somehow, because as she said, "Sounds like life. Taking each day as it comes."

"It is," Genie said. "Only much worse."

****

Becky had a tough time sleeping her last night in the Chateau LaMonde Hotel, partly because her roomie snored like a hibernating grizzly, and partly because Genie's warning speech had Becky tied up in worry knots. Could it really be that bad? Since she had no reference point, no experience to draw on or compare, she felt a bit lost at sea.

She'd already had interactions with a few people she considered unsavory, and she could readily imagine there might be others. She'd dealt with them so far, stood her ground when she needed to, and been okay. How much worse could it get?

Genie had put the fear of the devil in her. But who would those satanic shit-stirrers be as time went on? And would there be any at all? Had Genie maybe had one or two bad experiences and blown them up to keep her sanity and sense of self, as humans are wont to do? Or was there real trouble ahead?

Becky had no idea, though her mind ran through

endless scenarios of arguing, of tearful submissions and recantations, countless horrors of inappropriate sexual encounters and harassment—though she wasn't as concerned with the latter as the former. She'd fended off plenty of inappropriately aggressive men. That was easy—or had been so far. But what about being asked to do something she really didn't want to do? What about being asked to do something demeaning or ethically questionable?

Illegal.

Genie's talk had done nothing to make Becky feel anything but *more* out of her element. She began to question why she'd won the *stupid contest,* how it was even possible she *had* won, and of course how she felt she had no reasonable expectation that being chosen was the right result for anyone involved, especially her.

By four in the morning, she'd run through what felt like a thousand unpleasant circumstances, none of which ended well for her. She was drained. So, she made a decision. From that moment on, she would do as Genie suggested—or more, *instructed.*

First thing in the morning, she'd buy a notebook and start keeping a journal of everything to happen—every event, interaction—and she'd include her genuine feelings about it all. She made a pledge to herself to be on the lookout for anything that might result in a bad outcome of any kind. Not that she'd necessarily act on those feelings, but she'd be aware and keep a record if she ever needed to.

Mainly, Becky Darnell from just outside Auburn, Indiana, officially now the Sexiest Woman in the World, made a promise to herself. She would not back down no matter what. She would see herself, as Genie had said, as their queen.

No! As my own queen! Yes!

She would demand and receive respect, even if it meant being stripped of her title. What did she care anyway who was or wasn't wearing the actual Sexiest Woman sash? It meant nothing to her own sense of self or wellbeing. It was an honor—maybe—but in no way affected her opinion of herself.

Was she sexy? Sure. Why not? She knew her way around a hot date. She knew because she'd had few complaints and many compliments. So, as Becky's saw it, she was sexy enough. The title added little to her personal cachet.

What it *did* do, if she believed Genie, was open the door to a world of travel opportunities, new ideas and ways of looking at life, and never-anticipated experiences in general. The world would be her new oyster. She was not about to let any of these shallow people with their greedy little claims on her person take anything away from who she was.

Before the contest, she was Becky Darnell; through this coming year, she would continue to be Becky Darnell; and when it was all over, she would still be Becky Darnell. She had no intention of changing anything inside—or outside, for that matter. Makeup and wardrobe, hair and poise, were all surface distractions. She was herself, and nothing and no one was going to change her—not high water or Hell itself.

Becky decided right then, in the middle of the night in Beverly Hills. Nothing about her would ever change. She would be the same Becky at the end of this crazy ride as she'd been before any of it started, and she would defend that position to the bitter end, no matter whose head she had to bite off.

The She Beast had awoken.

Chapter Fifteen

Art Lane felt good for Becky, happy she'd won and would benefit in ways she probably couldn't yet calculate, being new to the pageant scene. But he also worried. Something didn't smell right to his investigative journalist's nose. Though he'd mainly written what most considered to be fluff pieces, like covering beauty pageants, his heart had been in hard journalism since college; but income needs had won out over integrity. He sensed everything was about to change even if he didn't know how.

But first things first.

Art had secured the first post-pageant interview with his favorite subject, and Becky Darnell did not disappoint. She delighted Art with stories about growing up in smalltown Midwest America, how she felt homely for most of her growing up until she reached eleventh grade and "sort of blossomed, I guess. You know: boobs." And she finally lost her baby fat and braces. Her hips filled out and her face thinned down. Her feet stopped growing. Suddenly, boys who had ignored her for years became *interested*.

"Yep," she told Art. "Lost my virginity in the backseat of Barry Lott's father's Ford LTD. At least it was a classic. Or so Mr. Lott said."

She had sex three more times in high school, "Technically."

"Technically?"

"Once in a treehouse. I forget his name. Once in a field out behind the spreader factory" where she would later work. "And then, shall we say, multiple times with John Miller." Which she categorized as, "Generic boyfriend sex with a generic boy with a generic name in his generic teen bedroom when his generic parents weren't home because they both worked generic jobs to meet their mortgage and pay for raising their two-point-five generic kids."

"Two-point-five?"

"Three dogs."

"Ah."

When Art asked whatever happened to John Miller, Becky said, "Married him. Got pregnant twice, had two abortions because kids with him? No thanks. I finally divorced him when he wouldn't stop drinking and hit me. Once. That was all it took for me to rent out my house to get away from it and move back in with my parents for six months." It didn't last long. "I love my parents, but…"

Being an adult, after nine years of marital displeasure, produced a quick need to move on with her life. During her brief stay, she moved up to line foreman at the spreader factory and a better salary. Two years later, she married hubby Number Two. Six years later, she found herself single again, wondering if she'd ever get serious about anyone ever again. She told Art the prospects seemed distant and "scary."

He asked why and she answered, "Men."

After she walked him through her journey to Sexiest Woman in the World and her many doubts along the way, Art concluded the interview by asking how she saw her future. She said, "To be honest, I have no idea. I still can't believe I'm here in the first place. If you'd told me six months ago I'd win, I'd have laughed in your face."

"Now, here you are."

"Here I am."

Tears welled up in her eyes, mostly due to gratitude, as Art saw it. She'd been humbled by the entire experience, unlike the other girls he'd interviewed who expressed anger at not winning or flaunted "sexy" attitudes to reflect their inclusion.

Cleavage.

Only Becky seemed truly humbled at being chosen back in Ohio, not to mention at the big show in LA. Art wondered how long it might last, but he thought if anyone would go unchanged, Becky Darnell had the greatest chance of any.

Finally, he said, "That should give me more than enough for my editor. I'll let her know tonight and get it put together for the weekend. Thanks for spending so much time with me and being so forthcoming."

"You're not going to print all that about losing my virginity in an old Ford, are you?"

"I'll try to work around that part," he promised.

Becky stood and gave him a hug of thanks that lasted much longer than he'd anticipated. It seemed like the most honest hug he'd gotten in ages. It felt good. She said, "Thank you for listening and...being a friend."

Art said he too considered her a friend and looked forward to seeing her again on her "road to success," hopefully interviewing her at the "next big stepping stone, maybe when you get your first TV series."

She laughed, but Art told her he believed she could go as far as she wanted. He had faith in her. She gave her genuine "aw shucks" response, but he assured her he meant it and wished her "all the luck in the world."

What Art *didn't* say lay closer to his heart. He thought he might be falling in love. Already. Not with a sexy winner's persona, but with her average downhome non-LA one. He went so far to think, but not say, how Becky Darnell fit his model of the perfect woman, one he had been cultivating since college, through his own two failed marriages.

He also guessed she would soon be beyond his reach as fame absorbed her; but he'd deal with it when the time came. Now, he had an important article to write.

****

Art Lane didn't tell Becky something else. Though he remained happy for her success and shared her wonderment at winning, some doubts persisted. He had covered a few other pageants and they'd all felt the same—contrived but honest. However, something about this one stood out.

Becky Darnell winning.

No one had seen it coming—not Becky, not Art, not any of the other women, and notably, not the sponsors or judges who had voted one for, four against. Her victory hinged on the support of the viewers at home, online and pay-per-view. Fifty-nine percent had voted for Becky, two times the closest second, Genie. Miss Hawai'i didn't even make the top four despite her alluring, even overt all-around sexiness.

As shock ran around the auditorium when the poll votes were announced, Art was as stunned as anyone but, being a journalist, didn't dwell on his own feelings. Instead, he searched the faces of everyone in the hall to assess their reactions.

Most of the girls onstage showed surprise then "joy" as would be expected and as they had been instructed; though some looked more shocked than others. The judges, who had voted four-one against her, appeared caught off guard but perhaps willing to accept the bad judgement of viewers. Heck, they were paid to run the thing, not be right.

What caught Art's eye, however, was the look on the faces of the many sponsors in the front rows and the wings where he had a view from his side position. All looked dumbfounded, eyes wide, several with falling jaws followed by shared looks of befuddlement—followed by what appeared to be rage. Several raced off to huddle.

Why? Was his publisher's tip correct?

Art Lane came to one conclusion which he later shared with his editor. "Kay," he said over the phone. "Something's rotten in Denmark. I smell a fix gone wrong."

He hated to bring it up, in essence to doubt Becky's win. Sure, he found it delightful and life-affirming. Even funny. He thought Becky was sexy for sure, but not in a "world class" kind of way. "We expect clichés there, Kay. Shoo-ins. Not outliers."

Kayla Folger, culture editor of *Online BuzzList*, agreed. "I trust your instincts on this one, Art. See what you can find out. In the meantime, we'll hold back on putting your article up."

Art protested. "No, no, no. Go ahead and publish it. Everything in it is true as of this point in time. She gave a great interview and was more than honest, I'd say."

"You're saying you don't think she's involved in any hanky-panky with the results."

"I'm sure of it," he said. "If some cheating occurred, I'd bet my career she had nothing to do with it."

"I'd be careful with that," Kayla advised. "Too many careers have been lost by writers who fell in love with their subjects."

"I'm not saying I'm in love, Kay," Art said, feeling pulled in another direction but knowing it was unwise to mention.

"I didn't mean it literally," Kayla said.

"I understand," Art avowed. "But run the article. There's nothing in it I'd be unwilling to defend, should the need arise—which it won't. She's a straightshooter, I'm sure of it."

"If you say so," Kayla said. "I know *you* are. But I'd hate to see this thing turn around on you if you're right about the fix and wrong about her."

"I'll take my chances," Art said. "Because you can bet your ass if I find out this thing is hinky in any way, that's my next piece."

Kayla said, "Okay. But if it *is* the case, don't put yourself in the middle of it by trying to defend your subject—not until you have absolute proof she had nothing to do with any unprincipled behind-the-scenes duplicities."

It sounded harsh, put that way, but Art held his ground and his opinion. "If there is something, like I said, I don't believe she had anything to do with it. But…if she did, you know me, Kay. I'll report it. I won't hold back."

"Okay then," Kayla said. "We'll run it as soon as you send in your polish."

"You'll have it tomorrow night," Art promised.

Art hung up, sat at his computer in front of his article, and the worrying began.

Chapter Sixteen

Unknown to Art or Becky, a secret meeting of sponsors, judges, and a few irate losing contestants who had been pegged for important runner-up spots convened in a twenty-sixth floor hotel suite high above the Las Vegas strip. Emotions ran high.

"What the hell *happened?!*" became the most common highly-charged refrain.

The main organizers claimed they didn't know. Mark Tindell, Amy Siderman, and Jessie Gambor all claimed they had, "No idea!" to which the aggrieved sponsors called, "Bullshit!"

Their notion held that anything so all-encompassing as to "ruin the whole fucking event" had to be a conspiracy so thoroughly all-encompassing as to be known to "every-damn-one" involved. But no one admitted any involvement or knowledge.

The six most aggrieved sponsors represented the companies who had spent the most on originating, convening, supporting, and advertising the event.

"Maybe you shouldn't have licensed it all for nothing," one of the judges noted.

That idea went nowhere when the sponsoring channel's sole rep reported the numbers. "We killed those two hours."

A sponsor hollered, "We came in third!"

"Right. Behind the two top cable news shows. You

beat every other entertainment offering."

"There was nothing else on!"

"Because we ran careful analysis for four months and chose the time slot least likely to have similar or even contrasting content. You won because you followed our advice."

"And now the whole world thinks this nobody from nowhere represents us!"

"She won fair and square."

"Did she?"

What followed was a less-emotional deep-dive into the design and making of the Sexiest Woman pageant, from its *brilliant* inception to unexpected conclusion.

The truth came out.

****

When Becky didn't return to her job at Indiana Littleman Implements, Floyd officially fired her. Since he was both embarrassed and chagrined at having given in to allowing her the time off, he hand-wrote a letter and mailed it to the address they had on record—Becky's first apartment post-community-college—so, it came back.

Not to be dissuaded, and hoping to bolster his self-idealized image of being a tough boss in control, Floyd posted it on the Company News corkboard. Someone took it down by the end of business with no one admitting to the theft. Floyd rightfully suspected Darla, Myrna, Briana, or all three co-conspirators, but had no proof.

He didn't care. He'd made his point. Cross him and receive harsh treatment! Though it seemed unlikely anyone else accepted that posture on his terms. Still, its effect was tangible. Morale plummeted along with proscribed chatter on the line.

Becky's besties showed up every day on time and did their jobs as well as they always had, but their hearts weren't in it. Without Becky's positive ministrations to keep them buoyed on tough days, their will to rise and shine—to joke and kid—diminished over the following weeks to zero. A reality had set in that their best bud Becky Darnell would not be returning any time soon—if at all.

****

Out in Los Angeles and back in New York, sullen pageant sponsors had reluctantly accepted their "loss" and were determined to make the best of a bad situation. They called Becky in for a makeover.

Of course, Becky objected. "I don't wear that much makeup. Ever."

"You do now," a sponsor's *cosmetological* representative declared.

"And why's that?" Becky demanded.

"Because we pay the bills."

The argument proved hard to dispute, because even a smalltown girl like Becky Darnell knew how cash lubed the fast-spinning wheels of success to prevent it all from seizing up—to prevent the benefits from *drying* up. For, though Becky was but a few weeks into her reign, she had already decided she liked the perks. At least enough to ignore the downside, which included trying hard to pretend to be something she was not and had never been. Had never imagined or wanted.

But now she was officially the Sexiest Woman in the World—even if she didn't feel like even *one* of them, much less *the* one. So, each late afternoon, she retired to her plush hotel suite to soak in a hot tub of bubble bath salts and sip a glass or three of white wine. All the fussing over her hair, her lips, her hips, tired her out. Not to mention the two hours of gym in the morning and late afternoon to get her "toned up for the tour."

Becky had never been a gym rat because she didn't like the atmosphere—or the work. She'd been blessed to have a fairly calorie-resistant body with a constant twenty one BMI. Her new *overlords* wanted her squarely at nineteen or less. She told Darla, "If I eat one more plain salad, I'm gonna start bleating at tin cans."

Darla mused, "They can't taste worse than Marcus's burgers," at the bowling alley.

"What I wouldn't give for one of those greasy wonders," Becky opined.

When she asked her new personal trainer why they wanted her BMI so low and what they expected of such a seemingly impossible result, he said, "They want you toned, girl! Hard as a rock but supple as a tulip."

She'd muttered, "Whatever the fuck that means, Cody."

He said, "It means you look soft and sensual but have abs under the thinnest layer of fat we can manage so you could lift a pickup truck with your legs while lying on your back in the mud."

To which Becky kvetched, "And what the fuck does *that* mean? I'm not a frickin' *mule*."

"It means," Cody said with his usual mix of cheery fascism and suppressed rage at skinny weaklings, "ten more sets of crunches, knee raises, planks, and Pallof presses. And before you ask what the fuck are those, let's get you to do twenty."

Between free weights, machine work, cardio, and other "whole body workouts," by the end of each day

Becky was ready to hand in her tiara. But after the wine, the soak, and a phone pep talk from Genie to remind her about the benefits of continuing to wear it, Becky relented and watched some mindless *Real Housewives of Paducah.*

Genie would laugh and predict, "Maybe someday we'll be those battling bitches."

Becky lamented, "Yeah, wow. Definitely gives me something to live for."

But she hung in and, at the end of her fitness month in Hell, felt better about herself, as well as the contest and title. Admiring her progress in the mirror, she told herself, "This could work out."

She'd never had abs before and hadn't felt so good about how she looked in general for a decade—maybe since senior year in high school. "Maybe now I could get Bart Kormley's attention." Bart being the Auburn Boattail's quarterback.

Then she decided, "Aw fuck him. He doesn't deserve this bod. He's probably as fat and bald and boring as Floyd by now."

Her smile carried back into the bedroom where she discovered someone had come in while she was showering and laid out what she supposed was her outfit for the day. "That's new," she said, checking around to make sure she was alone.

Though irritated and hesitant, she doffed the duds and decided, "Not bad." In fact, "Pretty cool." Someone had chosen well for a change.

Becky would never have spent money on such an outfit, even if she could have afforded the designer labels, but she had to admit the fit and finish felt incomparable. "High line stuff," she said, modeling in her mirror. "I like it."

What wasn't to like? Between the specialty lingerie, high-fashion slacks and top, and tasteful accessories, the cumulative price tag had to be equal to her every other week paycheck. "Yep. Not bad."

She strutted in front of the unit's wall of mirrors thinking she looked like a real model. Definitely less trashy than she had imagined. The only part of the ensemble that didn't match, she noticed, was, "Me."

She meant her hairstyle, which her overseers had yet to address, and her face. "No amount of makeup is ever going to make me into Venus di Cleo."

The notion so bothered her she called Genie, who said, "Becky, relax. You're the *sexiest* woman in the world, not the most beautiful."

"Thanks."

"It's not an insult," Genie said. "And hey, most of those women are so beautiful they're inaccessible. So, not sexy. Easy to look at, but not easy to get in the sack. At least they look that way. Of course, if you read their tell-alls, they bang every hot guy on the planet."

"You're not helping."

"Do you want to bang every hot guy on the planet?"

"Some of them. Maybe."

"And you will. Because you're the sexiest women anywhere. You'll see."

"I don't get it, Genie. I mean, under all this…fluff and makeup and these expensive clothes, I'm still little ol' Rebecah Darnell from Bumpinville, Indiana."

"So are we all," Genie said. "A lot of famous people came from small towns no one ever heard of. Big names. Tiny towns. Nobodies until they were somebodies."

"I never knew that—or at least never thought about

it."

"Because you're a normal person," Genie said. "It's what you've got going for you, so quit fighting it. Your looks are your looks and you looked good enough to win. So, quit queefing."

"Queefing? Isn't—"

"Yeah. Hot air from flapping lips."

"I get it."

"Good," Genie said. "So…"

"Quit carping and enjoy my day in the sun."

"That's it, girl. Trust me, *it don't last a lifetime*. Ask my mother."

"Was she a model?"

"She was a pin-up in the Eighties for those softcore man-mags. Then she had me and her tits deflated and abracadabra, no more phone calls. It really depressed her until I discovered I could make her laugh when I was six or so. Then she got over it."

"Was she okay about you modeling?"

"Oh, hell no," Genie said. "But I did it anyway. You might've noticed, I'm a little headstrong. Anyway, she's over it now I'm making money. But she always warns me my day will come and my phone won't ring and it'll be depressing as hell. So at least I have someone to warn me, unlike her."

"And you're passing it along to me."

"Just 'cause I love you, babe," Genie said.

Those words meant a lot to Becky—having someone out on the road who understood some of what she was going through, someone who could say, "I remember that," and commiserate and offer advice. Even if it was gloomy.

"Okay, I'll do my best," she told her glamorous

friend. "But I don't think I can stop thinking I don't deserve it."

"You don't," Genie said.

"What?"

"None of us do, hon. We happen to be a little luckier than some others, is all. Either because God gave us a good-looks gene or we're stronger or more determined or cleverer or more deceitful or whatever it is we exploit to get on top. But you always have to remind yourself, it ain't forever. It never is."

"That's pretty dire," Becky thought.

"It keeps me grounded," Genie said. "That's why I'm telling it to you, so you don't start believing all the lipstick-on-a-pig stuff."

"Genie!"

"I'm not saying you're a pig, girl! I'm saying, and believe me, this is true, that is exactly how these people look at us—every one of us. Sure, they may fawn over this one or that one, but what they really think is they made us what we are. They picked the dress or the jewelry or the makeup or the hairstyle or the hair color, and they made the calls to get us into this or that event, to walk a red carpet here or be seen with a bigger celebrity there. Their little egos require it. They have to believe they're better than us or they'd all hang themselves. They're insecure and they blame us for it. The minute we walk out the door, they bag on us. I've seen it and heard it when they didn't think I knew. So…"

Becky felt pulled in several different directions. "What's your point, Genie? I'm not sure I'm following it all."

"My point is: Don't believe any of it. You're you, you're fabulous, you're beautiful. And you're all that *because* you're you. So, don't forget it. Don't let them convince you you're more, either—something special and irreplaceable—because they don't believe that themselves no matter how sincere they sound or how much flattery they slather on. It's all fake. They hate you."

"Wow."

"Yeah. And the very second you stop making money for them—and by the way in the quantities they want and expect—you're out the door and they're on to the next beautiful sucker. So…"

"Don't be a sucker."

"And don't trust anyone. And I mean *anyone*."

Becky let her thoughts simmer a moment then said, "I know you think that and that I'm green to this and all, but everyone's been supportive to the point of being annoying. I haven't seen any of what you're talking about."

Silence lingered on the other end for longer than Becky would have liked. Finally, Genie said, "You will."

It didn't sound like a part of her prior speech, more like a separate idea—not a warning, but a prediction. Becky was left only with an, "Okay."

After more silence, during which she thought she might have heard Genie sniffling or even crying quietly, Becky said, "I'll heed what you say, Genie. I trust you."

"Yeah well," Genie said. "You shouldn't."

****

Determined to make the best of an odd situation, Becky bucked up. She remembered her father's advice years ago. "Go along to get along," he told her during a rough spot in high school when she butted heads with a mean teacher known for his insults and unfair grading.

169

Becky had made the mistake of standing up for a classmate who had done her best on a test only to be berated by that teacher for several minor mistakes. The girl, Alina Bastos, had brutal periods, but her father made her go to school no matter the flow or pain. On that particular test day, she could barely concentrate, but did well, considering.

Then the teacher, one Simpson Mallers, laid into Alina in front of the class until she fell into tears. Even though Becky didn't know Alina very well, she felt the girl's cruel diminishment and stood up to the brute, literally.

"Ms. Darnell. You have something to say in front of the whole class?" He had a way of cutting kids off at the knees by using his old Marine training akin to getting everyone else to attack the offender in their bunk. This time, it didn't work.

Becky remained standing and said, "Yes, I do, Mr. Mallers. Alina suffers from Dysmenorrhea, and I think it's inappropriate to pick on her while she's sick."

Mallers scoffed. "What is that? Some made-up something?"

"Not at all. It's a real condition."

"Well, I've never heard of it."

"Of course you haven't. You're a man. If you like, I can go ask Ms. Primm to come in and explain it." Primm was their biology teacher. Becky added, "Or I can explain if you like."

Mallers snorted a small laugh, clearly meant to demean, and said, "Pray enlighten us, Ms. Darnell, about this…awful medical condition that caused your classmate to flub her quiz so badly I thought perhaps she wasn't an American citizen."

"Number one," Becky said, "that's racist and xenophobic. You know full-well Alina is of Hispanic descent—third generation American as I recall from our first day introductions. I'd suggest you take your slur back before I call the principal in to hear you repeat it."

Mallers was taken aback. But rather than apologize, he said, "Go on. You mentioned a medical condition. What could it possibly be?"

"Cramping from menstrual periods. It happens when your uterus contracts to shed its lining and could be a warning sign for endometriosis. Which, in case you don't know that either, is when tissue that lines your uterus grows *outside* your uterus. It then breaks apart at the end of your cycle and causes more bleeding and pain and—"

"That's enough, Ms. Darnell. I get your point," Mallers said. "Though I have to wonder how you knew about it, yourself."

"I looked it up," Becky said plainly. "And saved you the effort."

"Well," he said snarkily, "I thank you for that."

"You can thank me by giving Alina a passing grade."

She looked over to see poor, shy Alina looking down and shaking her head no. But Becky told her, "You deserve it."

Then she looked back at their teacher and said, still referring to Alina, "And you don't deserve to be made fun of for having a serious medical condition that can lead to infertility later in life."

When Mallers didn't respond—but looked unsettled—Becky offered a solution. "How about this? Let her take the test again when she feels better, since she really shouldn't have been here today to begin with. Not that any *male* could understand."

Mallers squirmed. Becky could see it. So, it was time to use her father's advice. "You can give a slightly different test, so you don't have to worry about her cheating by remembering this one. That should make everyone happy. Even Ms. Childers."

Evelyn Childers, the female principal.

Though Mallers probably didn't want to give Alina Bastos a retest and was not happy about being called out by a student, he said, "Ms. Bastos, see me after class and we'll work something out for when…you feel better."

Alina said, "Thank you, Mr. Mallers. I'll do better on it, I promise."

"Well," was all he added.

Alina then mouthed *Thank You* at Becky who smiled then turned forward. "Sorry for the interruption, Mr. Mallers, I thought you might like to know the facts, as difficult as they are to digest."

She sat down.

After class, Becky lingered to further her father's "Go along to get along" philosophy, telling her gruff teacher, "I'm sorry to have caused a stir, Mr. Mallers. It wasn't my intention. I merely grieved for poor Alina. I could tell she was too weak to mention it, herself—and probably too embarrassed. You can understand that, it being a female issue."

Her male teacher looked queasy, as anticipated. So, she embellished. "I've had some really bad periods myself. Bled like a stuck pig, I swear. All down m—"

"Okay!" Mallers nearly shouted. "That's…I get the picture."

"Oh, it's awful being a woman, Mr. Mallers. If you

172

were married, I'm sure you'd be hearing about it all the time."

It was a well-known fact that the ornery Mallers had recently gone through a loud and dramatic divorce because his ex-wife had come to the school with a deputy to have divorce papers served during class. Rumor had it he'd been ducking the servers—which she let everyone know in a hollering fit in front of his fifth period class.

Becky finished her calculated toadying by offering, "If there's anything else I can do for you, Mr. Mallers, you know, regarding these intimate female problems that are often difficult for the male species to think about, you let me know. I'm here to help." She smiled large.

He seemed defeated. "That won't be…it's fine. Thank you, Ms. Darnell. You can go, now."

"Okay," Becky said, as chirpily as she could. "Thanks for your understanding. Alina won't let you down!" She grinned wide at Alina who seemed to be having trouble not laughing.

Finally, Becky said, "Seriously, anything you need, just call. I'm there for you!" With a last jaunty wave, she left—and later heard Alina aced her retest.

Mallers never bothered either girl again, and Becky learned a valuable lesson about lessons. They are meant to be taken literally, and often require some massaging to get right and make them work well.

So, when faced with a group of contest sponsors who still seemed frosty towards her, Becky knew what to do. "Brown-nose the fuck out of them," she told Genie.

"That's the spirit!" Genie encouraged. "And take them for all they're worth—every outfit, tube of toner, box of lashes, everything. And most important of all, every last dime you can get your hands on. You will never regret it."

Becky had to admit, the approach was sounding better all the time. They might fire her the next week or month or *hour*! But by God, in the meantime, she was going to milk it for all it was worth, and have a damn good time doing it.

Go along to get along, indeed.

Chapter Seventeen

Art Lane let the initial hubbub die down before asking Becky out on a "formal" date. She asked, "Formal?"

He said, "I expect a gown."

She said, "Well, you're not gonna get one. I had to give it back."

"Aw, crap. Then we better call it off."

"Fine by me."

He knew she was kidding, and the date went well. Becky even noted that she had never enjoyed a Louie's Pastaporium so much.

Over garlic rolls and salad, he said, "I thought you were kidding about coming here."

"Me kid? About food? Never."

"You don't look it."

"Thanks," she said. "And don't tell the pageant fascists I had anything more than water and a saltine."

"My lips are sealed. What about the wine?"

She held up her glass. "This swill? I don't think it counts."

"It shouldn't," he agreed, sampled a sip, and lowered his glass to the table.

"So," he said. "How's it going?"

"It's going," she said.

"Are they driving you crazy yet?"

"They were before I won. Now, it's off the charts."

"You could always forfeit your title."

"Are you kidding?" Becky said. "And miss out on all those free exercise programs and poise lessons and fancy underwear fittings where everything is two sizes too small? Telling me what to say and think? Nope. Wouldn't miss it for the world."

Art pointed out, "You don't seem overly stressed by it."

"Actually, you know what?" Becky said, leaning in and lowering her voice. "I'm having the time of my life. I've never had anyone fuss over me like this since nursery school. I kinda like it."

"Better than the manure factory, huh?"

"Manure *spreader* factory, thank you very much," she said, leaning back. "And no, except for my friends, I don't miss it for a second. Granted, it was easy— knowing what I'd be doing every day and then doing it. But…"

Becky stared off a moment, then looked back. "I guess I never realized how boring it was. How bored I was. How boring *I* was."

"I don't think you're boring," Art encouraged.

"You didn't have to follow me around the plant or home to my microwave dinners or to the bowling alley for 'beer and burgers' every weekend like clockwork. I guess I never realized because I was so used to it and caught up in my routines. But it was shit, Art. Pure shit. Nothing to it, boring as hell, nothing to look forward to, nothing different. The same old shit week in and week out for fifteen shitty years.

"This whole thing now is like a whole new me. They've given me permission to be someone completely different. To not be plain old boring Becky Darnell from

Hicksville, Indiana. I'm...I don't know...someone now. I'm *someone*."

Art wasn't sure he felt good about what he was hearing, but he decided being supportive was better than giving a lecture. "Well, that's great, then. I'm glad you're happy."

"I'm more than happy, I'm elated. Delirious. I don't ever want to go back to that life there. Ever."

"Already?" Art said, careful to keep his doubts hidden. "That didn't take long."

"Why would it?" Becky said. "This is like the greatest opportunity a person could ever have in my position. I clearly don't deserve it. But here I am. It's awesome."

She dug into her endless salad with gusto.

Art watched her eat and thought how without all the contest *hoopla* on her, Becky Darnell was the prettiest woman he'd ever known. But he also thought she was right. She probably didn't deserve it. The rumors he'd heard could very likely be true. It pained him to think he might uncover some dark truth she hadn't been meant to win—and if he did, how could he ever tell her? It would break her heart.

Wouldn't it?

****

As Becky saw it, she had behaved herself and eaten salad—along with three breadsticks, shrimp scampi, and half of Art's tiramisu. Then she excused herself to the ladies' room where she stuck her fingers down her throat until she barfed the whole meal into a toilet. Damned if she was going to show up to her morning weigh-in lugging even one new pound. It wasn't worth the humiliation from Cody.

When she returned to the table, Art noted, "That was fast."

"Quick pee," she lied.

"So, shall we order anything else or…"

"Let's hit the road," she said and reached for her purse.

"I got this," Art said.

"No way," Becky said. "With what they're paying me?"

Art said, "It's on my expense account. I can write it off."

"Oh," she said. "How?"

"Part of getting to know you better for a longer profile."

Becky felt offense. "So, this wasn't a date? You were *profiling* me?"

"No, it was a date. But why not have my editor pay for it?"

Becky's pique didn't leave immediately. "As long as you don't repeat anything I said here in any articles."

"I can't promise. You said some charming stuff."

He threw her a *charming* smile that didn't sit well. She said, "I don't know what that could possibly have been, but…as long as it isn't…"

"Isn't what?"

"I don't know," Becky admitted with some irritation. "But this whole being in a spotlight thing is gonna take some getting used to."

Art reached over and took her hand. "Rebecah. Becky. This is a date. This isn't an interview or a profile. I'll let you know when it is so you can be more oblique and political. I promise."

"I don't think I know how to do that."

"You will," he said. "In the meantime, shall we go for a drink, or should I just invite you over to see my etchings?"

"You have etchings?" she said with a wince. "Of what?"

"I was just…that old stupid pickup line. But I do have a nice Leory Nieman of Melrose Avenue."

"Oh," she said—trying to decide.

"Or we can go back to your room if you like," he offered.

"No, they watch it like hawks. Owls at night."

"So?"

"Are you suggesting, I don't know, hooking up?"

"I am," he said. "Did I mess it up?"

Becky had mixed feelings. For some reason she couldn't isolate—even though she had hoped for, even planned on, having sex because it had been way too long—at that moment, she felt detached from lust. In a way, detached from her own body. She knew she might regret it later, but erred on the side of caution. "If it's okay, maybe not tonight."

"I did blow it," Art said, retrieving his hand.

Becky said, "No. I don't know. Maybe. It's…"

"Please don't say it's you not me," he said somewhat pitifully—and possibly vexed.

"Okay, but yeah it is," she said, and debated sharing the inner conversation she'd been having with herself. But she chose a different tack. She reached across the table. "Give me your hand back. Come on." She gave as honest a smile as she could muster.

He took her hand, if somewhat reluctantly it seemed.

"Look, Art. I think you're terrific."

"And I think you're terrific."

"I know you do," Becky said. "But your…praise might be misplaced."

"I don't think so."

"I'm not all that, really," she said. "Just a little country girl at heart who got lucky out of the blue with something everyone, including you, is saying will change my life. Honestly, I don't know if I'm ready for a *life change*. I mean, I am, but…I'm not. Maybe."

"I think you're handling it very well and you'll continue to handle it very well and…I'd like to stick around and be a part of it. If you'll have me."

Becky winced. "Ooo. See? I don't think…that. It's all too new, too weird. I mean, I hear you saying it and…by the way, I had planned on us hooking up. I did. But when it got time for it…I don't know. I froze up inside. I don't know why."

"I do," Art said. Becky cringed, pretty sure she didn't want to hear his reasoning. But he said, "You're scared and you don't know who to trust."

Becky let those words sink in a moment then nodded. "Yeah."

"That's normal and it's fine," Art said. "I can wait." He gave her hand a squeeze and took his back.

She said, "You may not want to after this thing gets wound up. I have no idea where it's going."

"Wherever it is," Art said, "I think you'll be fine." He smiled and nodded.

"You're very sweet," she said. Then she blew out a sigh and said, "Now that we got that out of the way, what do you say we go back to your house and fuck like teenagers?"

He grinned and said, "Sounds good to me."

****

Becky Darnell left her reluctance at the Pastaporium and enjoyed two hours of the best sex she could remember having in a very long time. Maybe forever. Art was gentle when she wanted him to be, forceful when she craved it, and funny when a position or odd result begged for a joke. All in all, a hopping success.

After, he offered to take her back to her hotel suite, but she said she wanted to go on her own, to "savor this night." She said, "I can see myself smiling all the way back."

Which was exactly what happened after the two new lovers shared what felt to her like a delightfully honest long kiss on the sidewalk. Then she climbed in the cab, waved with a smile—and never looked back.

Chapter Eighteen

Over the next two months, both Becky and Art did a lot of traveling: Becky for model shoots, guest appearances on lesser-known television shows, and supermarket openings; Art for a superseding assignment covering meat packing plant violations. He missed his other "soft" assignments almost as much as he missed Becky.

He had not planned on falling in love, especially with a beauty pageant contestant, much less a winner. That was odd enough, but Sexiest Woman in the World? The whole thing felt surreal. He confided on phone calls—when he could catch her at night before lights-out—that their sexual escapade had been his most gratifying as well.

Privately, he still couldn't wrap his head around it being Becky for several reasons. He was a Southern California guy through and through; she was essentially a Midwest farm girl. He was a writer whose articles often ended up buried in the back of mediocre magazines; she was a pageant winner who had already graced the covers of three second-tier fashion magazines with rumors she would soon be featured in the top two—maybe on the cover. He watched talk shows and found she was already *on* them. Apparently, the late night hosts had called her personally.

But why? Why any of it?

Sure, Art thought Becky was terrific, because she had struck him as real and humble, self-aware of her smalltown presence, if not her overwhelming charm. But that all added to her appeal for him. She had surprised everyone, it seemed in recall, how she answered every question in an offbeat, unexpected, yet thoroughly appealing way. Honest. She made being sexy seem not lurid or pathetic but wholesome. No one else had done that. And she *won*.

So, Art Lane, sophisticated, worldly writer he imagined himself to be, came to one dark inescapable journalistic conclusion: Something really *was* rotten in Denmark. Which meant he had to do his journalistic duty and out someone. Whoever it was.

When he had time, Art put out feelers, hoping to hear some backroom gossip about what actually might have happened, but no one stepped up to the plate. Some of the losing girls still had harsh things to say about the contest and Becky's win—Art expected that—but none had confirmation of anything nefarious.

"Sour grapes," as he told his editor.

On the wild chance one of the sponsors or organizers might let something leak—maybe they too had gotten a bad result—Art made it a point to reach out to at least one of them every few days. But after a while, they got onto him and stopped taking his calls.

He knew this was the case when one of them said, "You're that writer trying to make us look bad. Fuck off." She hung up. Starting the next day, not a single one of the group picked up. Word had gotten around.

As Art put it to his editor, "I ran aground."

"It's a dead story," Kayla told him. "Focus on the meat."

Art joked, "I thought that's what I was doing."

"Ha," she said. "Don't let any of the models hear you say that."

"I don't plan on it," Art assured her. Then he noted, "At least some of them will still talk to me."

"Dead story," his editor reiterated.

"Got it."

Art let it go for the moment, but his reporter's sixth sense continued to nag at him that something was wrong—had been wrong—with the pageant. He felt conflicted when talking to Becky, careful never to mention his lingering doubts while continuing to support her victory and resultant happy ride. After all, this was the biggest thing that had ever happened to her. Why spoil it?

Why? Because he couldn't let it go!

But a Nebraska meatpacking plant beckoned like tartar sirens, so he put his qualms aside, flew to Omaha and picked up his rental sedan. He would be shocked to learn the plant in question had some twenty-six children under the age of fourteen working on dangerous slicing lines and cleaning bloody floors.

By the end of the year, his piece would win an award. But he never stopped thinking about that damned Sexiest Woman contest and what had eluded him, what improprieties, what unfair voting practices, and his beloved tainted *winner*.

****

Becky Darnell settled into her new routine and even came to enjoy it. Sure, some of the makeup people seemed rude, as if they didn't think she should *be* the Sexiest Woman in the World, but they never said anything aloud, so she didn't either. Still, that off-scent lingered—the odor of doubt and disrespect.

One day, while getting *prepared* for a county fair appearance in Arkansas, an assistant to someone said, "I think it's so great someone normal like you won the title."

It hit Becky wrong. "What do you mean 'normal'?"

"You know, not all glamorous and all. More…average like me."

Becky snapped, "Honey, I am not like you in any way, shape, or form, and you will never be like me. So, stop talking and do my makeup."

It was out of her mouth before she heard it.

The girl stared, clearly shocked—then started to cry. The sight took Becky aback some, and she said, "I'm sorry. That came out wrong. I didn't mean it that way."

"Yes, you did!" the girl cried. "You think you're better than me. Than us. Better than anyone!"

"Not *anyone*," Becky said, lamely.

"Well, you're not," the girl wailed. "You were like us and now you're not!" She trotted off to tend to her tears elsewhere. "I quit! I'm done with this bullshit. With *your* bullshit! Asshole bitch!"

Becky felt…relief. She thought, *When you're right, you're right.* She *did* feel better than the girl. *I won the damn contest, didn't I? That makes me better, doesn't it? You're damn right it does. It wasn't easy. I had to work for it, and I'm still working for it, and I deserve every bit of everything I got and am getting. This shit isn't easy!*

She called out, "You think I like coming to these damn stupid state fairs? I never went to them at *home*! They're stupid! This whole damn thing's stupid!"

Becky stood up from her makeup chair and told her government liaison, "I'm outa here. I'm not doing this."

She tore off her makeup bib and started for the door.

The matron said, "You can't walk out. There's a contract."

"Well, I didn't sign it!"

"But your organization did."

"Then have them come and parade around in this stupid dress with the Biggest Hog of the Year and the rest of this ridiculous crap. State fair. Jesus."

Becky walked out of the makeup trailer, told her driver, "We're done here," and got in the van.

The kid said, "But you didn't do anything yet."

"And I'm not going to," Becky told him. "Let's go."

He looked around, apparently feeling helpless, and said, "I don't think—"

"Good. And don't start," Becky said sharply. "Now, let's go before I smell any more cow shit and think I'm back home."

She slammed the door herself and sat in the back, arms folded across her chest, stewing mad. Boy, was she going to tell off *those contest assholes*.

****

Boy, did they tell *her* off.

"Who do you think you are!"

"Do not *ever* do that again!"

"You have a contract and you will abide by it!"

"In case you don't understand, you will do what you're told. Period!"

"You will write a full letter of apology and hand deliver it to the governor!"

"If you ever pull something like that again, your crown will be stripped!"

"You will never work in this industry again!"

Becky faced the red-faced group of sponsors and

said, calmly, "You apparently haven't seen my media numbers."

"What about them?"

"Every time I go on the radio or TV or do a podcast, their ratings go up. Way up."

"So?"

"So, they want me on there. I make money for them. I'm making money for you. Everyone's making money off me but me."

A sponsor looked shocked. "You'll earn close to two-hundred thousand dollars by the year's end!"

"And how much will you earn? How many teddies and bras and fucking 'invisible girdles' will you sell because people see me and hear me, and they *relate* to me?"

A nasty sponsor said, "They relate to anyone in the outfits we provide with a tiara on their head."

"No. They wouldn't," Becky said, remembering the poor crying girl at the fair. "These people, the people out there watching and listening, they like me because I represent them, not some phonied-up floozy they can never emulate. Just little ol' Midwest me who never should have won this stupid contest to begin with! Now, I'm your cash cow. Hmm?"

She mad-dogged the sponsors who went quiet.

"Uh-huh," Becky said, surmising their supposed guilt. "You guys put me in here to take advantage of all that. Skipped over Genie Vintier and Miami and Miss Hawai'i, whatever her name was, to pick me because I'm so plain and so boring so you can sell more sexy bullshit to the vast majority of women in this country who look more like me than them!"

Again, the sponsors stood still and voiced no

objections.

"I was your ace in the hole all along, wasn't I? Boring me. Well, let me tell you something, I see what you did. And I am not doing these ridiculous Podunk appearances anymore. You want me out there shilling for you? Then get me better gigs. I'll do all I'm supposed to do—play up the downhome 'You can be just like me, girls' crap, and get them to buy whatever ridiculous junk you're pawning off on them.

"But know this: I'm onto you. So, don't fuck with me or I'll bring this whole little crooked enterprise down around you. Then I'll sue you for everything I can get for emotional duress, physical injuries from wearing these damn high heels everywhere and having diarrhea from all the damned salads you make me eat. Not to mention the lost income I won't make because you keep me on a 'tight leash'—your words—and prohibit me from profiting any other way. The list is long, I'm sure. Ask your attorneys."

When the sponsors had no response other than to turn redder, Becky finished up her threatening rant, sure that Genie would have been proud of her taking a stand.

"You knew exactly what you were doing, who you were exploiting, who you were conning and fooling, who you lied to—like your entire viewing audience. Well, congratulations. It worked. I am now a household word. Like some kind of movie star. Who knew? I didn't see it coming, I guarantee. But you did. So…*here we are*."

Silence fell over the suite as the sponsors stewed, speechless—until it broke.

One of the sponsors, an older woman with too much makeup for the number of wrinkles around her tight mouth said, "No."

Becky said, "No?" making sure to sound incredulous.

"You have it wrong, dear," the matron said. "But, as you point out, we are here, and we plan to remain here. We will have a meeting, and I imagine we will agree to limit your, shall we say, lesser appearances. You have proven to be an asset we had not imagined. That said, be careful what you wish for—and what you say."

Becky was surprised by the woman's words, but claimed, "I've said it all."

"Let's hope so," the woman said, steelier than Becky had expected. Then the entourage walked out of the room, leaving Becky with her thoughts—and a middle-aged black woman who emerged from the bedroom.

Becky said, "Were you in there all this time?"

The maid nodded and said, "You laid it down."

Becky grinned. "I did."

The maid said, "You mind if I give you some advice?"

"I suppose not," Becky said cautiously.

"That bunch'a white people there? They're dangerous. Don't matter you white, too. That type don't care about race or color. All they care about is money and power. You take away one iota that, and you better run for the hills."

Becky thought about the sponsors' silence and said, "I think I'll be fine. But thank you."

The black woman said, "Mm-hmm," and started for the door. "I turned your bed down for you."

"Thank you."

"You're welcome."

She left and Becky never saw her again. But she never forgot the warning.

Chapter Nineteen

Two more months ground past to find Becky having lost all patience—with everyone. Even Art. "You need to stop calling me so much, Art. I'm super busy. I have to plan for my next appearance, get a good night's sleep, and deal with this endless stream of toadies and hangers-on. I ask for something, I get something else, usually with some rude sass. I swear, I haven't seen a professional in months."

Art pointed out, "You've only been *at* this for months."

"You see? Even you. I gotta go."

Rather than wait to hear his *whining response*, Becky hung up and went to soak in her suite's jetted tub before her masseur arrived. She liked it that he was a little handsy.

Her rant two months back seemed to have worked well—no more bookings at fairs or store openings. Then she arrived at one for an auto dealership and refused to get out of the van—until she learned she might be eligible for a free car—which turned out to be a used hatchback with "favorable lease rates." She screamed into her phone for a good five minutes, again threatening to out the organizers or quit. Not that she had any intention of leaving. She was having too much fun—when she wasn't complaining.

Being from a small town where everyone treated

everyone else with respect but no overt deference, getting waited on hand and foot had come to suit Becky. In one of her last regular calls to Art, she told him she'd "finally trained these people."

He asked what she meant, and she told him. "No more threats, no more lousy bookings, no more people looking down their noses at me. I demanded respect and I got it. These greedy bastards are making money hand over foot because of me. Every one of them is showing increased sales and profits, some by fifty percent or more. So, they won't be disrespecting me anymore or I'll—"

She caught herself. One thing she didn't need was to tell a reporter how she had accused them of making the contest go her way so they could make a princess out of a stable girl and sell more of their *sex crap* to the unsuspecting masses.

Art had said, "Or you'll what?"

"Nothing," she demurred. "It all worked out. Anyway, I have to go. The girl's coming up for a mani-pedi in ten. Ciao!"

Becky had become accustomed to weekly mani-pedis, nightly massages if she asked for them, hair color and trim weekly, and the rest. She'd demanded that her outfits be changed before every outing so as not to repeat. She told her wardrober, "You'd think they'd know. Nobody wants to see me in the same thing twice. I'm not a damn gameshow card flipper. Even Vanna gets a new dress now and then."

The wardrobe woman said, "Yes, ma'am," and went scrounging for something different. It seemed everyone had received notice that Becky Darnell who had decided she needed to be called Ms. Darnell or at least Rebecah when not onstage—their *star* Sexiest Woman—was to be treated like royalty, *or else*.

If anyone had expressed ire at her requests, Becky had not heard them. She rationalized how she likely *wouldn't* due to the nature of the situation, but it didn't bother her. She told Genie in a rare catchup call, "They can say whatever they like behind my back. I don't care. I'm used to it. I had two husbands talking shit all the time and dumped them like the dumb jocks they were. This is my show now and I'm running with a full head of steam, damn the torpedoes. Like you said."

Genie said, "I don't think I meant it quite that way. But as long as they're treating you better and you're happy, then I guess it's all working out. Anyway, I need to go. I'm doing a pageant this weekend in Bangkok."

"What's it for?"

"I don't remember. But I get two weeks in Thailand. Phuket, baby."

"Yeah, fuck it," Becky said. "Fuck all these assholes."

"No," Genie said, and repeated, clearly. "Phuket. It's a province in the south. Beautiful beaches and mountains. It's gorgeous."

"Oh," Becky said, making sure she sounded indifferent. "Have fun, I guess."

"Oh, I will," Genie said. Then she asked, "Are you okay, Becks?"

"Yeah, don't call me that," Becky said. "I never liked it."

"Okay, hon," Genie said, sounding icier. "Then, uh…we'll catch up." She hung up.

Becky said, "*G'bye*," sarcastically to her phone and threw it on the bed. Then she sulked. "Everyone. Every single one of them. All the same. I get a little fire, outshine them, and suddenly I'm the bad guy. Well, fuck them. *Fuck it*!" she repeated as mockery.

Then she said it correctly. "Phu*ket*." But it tasted bad in her mouth. "Who wants to go all the way to Thailand anyway. We have beaches here."

The bad taste continued—which reminded her. "I need a drink."

****

Becky Darnell grew up around alcohol, a central aspect of small town Indiana culture where bars stayed filled in winter when there was nothing else to do—and summer, because by May, boozing was a happy habit. She had never let it get out of hand except during those difficult post-divorce times; and even then, she managed to keep her drinking in check.

But the stress of being on the road with no one she felt she could trust, no one she liked, along with the grueling schedule, the fawning sycophants and *jealous bitches* everywhere she went, the strict diet—"No Beer Under Any Circumstance Unless Part of an Ad Campaign," her instructions read—night flights that left her wondering where she'd landed, vans with black-out windows that made it impossible to tell at night, and the rest that came with being "in demand," all led Becky back to vodka.

Sometimes, when the booze started to kick in, she'd think about home and miss her pals Darla, Briana, and Myrna. Even Floyd on occasion. But by the bottom of the third *installment*, she'd forgotten them and moved on to her growing state of resentment. The whole thing felt like a dog and pony show and she was both the pony *and* the dog.

It didn't seem fair. Everyone else in every town got to go home to their families, their friends, and their nice little apartments and houses, while Becky got to ride in another blacked-out SUV to the airport to be shuttled off to somewhere else that, because she only got to see it in the context of her Sexiest Woman representation, looked like every other place. With each new town, she felt more alienated—from her past and even her present. Hell, all of America. She felt like a damned traveling *migrant*.

She also felt more and more put upon as the sponsors and writers and TV hosts demanded more of her time, more of her energy, more of her soul. It all made her angry and resentful. But it also forced her to demand more of herself, to perform more and be better— to be more of what people expected of the Sexiest Woman in the World.

Whatever the fuck that is.

In doing all of it, Becky Darnell felt simultaneously demeaned and worshipped. To be reduced to a mobile sex object, further objectified by her hyper-sexualized looks, but be raised on a kind of celebrity pedestal at the same time was both confusing and invigorating—when it wasn't enervating.

In the end, that being the close of nearly every day and night, she was exhausted, mentally and physically, while at the same time convinced she had become *The best me I've ever been*. She saw it as what they were paying for—to see Rebecah Darnell, small town sex goddess, take a stage or smile on a page, showing confidence and glee, even when she didn't feel like it. Being all they wanted and expected her to be.

Genie had told her, "That's the biz, hon. It's what we do, what we get paid for. Keep that perspective and you'll go far. Forget it and you'll crash."

That may have been true for Genie Vintier, but for Becky Darnell, it meant hating herself every night, then arguing with herself, then having a few drinks to beat down those negative feelings, then building herself back up, even if it meant looking into a mirror and slurring to herself how she deserved every bit of praise, every moment in the spotlight, every charge on the sponsors' credit cards.

"You're damn right I'm worth it," she would tell herself every night. "Damn worth it."

Sometimes she would go so far as to advise herself: "I was born for this shit. Fuck all those naysayers. What do they know? I won, didn't I? I'm here, aren't I?"

This would often be followed by a laugh. "Yeah, you idiots fixed it for me to win when I didn't expect it, didn't want it. Then you made me *be* it so you could sell all your sexy crap to suckers all over the world. Hell, I'd'a been one of those suckers if I saw wholesome me all dolled up and some phony TV guy telling everyone how 'authentic' I am, and how I'm a 'role model for women everywhere.' What total bullshit."

Becky would slug some more vodka and tell her mirror image, "You know why it's bullshit, Mr. Late Night Fucking Emmy Award Winner? Because I *am* hot. It's not an act like yours. I'm the real deal. The sexy MILF with no kids. Which, by the way, makes me way sexier than some damn mom with screaming kids in the backseat, right?"

Cue stage laugh.

Becky often asked herself questions so she could give herself answers she wanted to hear—the one that lifted her up, eased her conscience, and made it possible for her to finish off her last glass of clear fortitude with a laugh and turn out the light. Otherwise, she wouldn't sleep a wink.

Chapter Twenty

Becky might have been believing her own press, even though she knew it was reputed to be a bad thing. But so were the press believing themselves. During the first four months of her reign as Sexiest Woman in the World, via Auburn, Indiana, media coverage of Becky had gone from doubtful to amused to fawning. No longer did they write her up as the unlikely face of lust but rather the "new look of sexy." For a reason.

Sponsor companies initially less than thrilled with her victory began noticing their numbers rising. Sales of products pushed by Becky in ads in magazines and streaming platforms had begun to climb. About the time Becky began to see herself as a sex icon, so did her sponsors.

Money talked.

Whether her new accolades came as a result of advertisers reporting increased sales numbers or the reverse, Becky had captured the sexy imaginations of women everywhere—not just in Indiana, South Carolina, or California, but all over the world. Women in Europe and India had started buying the products she plugged and claimed to use. Only Japan, forever enthralled with younger demographics, remained flat.

The sponsors didn't care. Becky Darnell continued to generate revenue wherever she went, whatever she pitched or wore no matter the venue. As for the bottom line, on all fronts, Becky, the doubted contest queen, had become a selling machine. A true winner.

Once the sponsoring companies realized and then understood, they changed their tune. They stopped bullying and haranguing and began heaping praise on Becky in person as well as in their own interviews. They *got* it.

No one walked.

"Becky Darnell represents every woman in America, real women, not high-fashion models and celebrities. She is the collective *us*," a less-than-attractive corporate woman told reporters in an "exclusive" interview. "She has given every day, average women permission to be the sexiest we can be while still being ourselves."

Another claimed, "We don't need to be glamorous or even *strive* to be glamorous. We can all relax and be ourselves—don these apparels and treat ourselves to these products with confidence because we know we are sexy and terrific because of who we are underneath them: ourselves!"

A third said, "We are merely enhancing who we truly are. We longer need to try to be sexy. Becky Darnell has shown us we *are* sexy, deep inside where it starts and where it matters. Everything else is window dressing."

Said the corporate booster selling that window dressing with a knowing smile.

But everyone everywhere picked up on the real message that anyone anywhere could be the sexiest woman in *their* world. It didn't matter where they lived, where they came from, what they did for a living, or how they looked. Every woman everywhere was fine the way she was, which proved to be a strong message of empowerment.

Becky didn't see it that way.

"It sounds like they're saying I'm a dog," she complained to Genie one night.

Genie said, "I hear what you're saying, but I don't think anyone outside the business is taking it that way. I think you've made a real difference."

"Yeah, outside the business," Becky said sourly. "Inside? They think I'm homely."

"Who cares?" Genie said.

"I care!" Becky shot back.

"Becky, you're making good money off your average looks. Don't rock the boat."

"Gee thanks, Genie."

"I'm not saying anything you haven't said about yourself."

"Well, that was before I realized I have something. Something special. Yeah. That's what's selling all this merchandise. Not my fucking 'average look.' It's my special purpose."

"Yeah, I remember a movie where a guy had one of those."

"What was it?"

"His dick."

"All right," Becky said, rising from her plush king bed at the Waldorf. "I have to go. "I'm doing *'America's Top-Rated Morning Show'* tomorrow." She made it sound silly.

Genie said, with obvious surprise and reverence, "You mean—"

"Yeah, whatever. Doesn't matter."

"I…no," Genie said, though Becky didn't think she meant it.

"I know what you're thinking, Genie. You think I'm not up to it. That this is the biggest interview I've done and I don't deserve it."

"I didn't say that."

"But you were thinking it. Because of my boring plain face."

Genie sighed on the other end. "Beck, listen to me."

"I told you not to call me that. And don't be condescending. I worked hard to get here."

"Yeah, for what, six months? I've been doing this since I was three and I've never been asked to do a morning show."

"Well, maybe you should think about doing something else."

Becky heard a long silence and couldn't decide if it came from shock, fear, anger, or harsh reality. Then Genie said, "I thought you said you had to go."

Becky said, "Don't be a bitch. I'm just—"

Genie hung up on her.

Becky shouted at her phone, "Really? Fuck you, Genie!" and threw her phone on the bed. "Bitch!"

Then she saw her bottle of clear liquid remorse remover.

****

Though the morning show makeup guy had some thinly-veiled comments about the bags under Becky's eyes the next morning, he managed to cover them well and make her look, as Becky saw herself, more like a movie star-sized celebrity than a near-farm girl from the Heartland—which suited her fine.

The interview went well. She'd learned to relax in high-pressure situations and project an air of "easy confidence" as the magazines claimed.

She talked about Indiana, the Midwest, her "normal" friends back home, her old job at the spreader plant. A guest celebrity host asked if she missed it. Becky said, "Hicksville? Hell no! Not a bit of it!" to roars of approval from…somewhere. Which delighted her and justified her presence.

Becky had never thought she'd have anything to do with TV except watching it, much less being on the other side of the screen as a *celebrity*. As far as she was concerned, she'd entered the Pearly Gates—and felt right at home. To Hell with anyone who didn't agree.

****

Becky's phone rang as she climbed into her limo. She saw it was Darla and almost didn't answer. But then, figuring Darla and the girls were probably calling to gush over her appearance on *the most popular morning show in the world*, Becky answered. "Hey, girls."

Briana said, "What the fuck was that 'Hell no' bullshit, Rebecah? That ain't what you been tellin' us! How you miss us and everyone at the plant and even Floyd and what the hell is that shit?!"

Taken aback, Becky said, "You don't have to go all angry black girl on me, Briana. And why are you on Darla's phone?"

"It don't matter and don't you 'black girl' me, Miss Becky Whiter Than White Ingrate. All we done for you? All that cheerin' and breakin' our fuckin' backs to make sure you got where you had to be and won that stupid-ass piddly contest bullshit. You better watch it!"

Becky…laughed.

"What was that?" Briana said sharply. "Did you just *laugh* at me?"

"No," Becky lied. "Not at you. At…you know, what

you said."

"What the fuck is funny about anything I said? Have you lost your fucking mind out there in TV celebrity land?"

"Okay!" Becky blurted. "I get your point, but—"

"No! I don't think you do," Briana said. "Or you wouldn't'a just said 'but.' "

Becky claimed, "I was going to say: But I'm here at the Waldorf and I need to get off the phone."

"Oh, it's the 'Waldorf,' now. Not the Waldorf Astoria. You two on a first-name basis now."

"Okay, Briana—"

"No."

Becky waited, then asked, "No?"

"No," Briana said—and hung up.

Becky stared at her phone. "That was weird." Then she added, "Bitch."

She put her phone down and leaned forward. "Driver, are we close to my hotel?"

"I'm pulling in now, ma'am."

The ride took four minutes. The ruination of a long-term friendship, three.

****

Since Becky had helped herself to the studio breakfast table before and after her segment, she went straight into her bathroom and stuck her fingers down her throat. She'd gotten so used to it that it didn't bother her anymore. Didn't even give her pause.

She then washed down the foul taste with her first vodka of the day and felt much better. She figured Darla and Myrna had been listening to the call on speaker, which neither gave her pause. She didn't think about it, didn't feel bad about it, and knew that the next time they called, she wouldn't answer. She'd moved on.

Chapter Twenty-One

Art Lane saw that the "most-watched" morning show had Becky on their schedule and tuned in to watch. He almost didn't recognize her. The Becky Darnell he first met and fell for had, as far as he could tell, checked out to be replaced by a clone designed in an AI lab—only less real. He wondered, "What happened?"

But he knew. She had fallen prey to the ever-lurking "current trends" beast that showed up weekly to devour anything in its path—then abandon it the next week for a new PR meal. For the moment, Becky Darnell was somewhere in its alimentary canal.

Art felt bad for her, as he did for everyone consumed by belief in the inebrious nature of instant notoriety, because he knew it would be temporary. All fads are, with sex fads especially vulnerable to irrelevance as soon as the next "hot thing" comes around. He recalled edible panties that "melt in your lover's mouth!"

"Is that strawberry or liver and onions?"
"I'm not sure. Wanna try Hot Lube in the City?"
"Nah. Let's just…"

Art was certain Becky's relative fame would be no different, sadly. He'd seen it a thousand times before in every area of popular culture from music to sports to hem lengths. The shine is bright when new, but fading from the spotlight is assured.

Worried specifically about Becky's blithe

comments regarding her roots, Art contemplated asking if she'd gotten any blowback from home, which seemed likely. He knew he'd have to be careful broaching the topic, especially after their last tense conversation, but thought he should brave it. He still cared about her and felt somewhat responsible for her initial success due to his infatuation and strictly positive reportage.

He had second thoughts. "Maybe I'm overvaluing my contribution," he chided himself. "She did win. I only reported on it."

Art waggled his head to shake out lingering doubts regarding his writing standards and aptitude as well as his misgivings about Becky's deservedness to be the Sexiest on the planet. Even if he felt she deserved it, others clearly thought someone else should have won. Someone more traditionally "sexy." But her wholesomeness won him over and took the day. "Now look at her."

He almost hadn't recognized her. To Art—as journalist and admirer—Becky now looked cheap. And no different than any other attention seeker on social media or one of the endless, disingenuous, ridiculous *Fake Wives Freak Fests*. "Ten years from now, she'll be pumping her lips and tits with silicone at Mar-a-Lago, courting a platinum bachelor."

He decided to call for a show of support—and personal responsibility. To at least check in and make sure she hadn't wholly gone off the deep end. See for himself that she remained the nice person he remembered from six months before.

At least on the inside—under that new plastic veneer.

To be sure he wouldn't come off wrong, Art made

crib notes. He didn't want to offend or fan Becky's recently flammable ire—sound like a naysayer or someone making wrong assumptions. After all, she could just be reflecting what the sponsors wanted, saying the things they wanted her to say. Looking and playing the part.

He hoped so.

His first note read, "How are things back home?" That should open the door to a conversation about any repercussions from dissing her Indiana roots. But on a third read, Art decided the question might sound too confrontational right off the bat.

He'd move it down the list.

Next, he wrote, "So, how's life on the road treating you?" That sounded better and would give Becky an opportunity to rave or gripe. He knew life on the road couldn't be all fun and games, and maybe she'd appreciate a chance to vent. Or praise it. Either way, that opening gambit felt neutral and safe.

Another question that seemed benign, coming from a journalist like him, was, "Are you enjoying all the coverage?" with a side note of, "Are they getting it right?" That one might even get him a quote for a new piece—if she would approve one. Which brought up another, larger concern.

Was he calling as a concerned friend or a hungry reporter? Art wasn't sure. And worse, he wasn't sure he could even tell the difference anymore, at least as it concerned Becky. She had become a hot property, not just an object of his fancy—and certainly no longer a puff piece for a Page 62 sidebar.

Art worried for a moment Becky might see his approach as a thinly-veiled *ask*. He could always demur and stick to the questions as from a friend, not a writer-friend. He could mention he'd read some pieces about her—without mentioning it was *every single one he could find*—but decided he'd be better served to seem out of touch. *I've been on the road constantly—this meatpacking story and the like—so I haven't had a chance to keep up on your—*

No! That sounded even worse. Like he didn't care. Wasn't interested. So, maybe something about her favorite location so far, a hotel, a restaurant, a tourist spot, a…

When Art Lane finally looked up from his list writing he saw that four hours had passed. He couldn't remember the last time he had spent so long preparing interrogatories—and for a *social call*. Clearly, his nerves were frayed, and he doubted his own intent.

He threw away the list.

"Just call her and chat," he told himself. "It'll work itself out."

After all, they'd had some fun times together even without the great sex, which now felt like more of a lovely bonus from another lifetime. It certainly hadn't been his main driver, and it had come about easily, comfortably. "Don't bring it up," he advised himself and restarted the thinking process—

"Jesus, Art! Just call her for fuck's sake. What the fuck's wrong with you!"

Art looked at the publicity still and had the answer. The Becky Darnell in that shot in no way correlated to the Becky Darnell he'd met and fallen in love with.

Love.

"Crap."

****

Art's concerns proved to be irrelevant when Becky didn't return his call. After five days and a text on Day Three to make sure she'd gotten the message he left on her voicemail, Art gave up and faced the truth that she obviously didn't feel the same way about him. Their romance was officially over.

Such a realization is never easy, and Art didn't want to face it. But as a grown man with a fair number of notches on his bedpost, he knew he had to let it go and move on. So, he tried.

It didn't work. He had felt something special and knew Becky felt it, too. He seemed certain *because* he'd been around. He'd dealt with infatuations before and knew how they worked. How they receded then vanished.

Becky had stayed with him, lived inside him, even after ignoring him. So, even though he knew he was treading on thin, dangerous ice, he decided not to give up on her, not to let it go. He'd wait it out and see—which led to many uncomfortable internal dialogues.

He wondered why she hadn't called. *Really*. When she *might* call. *Any time, now*. When she'd be in LA again, or when his schedule might overlap hers and they'd be in the same city. *Call for drinks.* Or should he forge ahead and see about writing a new piece. *Call my editor*.

An answer to the last question arrived in the form of an anonymous email. It read, "You need to hear this." Art found an audio file attached. Before opening it, he tried to reply but got an "undeliverable" notice saying the user didn't exist.

Being "investigative journalist adjacent," as he told anyone who asked about his credibility, Art had received a few such emails and knew what to do—run every virus check he had before opening it.

He suspected a zillion pop-ups warning him to stay away like the plague, but none arose. The attachment appeared safe. He opened it and listened to forty-five sometimes hard-to-hear minutes that would change his life—and Becky Darnell's.

****

Though Art couldn't be sure who was speaking at the secretly recorded meeting, he had no problems understanding the main topic of what they obviously thought was a private discussion: They *had* intended to fix the contest—just not the way it turned out.

From the often-heated exchanges, during which blame went back and forth and all around the room, Art learned that the girl from Hawai'i was supposed to win, with Genie coming in second. Organizers saw those two as best representing "sexy."

But something had gone wrong with their scheme. The idea had been that once the regional winners accepted their entries into the main pageant, organizers would review those results and choose First and Second Place based on looks, history, and "hotness." They wanted pros to represent their products.

To accomplish this, they sent out feelers for an experienced programmer/hacker who could alter the audience call-in algorithm results to guarantee their favored competitors would win. For some reason they couldn't figure out, the fix failed.

But they had a clue.

After the initial shock of Becky's win, they angrily called their dark web hacker in for a follow-up consult to find out what the hell had gone wrong. He answered their email but didn't show up. No one could find him anywhere.

They smelled a rat, but couldn't complain too loudly, lest their plan be exposed. Further, they could hardly change or reverse the results after the fact. So, they were "stuck with *fucking Miss Midwest Nobody.*"

But then, after the initial shock and rage settled and they reviewed tapes of the show, they began to see how and why the crowd warmed to Becky—her downhome easiness and humility, her honesty and humor, and her self-deprecating acceptance based on redefining "sexy" which then caught fire with average women everywhere.

At one point on the tape, organizers groused about how they had "crowned the homeliest girl in America," but they might be able to "fix" her with enough makeup, hair extensions, and pushup bras "before we all go out of business trying." A roomful of cruel laughs followed.

Art seethed. He didn't see Becky as homely in any sense. He saw a fit and healthy young woman with wonderful girl-next-door looks and a great outlook on life. At least when she'd won. He took umbrage at these *arrogant assholes* belittling her, mocking her, and thinking how, by making her fake, they could fix her and make her better somehow. But mainly, he was livid because he knew he had to write a new article, and at some point he'd have to tell Becky—which might be the hardest conversation he'd ever had in his life.

He didn't know the half of it.

Chapter Twenty-Two

"You sonofabitch! What the fuck are you trying to do to me?!"

"I'm asking you to tell your side of it before we put it out there."

Becky was beyond angry, beyond furious, all the way to apoplectic. "You rotten cocksucker! How could you fucking do this to me?! You fucking bastard!"

Art said, calmly, "I'm not doing it *to* you, Becky. I'm doing it *for* you."

"*For* me?!" Becky howled. "Ruining my fucking career!"

Art steadied himself. "Becky. They lied and they cheated."

"So?" she yowled.

Art said, "What about the other girls?"

"Genie and that bimbo from Maui? Please. They're gonna win contests all over the fucking place. I had one chance. *This* chance, you shithead!"

"Becky—"

"They gave me a life I never had, and you're gonna take it away!"

"Maybe not," Art said, hearing what sounded like suppressed tears. "You're doing pretty great by your own admission. Maybe you've brought something to the table they didn't expect. Maybe you'll do even better."

"Don't try that shit on me, Arthur. I didn't get off

the turnip truck yesterday."

"That's not the tale you've been telling all over the media," Art said, not feeling great about saying it. "And it's not Arthur. It's Arturo. My mother was Spanish."

"Same difference," Becky scoffed.

"And?"

"And I don't need you saving me!"

Art took a steadying breath. "Look Becky, this isn't just about you. I know it feels that way, but it's much bigger than you."

"Please don't say it's bigger than both us."

The exact phrase Art was about to use. He regrouped. "They need to be held accountable, Becky. They ran a fake, rigged contest."

"And it backfired!" Becky shot back. "I won!"

Art used his calm reporter voice. "Knowing what you know now, do you think you deserved to win?"

"It doesn't matter! I won! I'm the 'Sexiest Woman in the World' now," she said, not without sarcastic irony. "I've got six more months to be that, to be her, then I have to start all over again, and it may not be as easy if someone else doesn't cheat. So…back off. Please. Let me have my hour in the sun."

Art blew out a sigh. He could hear the desperation in her voice, the fear of losing her new identity. Even though she now knew it was fake, it was all she had.

More likely: all she had left.

She admitted, "I burned a lot of bridges, Art."

"I noticed."

"With you too, maybe."

"Maybe."

Becky huffed. "Jesus. Do you have to agree so fast?"

Art held to honesty. "You changed, Becky.

You're…I don't know, not you."

"As if you knew me at all."

"I did enough to know this new you, this…glossy, shiny, slick—"

"Those are all the same thing, Mr. Writer."

"You know what I mean," Art said darkly.

"Yeah, I changed. So what?" Becky said. "I'm not the stupid barnyard idiot I was. I learned how to play the game, did what they told me—every last fucking bit of it—and I *won*. I'm in control now. I own *them*. They don't own me."

"I wouldn't think that if I were you."

"Thanks to you," Becky countered. "And what you're about to do."

Knowing she was probably right, Art didn't respond.

"Art, I'm begging you. Don't do it. Wait. I don't know…six months. Let me live out my little fantasy dream world here till the end of my reign. Then you can do whatever you want. Just…let me have my fifteen minutes. I can prove my worth by then. That I'm more than a…straw-sucking rube from Nowhereville. I'm somebody, and I can do the job—whatever they ask me to do—and I can do it again. Please."

Art heard her and understood her grief and fear. But he had a greater truth to face. "Becky, my job is on the line, too. My editor knows what I found. We asked the organizers and sponsors for comment, but they haven't returned our calls. So, we're running it. Kay only agreed to hold off long enough for me to give you a heads-up."

"And now you have," she said darkly.

"Yeah."

"Well then fuck you, Art Lane. I never want to hear

your shitty voice ever again. And by the way, don't think I'm gonna take this lying down. I'm not some weakling pushover. That much *hasn't* changed, I can promise you. The same fight that got me here is gonna make sure I stay here. So, buckle up, buttercup. It's gonna get rough."

She hung up.

Art put his phone down. He'd known this conversation wouldn't be easy, but he hadn't predicted the towering height of her fury. That she would *threaten* him.

On the other hand, what could she do? He hadn't painted her as complicit in any way. All the blame went to the sponsors who deserved it. As for hearing back from them, he didn't expect to. They'd referred him and his editor to their lawyers who had already threatened to sue if the piece got published.

Tellingly, they hadn't refuted any of the charges. His side's lawyers did a close reading, as lawyers do, and signed off. Art had been careful, and his article reflected his circumspection.

"We're good to go," Kayla told him. "As soon as you get a response from Little Miss Homespun Sex Bomb, we're up like morning wood." She had a way with words.

Art could have called to say he'd spoken to Becky and to go to press, but he held some hope Becky would reconsider, knowing what was coming, and call him back to give her side of the story to round it out. Place blame where it belonged.

For despite her raw response, Art reasoned that inside she was still the Becky Darnell he'd crushed on and she would ultimately see he had no choice but to publish the truth about the cheaters and sit down for a

calm interview to set her side of the story straight.
Boy, was he wrong.

Chapter Twenty-Three

Art's editor woke him at six a.m. "Did you see the *Times* piece?"

"No, I was asleep. Did we go back into Bataan?" He'd been having a dream.

"Much worse," she said. "Ms. Muffet told them you sexually assaulted her tuffet in your house and wrote a false article to 'get' her for threatening to tell the cops."

Art sat bolt upright. "What!" The South Seas were instantly replaced by his Leroy Nieman lithograph of Melrose Avenue.

Kayla said, "She really put on the tearful act according to Carly Stewart over there."

"Oh jeez. Not Carly."

"She's got the ear of everyone in the Me Too *Plus* movement on the Hill and every courtroom in fucking New York. So, is it true?"

"Of course it isn't true. Kayla!"

"Did you fuck her?"

"Well…"

"I'll take that as 'Yes I fucked her in my house, Kay.' Let's hope she doesn't have a blue dress."

"Jesus."

"Yeah. I need you to put out a statement in the next hour denying everything."

"Can't we wait and see how it plays out a bit?"

"If you want the cops rummaging through your

underwear drawer."

"They won't find anything. I didn't *do* anything."

"Anything?"

"Not *that*," Art specified. "Come on, Kay. You know me."

"Do we really know anyone anymore?"

Art sighed. "I get it. But seriously."

"It's fucked up, Arturo."

"Very fucked up," Art agreed and thought a moment. "Can I expect a call from our lawyers?"

"Our?" Kayla said.

"Yeah," Art said, unsure of her apparent dodge. "What?"

"Art, honey, unless she includes us in it, you're on your own, here."

"Kayla!"

"It's not the way it works, Art. It's a he-said she-said thing at this point."

"And you don't believe what *he* said? What I say?"

"It's not for me to believe or not. I need you to deny, deny, deny. Whether you did it or not."

"Kay!"

"It's the protocol these days, Art. I'm sorry."

"Christ."

"Right. I'll be watching the news for your response."

Art could tell his editor was about to hang up. "Wait, wait, wait. What about my piece?"

"It's on hold, probably forever."

"But it's true. It needs to get out there."

"Not as long as your girl is screaming rape. It's not a good look."

"Did she really call it rape?"

218

"What's the difference?" Kayla said. "It's what everyone hears."

Art sagged, thinking maybe if they didn't run it, Becky would *Back off and tell the damn truth. Rape! Jesus Christ!*

He said, "Maybe I can talk to her."

"I'd avoid that," Kayla recommended. "Stay as far away from her as you do your crazy ex-wife."

Art thought how even his *crazy* ex wouldn't go so far as to cry rape—or even sexual assault—but he agreed. "You're probably right. But…shit. What do I do?"

"Issue the denial," Kayla prescribed. "Be firm and specific without being accusatory or providing any lurid details."

"That sounds contradictory."

"You're a good writer. You'll figure it out. Just be careful not to leave any doors or windows cracked. Don't leave her or her lawyers an opening to challenge or hype up anything you release."

"Her *lawyers*?"

Kayla said, "You don't think she's going this alone, do you? The sponsors are against the wall more than she is. They want your neck in a noose. How much did you tell her?"

"Too much, apparently," Art realized—and what that now meant. "So, she gets their lawyers but I'm on my own."

Art had expected trouble from the "Greedy, lying bastards." But not Becky.

Kayla said, "And you nailed them to the wall with their pants down to mix metaphors. But if I may quote an *anonymous* email I received at five this morning, 'We don't intend to get fucked in the ass by a third-rate hack writer.' "

"That hurts," Art said ironically.

"On the upside," Kayla pointed out, "if they're worried enough to send a shitty—and I should point out *stupid* email like that—they're worried."

"They should be," Art said, and something occurred to him. "Do you think they put her up to this?'

"Could be," Kayla allowed. "Wouldn't be the first time. But they'd be treading on dangerously thin ice, lawsuit-wise. So no, I think she brought it to them. Or maybe she casually mentioned your tryst and they ran with it. Who knows? At this point, it doesn't matter. You're fucked if you do and fucked if you don't."

"Thanks for the kind words of support."

Kayla said, "Art, you know I love you and your work—your work more than you."

"Ha. Ha."

"But."

"I'm on my own until we see where this goes."

"And perhaps beyond."

Her suggestion had an ominous dark, lonely-future tone to it—a dire warning as Art heard it—but the message came loud and clear. "You're expecting me to fix this on my own before it comes home to roost in the magazine's henhouse."

"That would be what I'm told."

"And you always think and do what you're told."

Art knew he'd crossed a line with his old editor, so he wasn't surprised when she said, "I need to run. Ta." But then she added, "Be careful, Art."

"Okay," he said, dispirited. Then he hung up and said, "What the fuck, Becky?" He clearly had not seen it

coming. Now it had arrived…
****

Art made coffee, drank half a pot, and mulled over the situation and his response, writing some twenty drafts before slapping his laptop shut and declaring, "This is bullshit." It may have been, but it was also real; and he had no idea how to proceed.

He knew Kayla would be waiting for his measured and *debilitating* response, something to take the wind out of the sponsor's sails while totally destroying Becky's credibility. But what could he say to accomplish that? And did he even want to? He *liked* Becky Darnell—had thought he might love her. Now *this*?

"Jesus fuck," he said to himself and let his head drop back to stare at the ceiling.

He tried to remember anything from that night which could be construed, or misconstrued, as nonconsensual or inappropriate, but nothing came to mind. Every memory he had felt *good*. He couldn't conjure a single negative. As he'd said at the time, it was the best sex he'd ever had. So, how could this be?

He sat up and reached for his phone. "This is total bullshit," he said aloud. "She felt the same way I did."

His impulse was to call Becky and remind her of her own words. To go over the night's events one by one, asking her to pinpoint where she thought he crossed a line. Any line. He felt certain she would not be able to name one instance.

He started to dial—then stopped.

In his mind, he could hear the entire confrontation, his denials, her…what? Evasions and accusations? His demand to know what the hell she was doing, what she was thinking, why she would do this to him. But he knew the answer.

Becky had come from nothing to sit on top of the world in six short months. She suddenly had long limos and fancy hotels, first-class travel, people waiting on her hand and foot. The moment his article hit the street, she would be reduced to nothing. Back to being nobody in less time than it took to read the article. In a way, he couldn't blame her for fearing such a loss. But why did she have to do it back to *him*?

He had an answer. "Because I wrote the damn story."

For the first time, Art Lane wished he hadn't been so driven to find the truth. But he had. And now he had to fight for his livelihood—his career and his standing in it. Maybe his savings. Maybe his house. Maybe his ability ever to work again. The court of public opinion, especially when it came to men sexually exploiting women, showed no mercy. And rightfully so. But he had done nothing wrong.

Or had he?

Art got up, had another cup of coffee, and paced, forcing himself to go through every moment he'd been alone with Becky Darnell, searching for any touch or kiss or suggestion that might have caused her to push him away or even recoil. He couldn't recall one.

Half an hour later, armed with renewed confidence, he picked up his phone again and this time dialed. He'd been blocked. "Shit!"

Who could he call? Not the sponsors or organizers. They wouldn't touch him with a ten-*mile* pole, knowing the gist of what he'd written, much less the specifics— names named. He figured to be served within weeks or days or even minutes. They had to be planning a big, splashy lawsuit. Those kinds of people knew how to use the press.

For a moment, Art shook in his boots. Then, he relaxed. He knew he'd written nothing speculative. He made no charges not mentioned in the purloined recordings. He'd suspected all along something was amiss with the pageant but held off writing a word until he got that recording and pored over it carefully. *Then*, he started to write.

He really wanted to have a conversation with whoever sent him the recording. That could solve everything, especially if they were in the know, on the inside. They would likely have more proof of the scam. But he had no idea who it was, no idea of where to start looking. So, his ultimate endgame was a non-starter.

Who, who, who could help him? There had to be someone.

Then it him. He rushed to his phone and dialed Genie Vintier.

She answered, "I was wondering when you'd call."

"Genie. This is insane." He told her the gist of his article.

She listened, then asked, "Did you do it?"

"Rape her? Hell no!"

"I didn't think so. You don't seem the type. But those types never do."

"Well, I'm not the type that does and I didn't," Art said firmly.

"I get it," she said, sounding cautious if not aloof.

"So, why did she say it?"

"Why do you think?"

Art had to subjugate his reflexive *I don't know* to say, more aptly, "She's afraid."

"Of you?"

"No! Of losing it all."

After a pause, Genie asked, "What's in the article? I heard the rumor but not the specifics."

"I can't say," Art said for two reasons. One, his publisher wouldn't allow it; his contract stated such in no uncertain terms. And two, Genie played prominent, having been pegged to come in second to the Hawaiian girl who didn't even Show. Genie was a big part of it all. For the briefest moment, he considered telling her all that, but sanity prevailed.

"I'm contractually bound not to reveal any details. Sorry."

"But you basically are busting the shits for cheating if I'm guessing right."

"Something like that," Art said.

"So, what do you want from me?"

"Some clue about why Becky would say something so vile and untrue about me. I thought we got along pretty well. At least before she—"

"Let it all go to her head?" Genie said.

"You too?"

"Big time," Genie said. "Called me a bitch then blocked me. You?"

"The last part," Art confirmed. "So, why do you think? Really?"

"I think what you said," Genie said. "You threatened her new existence. She's gotten pretty cozy with it all. If you can take it all away in one article, she's gonna fight back."

"But accusing me of assault?"

"Yeah," Genie said with a sigh Art could hear. "I didn't expect it from her."

"*You*? I about had a heart attack this morning. I've never been accused of anything worse than smoking in the boy's room—speaking truth someone didn't want to hear. And even then, only once or twice, when I was writing over my depth. This is a real shock."

"So, it's not true," Genie said again.

"No, Genie. It's not true."

"Did you—"

"Yes, we had sex. In my house. But it was wonderful as far as I knew."

"No weird shit?"

"No weirder than anyone else."

"I won't ask."

"She…" He started to say how she'd made specific requests, but decided it was irrelevant and no one's business."

"Yeah?" Genie said. "You started to say."

"She was a delight, and we had a great time. Which is what she said at the time, so I have…" He almost said, *No idea*, then changed his mind. "What I don't understand is why it had to be so extreme. She could have denied what I wrote as fiction like a normal person. Not put me in jeopardy of going to prison."

"Maybe she didn't," Genie said.

"Didn't what? *Say* it? She said it," Art said.

"Maybe she didn't," Genie reiterated.

"What do you mean?"

"Did you hear her say it?"

"No. I gave her a heads-up about the piece, and she blew a fuse. Ten fuses. She…I guess she threatened something, but she wasn't specific. Then hung up."

"So…what? The papers are saying it?"

"The *Times*, yeah."

"Was it a direct quote? Because that's not how I read it."

"What are you saying?"

"You're the investigative journalist. What do you think I'm saying?"

Art hated to be pushed around intellectually, but he didn't want to chance angering Genie, getting her to hang up too soon. So, he said, "You're saying maybe the sponsors said it for her?"

"Weirder things," Genie said. "Especially with those sleazebags."

"But that would be slander. I could sue them."

"Maybe you should," she said.

Art's brain felt like it was rolling around inside his skull, untethered. "I don't think we're there, yet."

"Just a thought," she said.

"Okay, but for a moment, let's assume she did say something like that, and for whatever reason felt like she needed to for her…I don't know, survival. It's just…not any Becky Darnell I ever met or knew."

"She changed," Genie said.

"I'll say," Art said without malice. "But still."

"Maybe she was—" Genie stopped.

"Go on."

"I don't think I should."

"Genie, please. My career's on the line here. My life. Maybe my freedom. If you know something, I need to hear it. What were you going to say? She was what?"

After a painfully long lull of silence, Genie finally said, "Tipsy."

"You're saying drunk?"

"She's drinking a lot," Genie said. "And…"

"And what? Coke? Pills?"

226

"Pills."

Art quickly slid into reporter mode—calm and careful to ferret facts without upsetting his *confidential informant*. "Did you witness this?"

"I heard about it."

"From?"

"My sources," Genie said. "You're not the only one with a vested interest in this."

Art thought, *If she only knew what her vested interest was!* But he said, "Okay. So, someone on the inside."

"You could say that," she said.

"And it's affecting her *how*?"

"I don't know if I can speak to it directly, but I've heard she's become…'disagreeable and demanding,' to quote. That she's taking this gig maybe more seriously than she should."

"More than it deserves?

"All of this comes to an end at some point," Genie said. "The trick is knowing how to make it to the next phase, even if it's lateral."

"To know how to survive."

"How to make a living through longevity."

"And you don't think she's handling that part well?"

"I know she isn't."

"I'm guessing you tried to talk to her about this."

"I tried."

"But she called you names and blocked you."

Silence.

Art guessed again. "You've seen this happen before. With other girls. Women."

"Oh yeah."

"And it doesn't turn out well."

"Never."

Art let the weight of that sink in then said, "Is there anything we can do?"

"If you find out, call me back."

Art sensed she was ready to hang up and cut in. "Wait. One more question."

Genie said nothing.

"You hinted that maybe the sponsors put her up to this or maybe made it up on their own and maybe Becky is too invested in the gig and too dependent on…whatever she's ingesting to refute it or say no to going along. Can we prove any of that?"

After a long pause, Genie Vintier said, "Goodbye, Art. Good luck with your story." Then she did hang up, and Art was left holding some heavy baggage.

He felt Genie was supportive of his side of the story, perhaps downplaying Becky's part in it all or her ability to do him any real harm—if he could get to the root of the problem, and all it meant. Use his investigatory skills to follow up.

Unfortunately, Genie hadn't given him anything definitive or provable. She'd made some vague accusations without specifics or attribution. A start. At least she'd said *something* in his defense. More important, she *hadn't* said he was mistaken or wrong. All he had to do now was prove it.

But how.

****

After talking to Genie Vintier, Art felt on surer ground, at least as far as his original story. If the sponsors were putting out lies about him, he must have been right about their possible complicity in a cover-up of some sort. A fix. Given that confidence, he asked Kayla to run

228

the piece.

She still had reservations. "Let's give it another week to see what else pops up."

"I don't know what else could," Art said, more hopeful than prescient. "But okay."

What else could he say? If his editor wouldn't publish his piece, he was high-centered, teetering while waiting for the next bit of bad news to come out.

That sent Art to his own bottle. The Canadian whiskey helped for ten minutes, then the worry returned. What if Becky *had* said something so vile? What if she planned to sue him for assault? What if the sponsors had already assembled a topnotch team of tort lawyers to go after him? What if the cops were outside his door that very minute!

"Jesus. Get a grip," he told himself. But a grip was not had.

Art spent the next week lolling about in a mental cesspool of confusion, anger, fear, and depression. He begged Kayla for another assignment. Anything! But she held hard to her wait-and-see approach.

"We can't take any chances on you right now, Art. Sorry."

He understood. A writer friend of his had gotten caught up in a similar snarl of accusations, lawsuits, and countersuits that played out over four years, during which he couldn't get an assignment to save his life. He ended up writing phony sex letters for a website—fake people "writing in" to ask questions about their particular kink. He called it his "Is this normal?" phase. It got so bad he went back to teaching.

Art stared at his MFA on the den wall and considered the same. Weeks of doing nothing was having an effect. He'd tried tending to his work-in-progress, historical fiction about Los Angeles in the 1940s, but he mostly stared at a blank screen. He drank more, wrote less, and fretted so much he felt certain he'd developed an ulcer.

Then he got an unexpected break.

The caller ID showed an "unknown number." He almost didn't answer, thinking it was probably another Medicare Advantage salesperson he'd have to let know he was *forty*. Then he threw caution to the wind—if with no enthusiasm.

"Yeah?" he said, making sure to sound as surly and unwelcoming as possible.

"Is this Art Lane?"

"Yes. And you are?"

"The dude who sent you the tape."

Chapter Twenty-Four

The man on the other end of the call sounded young, in his early twenties or maybe even his late teens. He wouldn't give his name, but he provided enough details from the original recording to convince Art he was the one who sent it.

"Okay," Art said.

The guy said, "I saw what's happening."

"What's happening?"

"The assault charges."

"They're not charges yet. Just accusations."

"They will be soon."

Art felt the blood drain from his torso. "You know this or suspect it?"

"I know a lot more than anyone thinks I do."

Art bristled. "Yeah, pretty cryptic and all, but what are you actually saying? They're preparing to file charges? How close?"

"It doesn't matter."

"It does to *me*."

"You're gonna stop them."

"I am?" Art said, not eager to play any games. "How?"

"With what I'm going to tell you."

"Okay," Art said again.

"I know who rigged the contest."

"You do," Art said, not wholly convinced. "Who?"

"Me."

Art had not expected that. "Why?"

"Because someone paid me a lot of money."

"So…you recorded them admitting it and sent the tape to me."

"I did," the young man said. "Once I got into it, I saw what was really going on and it pissed me off. I thought someone should know."

"Kind of late in the game," Art said as accusation.

A pause hung. Then the guy said, "I was wrong."

"About?"

"Cheating."

"Isn't cheating always wrong?"

"Not if you think you're doing something to help someone lower on the food chain."

"Okay," Art said again. "Who and why?"

The guy said, "Look, man, I could get in big trouble talking to you. You understand."

"I do. But you *are* talking to me."

Another pause led into, "Because there's more to be told."

Art wasn't born yesterday. "I'm guessing someone tried to screw you."

"No," the young man said. "Someone tried to screw *you.*"

"They're trying now."

"They are," the *kid* said. "But it's bigger than you and me and Becky Darnell."

"Does she know any of this?"

"No, but she will."

Art asked carefully, "Do you know what she has to do with these…allegations?"

"No," the young mystery man said. "But I doubt any

232

of it happened. I've watched you and read your stuff and, I could be wrong, but you don't seem the type."

"That's been said," Art recalled. "But it was also mentioned how those types don't always look like those types."

"True," the guy said. "But I'm going on a hunch. Plus, I know other things."

"You mentioned that," Art said. "And what are those other things?"

"Do you have a pen and paper?"

****

What the young man conveyed proved to be a revelation Art had not expected. First, the anonymous *dude* said to call him Bob. Art assumed he was not a "Bob," but agreed. Mystery Bob then confirmed that the contest had been rigged by the organizers and sponsors, as the recordings revealed. But it didn't start or end there.

Those unscrupulous promoters had indeed sought him out through the dark web where he had advertised himself as a computer whiz capable of turning any program around any way a user wanted—legit or not, the notice implied carefully.

Bob intentionally played coy, making it difficult to contact him directly to add to the mystique and the secret mission. When he figured he had them on a line, he reeled them in, pretending to be hearing their request for the first time.

In fact, he knew all about their plan before they ever contacted him. He knew what they would request, what he would respond, how much crypto currency he would demand for his services—and what his real job would be.

Who had hired him *first*.

Art listened in amazement as Bob revealed that he

was originally hired by a small group of lesser players in the "How to be a sex bomb business." New players on the block who sold the same products—clothing, lingerie, body creams, makeup, hair extensions—but were having a hard time breaking into the business because the old guard contest sponsors had formed a tight, likely illegal, coalition to keep a tight grip on everything to do with convincing women how to be sexy in every commercial area.

So, the lesser group searched the dark web, found Bob, and pitched a plan that entailed a complicated double-cross. They would wait to see who won the regionals then choose the least-likely contestant to win the pageant. Bob's job was to fix it so they did.

Enter Becky Darnell, the perfect candidate for their nefarious plan.

There rose the double-cross. Because by then, the real sponsors had already hired him to help them rig the results so Genie or the Hawaiian girl would win. He convinced them he did it, then sat back to watch the fireworks.

When the votes started exploding and they called him for an explanation, he told them—using a voice modifier—he had *no idea* what went wrong. Someone must have messed with the algorithms—someone *else* from the dark web.

He claimed innocence, even confusion, but promised to look into it and fix whatever he could. Of course, he had no intention of doing that. And it was too late, anyway, as he later explained.

A shocking truth arose after.

When Bob went back to check his input and the results, he discovered that Becky would have won, anyway. The at-home audience responded so well to her natural good looks and honest answers they would have pushed Becky over the top without his help. The irony was not wasted on him, which he found hilarious. "Dude. Right?"

"Unbelievable," Art muttered, in agreement if not equally amused. "Suckers suckering the suckers. And it all backfired."

Not realizing this, the contest sponsors had their meeting to bemoan the failed fix and decide how to proceed. Stuck with Becky, they knuckled down and, to their shock—while ignoring her obvious appeal—turned her into the sex bomb cash cow they had wanted all along. Sales soared, but with attendant headaches.

Becky became a pain in their cumulative ass—not that anyone on the inside admitted it. Everyone continued to put a happy face on their situation, especially to the press. But they had begun making plans to rid themselves of their self-created *sex diva* by exploiting the exposé.

Hacker Bob felt bad—and guilty—on realizing he had helped create the Becky monster as well as facilitating the products war between two equally undeserving groups of marketing monsters. So, he catalogued everything and called Art.

They said their goodbyes and Art reviewed his notes, mind racing. The evidence was overpowering. They could no longer hold the piece back. His editor and publisher would no doubt be frothing to get it all out there and crush their own competition with the massive scoop. Art might win a Pulitzer!

But what about Becky? What would this do to her?

****

In a hot tub on St. John, Becky stayed submerged under the bubbles to give the illusion of being nude while being interviewed by a "reporter" from *Celebrity Night Out*. In the day. The new guy, a pointlessly handsome *replicant* fitting their "style," managed to make several thinly-disguised lustful double-entendres without crossing any network censor boundaries. Becky played it up.

While sipping a "devious rum concoction," she gave overly perky answers to questions about her new life as Sexiest Woman in the World. "It's fabulous, Brody. I never dreamed life could be so grand! I was a smalltown girl from middle-America with no dreams of ever becoming anything more. Now, here I am!"

She went on to extoll the wonders of living in the lap of luxury with men all over the world slavering over her and women wanting to be her. When asked if she missed anything about her past life, she said, "Are you kidding? No way! It was holding me back from being someone with a *real* life. Look around.

"I wouldn't trade any of this for any of that if my life depended on it. Those places, those days, those *people* are as dead to me as ancient Rome. No, I happily left all that behind and have no desire whatsoever to go back to *any* of it. I'm free of my past, living for my future, and it's fabulous. Screw my past. I'm here now and loving it like the End Days on acid. Everyone else can go to Hell."

She minced no words—and slurred several.

****

Though the *CNO* interviewer, editors, and in-studio hosts played along, showing nothing but exaltation for "Becky Darnell's incredible worldly success!" not everyone shared their view.

Outside Auburn, in the spreader factory, Floyd sighed and hung his head. He'd been following Becky's sojourn to fame and silently supported it, happy for her. Darla saw his dejection, patted him on the back, and threw her safety helmet at the TV.

****

Art Lane didn't throw anything at his television in his den in LA other than invectives. "Jesus, Beck. What the hell happened to you?"

He knew the answer—money, fame, global adoration. Any one of those factors would generally be enough to ruin anyone. Put it all together with a glistening sheen of sex, then add booze and pills, and Becky was a goner.

He hated to see it. He hated it for her and her old friends. For himself. But he no longer had any reason to hold the article back. If anything, he had a new reason to put it out: he hoped to save Becky Darnell from herself.

It presented a high bar, one Art didn't fully believe he could leap, but he knew one thing for sure. He could bust her bubble along with the many bubbles of the cheating sponsors, and maybe bring some truth into, "This squirrely eddying pool of shark-in-the-water blood-lies."

He said it aloud. Then he said, "I don't even know what that means." But then he wasn't sure he knew what anything meant anymore. Except for one thing, his one responsibility: Tell the truth.

****

The truth for Becky Darnell was that she didn't really think life had become easy at all. Though she would never admit it, fame kind of sucked. Every aspect

237

of her life had been shuffled under the constant eye, and reproach, of her handlers who controlled everything she ate, said, and wore—everywhere she went, how she got there, with whom she traveled, and to whom she could speak once she arrived. Everything they expected her to say had been laid out in bullet points on an official memo left in the limo for her.

The further truth was that, had she been a "normal" model, doing normal model things—working for more traditional outlets, doing shows with other women who would become familiar faces with similar sympathies and enlightening advice to share—Becky's outlook and experiences might have been different.

But because she was a "one off," working in a singular sliver of several industries rolled into one, with an even smaller window of modeling opportunities— only the ones her sponsors arranged that featured her— Becky was on her own. No other models ever accompanied her appearances. She had no one to talk to outside her dictated path.

She walked alone.

It proved to be a lot for the small town, Midwest average girl turned international fashion plate, and could have broken her on its own merit. But what really did it was the moniker. The title. Being the Sexiest Woman in the World held with it other pressures less seen. In short, every man she came across wanted to fuck her.

Every. Single. One.

Some women, too, though that wasn't her thing. One time trying it while drunk and on pills, to make it easier to swallow, convinced her. She had nothing against it or the beauty who seduced her. But it wasn't her thing.

On thinking back, she supposed she had hoped to

find it *was*, since that would give her an excuse to ignore all the horndogs who crept out of the woodwork everywhere she went, in every city and port around the world. They all wanted the same thing—to say they conquered the Sexiest Woman in the World. It took her a few dozen times to learn that lesson—and herpes. Which gave her an even better excuse.

But the unwanted advances continued. And though she had an occasional hope of meeting someone special, some guy who wasn't all about her title to gain his own, she only met "sash suitors" as she dubbed them. And, when she could be honest with herself, she missed Art Lane.

That was about to change.

Chapter Twenty-Five

Armed with "Bob's" new information, Art reworked his article to include the Escher-like contortions of the intertwining plots: How the main sponsors searched for a dark web hacker to rig their contest for "Maui Wowie" to win and Genie Vintier to place; but that Bob had already been secretly hired by the lower-tier "sexy beauty" product makers to sabotage the rigging for a "homely" girl like Becky Darnell to win so the hotshots would look stupid and lose clients; but how Becky won over the viewing audience thereby flipping the fix backwards and causing the lower-tier merchants to fail after all; how it all compounded when the original sponsors realized their mistake via Becky's popularity and flipped their own script, choosing to support her and cash in on her homespun humor and good looks by remolding her into their timeworn archetype of sexy; and how those moves had two devastating effects.

One, after achieving such unexpected success, Becky became insufferably vain due to her newly-acquired drinking problem, turned on those same sponsors and, once the public heard about it all, everything in turn turned upside down, which brought about Two, when Bob had an about-face and gave up the entire dirty plot to Art who told his editor, "The shit's about to hit the fan club," and Kayla revoked her "no-run" edict.

****

Art's article went live on a Friday morning. By ten a.m., phones were ringing all across the country and the world, most everyone calling for multiple firings, including Becky. Three members of Congress demanded an "immediate investigation," and the fashion world fell into full tizzy mode. Most who had been at the pageant got a good laugh with a few adding, "I told you so."

Art Lane found himself back in his publisher's good graces, being touted for a Peabody Award, which he thought highly unlikely; but it had its appeal. Still, he didn't feel good about his exposé. If anything, he felt fairly awful. His fondness for Becky had been tested and, as he saw it, he had failed. At least he'd failed *her*.

"She's toast," Kayla said, sounding gleeful.

"Hopefully, they all are," Art said as a self-ameliorative.

Kayla offered a hard dose of reality. "She isn't a David to their Goliath, Artie hon. She's Lot's wife looking back and crystalizing while the desperate sponsors and their coterie of highly-paid lawyers conjure how to spin this so they look good and she looks like some sad and desperate Diablo incarnate."

"That's quite a jumble of demonically mixed metaphors."

"If the foo shits," Kayla said. "And yours does. Get ready for some plum assignments. That should be a balm for your chafing guilt trip."

"Yeah, great, thanks," Art said, not feeling in agreement, great, or thankful. Of all the calls he had feared in his life and career, the one he saw coming from Becky worried him the most because he knew it was coming, and it would be volatile if their recent history

Glenn A. Bruce

was any indicator. He braced for a pike-headed cul-de-sac.

****

After a six-island promotional tour that featured her in various skimpy outfits on a dozen "uniquely quintessential" Caribbean beaches, Becky's enthusiasm for her new career had flagged. She had no idea it would be so much *work*. Despite the exotic locations and lush accommodations, she felt more detached than ever—not to mention exhausted. The one thing that brought her comfort was the rum, which she allowed to comfort her in great quantities.

So, on "The Morning Of," as it would come to be known, Becky Darnell was asleep in business class on a Miami-bound jet, heavily hungover. A flight attendant apparently thought she had died in her seat when she didn't respond to several gentle nudges and gave her a sharper one.

Becky awoke on fire. "Goddammit, what the fuck?" she shouted, thrashing in her seat, unable to move due to her still-fastened seatbelt.

The flight attendant, a gay man from St. Petersburg, said in his best, practiced chilly way, "We've landed, sweetie. You're back on earth. Time to wake up and scoot."

He scooted himself away and left Becky to gather her senses. Since she had alienated everyone on the shoot save one young production assistant, also a gay man from Florida, she got no help until he made his way up from coach and found her still struggling with her seatbelt. "Let me help you, hon," he said and reached down.

"I can do it!" Becky snarled, but couldn't find it

242

under her shirt and hoodie.

"Rebecah," he said patiently. "It's me, Ben. Let me help."

She looked up, recognized the young, sympathetic face, and let her body go limp. He reached down, unhooked her, and said, "Let's get you up and out of here. Okay?"

"Okay," she said quietly and apologized. "I was having a bad dream. I guess I…"

"Didn't remember where you were?" he finished for her as a question.

"Yeah, that," she said and stood quickly.

"Watch your head," he said and put his hand over it to prevent contact with the luggage bins.

"Thanks," she said. "I think I can get it from here."

"Are you sure?" he asked kindly.

"We'll see," she said, her old smile peeking through, and started up the aisle.

"Wait, you forgot your bag," he said and reached down to retrieve her shoulder tote.

"Thanks," she said, taking it and reflexively checking her phone. "Wow. There's like a hundred messages. Did the world end while I was asleep."

"Not that I know of," he said, apparently equally unaware of any bad news. "I check out on airplanes. Turn off the ugliness of the world at large."

Becky chuckled as she started to check her messages. Impatient passengers who'd had to wait for her to get in the egress line pushed ahead. Someone called out, "Let's move it, people!"

"Yeah, yeah, yeah," she said. "I'm going."

She made her way past the flight attendant who smiled emptily as she passed. Then she heard him say,

"Thank you for flying JetBlue. We'll be sure to restock the liquor cabinet."

"Ingrate," she said over her shoulder, knowing she'd spent a hefty sum.

Though Becky reflexively felt the need to check her phone, other passengers continued to push and shove their way through the jetway, possibly for other flights, possibly happy to be back in Miami, possibly just wound up and rude.

Becky wished she had her makeup and wig, some clingy and revealing outfit to ID her as Sexiest in the World, but she'd chosen to forego "dolling up for an airplane ride" as her handlers had requested, since they never knew who might be waiting with a camera.

Apparently, they had checked their phones. On exiting the ramp, they scattered like roaches in daylight, all but running for the escalators.

Becky moved to one side to linger and check her messages. Ben passed by with a, "You okay, hon?" while checking his phone.

"Sure. Thanks," she said, unable to remember his name.

Then she heard him say, "Holy shit." He looked up from his phone and back, wide-eyed.

"What?" she said.

****

A full gaggle of local and national reporters waited at the base of the escalators in baggage claim armed with enough cameras to capture a presidential prison surrender. Not the usual claque of adorers, this was a shouting mob. Becky knew why after checking her messages. Though she hadn't read Art's article yet, she figured it was bad.

As the reporters started shouting questions, Becky said, "No comment," pulled her hoodie tight, and looked at the ground, hoping she could find her limo with no problem. Her regular driver was nowhere to be seen, nor was anyone with her name on a piece of cardboard.

As she made her way for the double exit doors, reporters crowded around and shouted hectically. "What happened, Becky?" "Did you know about this, Becky?" "Did you have anything to do with the rigging of the contest, Becky?" "Are you *complicit*, Becky?"

She shouted, "I said no comment! Move!"

The questions continued, becoming more combative and accusatory as Becky moved out into the humid morning air of Miami International and looked for her limo—not finding it. "Shit." Had they abandoned her *already*?

The horde surrounded her, shouting and shoving, sticking microphones and iPhones at her face. "Leave me alone! I don't know anything about anything!"

She searched desperately for anyone on her "team" to come to her aid. What she saw gave her no reason to hope for reprieve. One of the sponsors' traveling photographers and a makeup girl stood off to one side, silent and glaring.

Becky looked for an exit, but saw only the crush of reporters. "Move! Move, dammit!" She shoved two out of her way and heard one say, "I've just been shoved by Rebecah Darnell! Assaulted here in the Miami airport Arrivals lane!"

Becky shouted, "I didn't assault you, bitch! Get outa my goddamn way!"

She pushed ahead until she saw the line of waiting taxis and broke for it. The throng chased after her. "Stop it! Leave me alone! Go away! Stop! Move! Fuck!"

She whipped open the door of the first cab, jumped in, and tried to pull the door shut, but two reporters had their hands on it, holding it open.

Becky shouted at the driver, "Go! Go! Get us outa here! Go now!"

The driver looked momentarily unsure then put his Ford in gear and inched ahead, freeing the door for Becky to close it—which brought some semblance of peace and quiet.

As the taxi pulled away, Becky didn't look back. She knew the reporters were either running after her or scrambling for their cars and vans to give chase. Reminded of Princess Diana's final hours, she closed her eyes, fearful, nearly tearful.

The driver asked, "Where to, ma'am?"

Becky looked up, realizing she didn't know. Local travel and destinations had always been arranged for her ahead of time.

Now on her own, a stranger in a strange town, she said, "How about a motel where no one will know where I am."

"I think I know the place," the driver said—and stepped on it.

****

As it turned out, he did know a place. The small motel sat off Okeechobee Road just north and west of the airport. As he pulled into the small parking lot, Becky looked back to confirm no one had followed. "Wow. Good job," she complimented.

The Cuban American man nodded. "It's what I do, sometimes," he said.

"What do I owe you?" she asked, digging in her

purse for the company card.

"For the ride or the experience?" he said.

She chuckled. "Both. You earned a nice tip."

"Excellent," he said and gave her his rate for both.

"Wow," she said again. "Okay." It seemed high, but he'd apparently succeeded in getting her into hiding, so she handed the card up.

He ran it and found it had been, "Declined."

"What? Run it again."

He did. "Declined."

"Shit!"

Fortunately, she had enough cash for the ride and a more modest tip, which he accepted with a grimace down at the money.

"Sorry," she said. "I guess they cancelled my *fucking* card already."

"Mmm," he said. "What'd you do?"

"Nothing," she said. "But someone else did."

"Mmm," he said again. "You're going to need more to survive in Miami, mija."

She said, "It's okay. My personal card's in my..." Then she remembered, "Shit. It's in my suitcase."

He understood. "The one you left at Baggage Claim?"

"That one," she said, mournfully.

Becky looked around, not recognizing anything since she'd never been in Hialeah, Florida before. Then she noted the motel office and realized she had no way to pay for a room. "Fuck me."

"You're stuck, huh?" the cabbie said.

"Very stuck," she assessed.

He thought a moment then said, "Maybe we can work something out."

247

She looked up sharply. "Whoa, whoa, whoa, dude. That ain't happening."

He looked at her in his mirror. "I didn't mean that, mija. I'm married and happy."

"I'm sorry. I thought…" Becky faltered. "I'm sorry. What were you going to say?"

"If you give me your baggage claim check, and you can use your other card to pay me for my service, I can go back and get your bags for you."

"And bring them here?"

"Yes. Here."

"You won't steal them?"

He chuckled, perhaps darkly, and said, "You can go in there and ask the lady at the desk if you can trust me. Her name is Olivia. She's my cousin, and she'll vouch for me. She's very honest. Or…you're welcome to go back to the airport with me if you like."

An image of the rushing reporters convinced Becky she didn't want to go back, maybe ever. "Okay, but how do I know this isn't a scam and you'll really come back with my bags?"

"I guess you don't," he said. "But I guess you don't have a choice, either."

Though still in a mild fog, Becky said, "Okay. Let me…here…"

She opened her tote and dug around, finding her ticket and claim check easily, but she continued to dig. Then she stopped and looked up. "Shit. I don't have it. One of the production people must have it. Or one of their assistants."

"Then call them," he said. "Have them meet me there and I'll get your bags and bring them back here."

That sounded reasonable to Becky, but it still didn't

feel right. Something about her old ability to read people told her to pass. But how?

She came up with, "That could take a while. I'm not sure where everybody went. I mean, some live in Florida, but I don't know where. And Janine, she's from New York, and Olive…" She had started to use the name Olivia but caught herself. "Olive is from LA, so she's probably already on her way to Atlanta or O'Hare."

She said all that, but she thought, *They probably all ran for the hills*. She had little hope of reaching anyone but wasn't ready to fall prey to some scam theft ring that specialized in stolen luggage.

So, she looked up and put on her most sincere face. "I'm sorry. This sucks. I guess I'll have to figure it out on my own. But thanks for the offer. Really."

The way the cabbie looked at her made Becky uncomfortable, as if he saw through her ruse and couldn't decide how he wanted to play it. Finally, after what felt like days, he smiled—not genuinely, she noted—and said, "Up to you."

He turned away.

When he didn't get out to open her door for her, Becky let herself out of the cab and closed the door. He drove away without another look at her.

Becky sighed and glanced around again at the unfamiliar sights. Heavy morning traffic continued along Okeechobee Road between her and a wide canal. Finally, she turned back toward the motel office and walked inside.

A man stood behind the desk. He didn't appear to be Hispanic, but when he spoke, his heritage came through. "May I help you?"

"Is Olivia here?"

"Who?"

"Olivia. She works here?" Becky turned toward the driveway. "The cab driver. He said his cousin Olivia works here."

She turned back to find the youngish man shaking his head no. "Not here. Would you like a room?"

Becky sighed, both because she felt safe from surviving a scam heist and because she was in off the street away from the throng of nosy reporters. At least her cabbie hadn't lied about the location, even if it was likely part of his con.

She told the young clerk, "I would. But I left my bags at the airport and I'm gonna have to find someone to get them. Someone I trust, because…" She started to mention her credit card and other valuables but opted to stop there.

He said, "So…you want a room?"

"I do," she said. "But I guess not now. I don't have a card that's working and I gave my last dollar to the driver." Again, she held herself back from sharing her thoughts on the driver and his *idea*.

The young man said, "Are you alone?"

Becky cringed but said, "Yes."

He said, "No one's gonna come visit you?"

"Huh? No," she said. Then she realized what he was implying. "No! I'm not…no. I'm a working girl." Then her eyes went wide. "Not that kind! No! I mean…shit. I'm kind of a model. I work for several companies that sell makeup and clothes and stuff and—"

"Yes. You're that woman," he said. "The Sexiest one." He sounded happy about it.

Becky weighed her options. "That depends on whether you've seen the news this morning."

"I did," he said. "Sounds like a mess you're in."

"Oh, I think it is," she said. "But I didn't have anything to do with it."

He seemed to understand, "Perhaps why your card isn't working."

"Yeah, I think so," she admitted. "It's—" She shook her head. "—I don't know what it is. I was on the plane, then I got off, and…I don't know." She looked up, feeling lost.

He nodded, apparently understanding her unstated need. "I tell you what. I'll put you in Room Six. We keep it open for last-minute situations, you know, from the airport usually. You can hang out there until five, when I go home. I don't know if Raul will let you stay past then when he comes in. He doesn't watch the news like I do. But you're good until five. Okay?"

"Are you kidding? Yes! Thank you!"

Becky almost couldn't believe his kindness and her good luck. So, she wanted to make sure. "There's no strings attached, right? I mean, I need to ask. The taxi…he was…I need to ask."

The clerk smiled and said, "No strings. You're safe. You can lock the door with the latch on the inside. Okay?"

"Okay," Becky agreed. "And thank you so much. I'll make sure you get a nice tip."

"You don't need to," he said. "I got a great story to tell." He grinned.

"Don't tell it till I'm gone, okay?" she said. "You should have seen the reporters at the airport."

"I did. It was on the news," he said. "One of them said you punched her."

"Oh, Jesus. I'm doomed," Becky said.

"Not here," he said. "Sounds like you got the shaft. I don't like that. Rich high-and-mighties. You seem like an honest lady. My wife really likes you."

"Thank God for the girls," Becky said, and he led her to her temporary safe house.

Chapter Twenty-Six

Over the course of the day, Becky made so many calls in the transitory motel room she had to charge her phone in between, though she wasn't sure why. She muttered, "Probably some cheap knockoff those assholes gave me instead of a real one." She was also simultaneously amazed they hadn't cut it off as well.

One of the longer sequences of calls had to do with locating Ben the PA. Since she didn't know his last name, her only way to find him seemed to be by going through the main makeup artist, but Becky also only knew her by her first name, Melanie, from NOLA.

Becky left nine messages with the main production office asking for Melanie's contact number but no one returned those calls. Finally, exasperated, she tried searching for makeup artists named Melanie—and struck gold. The website page read, "Look your best everywhere with Mellani, New Orleans' premier face artisan."

"Seriously?" Becky scoffed as she found the number and dialed.

Miraculously, after hours of nothing, Mellani answered on the second ring. "Mellani's face. How can I make you better?"

"Mellani, it's Becky Darnell, please don't hang up. I'm in a real bad place."

After a moment during which Becky assumed

Mellani was seriously considering hanging up, the mixed-race vivacious woman said, "I can imagine."

Becky said, "It's not all what you think, I promise."

"It doesn't matter what I think," Mellani claimed. "It's what my employers think, and they specifically ordered us not to talk to you no matter what."

"Well, I appreciate you violating the gag order," Becky said, not without some snark, "but this is way more complicated than whatever they're telling you. They want to save their own asses. But I promise you, I swear on my mother's life, I had nothing to do with anything in that damn article."

"It says you were fucking the writer."

Becky had read it by then. "No. He wrote that at the bottom in the course of full disclosure that we had a fleeting relationship. One night. Nine months ago."

"That's all it takes," Mellani said. "And I saw you two together more than once."

"For interviews and stuff."

"Lunch?"

"Part of the interview. On his expense account," Becky said. "Which is part of why I'm calling. They killed mine. The AmEx doesn't work, and my per diem account has been blocked. I can't access any funds and I'm stuck in a seedy motel in Miami with no cash. They're gonna throw me out at five if I don't get some money."

"Sounds not good," Mellani said. "But I can't send you anything. If they found out, they'd fire me too. And I mean like forever."

"I'm not asking you to," Becky said. "I want to get ahold of your assistant Ben. He lives somewhere around here. I need him to go to the airport and get my suitcases out of baggage claim. I've got my personal stuff in there, you know, my card and account info and…whatever."

"I can't do that, Becky," Mellani said.

"Why not?"

"I don't want to get him fired."

"You won't," Becky said. "It's his decision, not yours. And besides, I'm not going to tell anyone you helped me. That would be rude and unappreciative."

All Mellani had to say was, "Well…"

Becky let go a heavy sigh. "I've been horrible, haven't I?"

"Yes, you have."

"To you, too?"

"You don't know?"

"I…" Becky blew out another sigh and felt tears coming. "I don't know. I'm sorry. I've…I've been in a fog for I don't know…awhile, now, I guess. It's not me. I don't even know who I am, anymore. None of this was me. Is me. I don't know. Fuck. I'm sorry. I'll let you go. I don't want anyone else getting in trouble over this crap."

Becky reached for red button.

Mellani said, "Wait."

"Yeah?"

"I didn't give you this," Mellani said. "And don't tell Ben I gave it to you, either. Tell him you had it on your phone. He won't question it. A lot of us have everyone's number. But this is on one condition."

"Sure. Anything."

"Get out of this business. Go home. You aren't cut out for it. Your skin's too thin and you believe your own bullshit. It's a recipe for disaster. And it looks like what's happened—or is happening."

Becky sat with those words.

Mellani asked, "Is that a yes?"

Becky measured her reply carefully. "Mellani, I appreciate what you're saying and on the face of it, I can't disagree. But I honestly have no idea what's going to come out of any of this. I love it and I hate it and…I certainly never thought it was possible or would ever happen to me. But it did."

"Because someone rigged it," Mellani said icily, referring to Art's article.

Becky had read about her winning anyway, unless Genie had won. "It's all very confusing," she allowed. "But I promise you I had nothing to do with any of it. And I plan to have a very nasty conversation with a certain writer about it."

Mellani stayed quiet a moment then said, "Go home." She read off Ben's phone number and hung up.

****

Becky took a steadying breath and dialed. "Ben? Becky Darnell. Don't hang up."

Ben didn't hang up. He said he was as shocked as everyone else about the article, but it didn't surprise him as he didn't think much of the pageant organizers and sponsors individually or as a whole. He agreed to help.

Ben lived in north Fort Lauderdale and said it would take him a little while to get his shit together, borrow his roommate's car, and drive back to Hialeah—probably about three hours. Becky checked the clock—11:14 a.m.—and only worried slightly.

While waiting, she girded her mental loins for the call she knew she had to make. It wasn't that she didn't want to make it. She did. But she wanted to be sure not to back down in any way, not take any responsibility for

256

anything, and let Art Lane know what she thought of him. "This ain't gonna be pretty," she told herself.

To make sure she was as up to it as possible, Becky took a shower hoping to wash away the ick of the trip and the truth. She worried that the motel people might be angry for her using their towels before paying for the room, but she planned to tip them well as soon as she had her money.

The shower didn't help.

****

"Hello?" Art answered.

"It's Becky, you rotten son of a bitch."

"I've been expecting your call."

"Well! You ruined everything. My whole fucking life."

"I hope not."

"Well, you hope wrong," Becky said, instantly feeling sorry for sounding dumb.

"You've made things pretty awful for me too, with those…accusations. I know you know none of it's true. We had a nice time. Both of us. So, look—"

"No, you look, *Arturo*," she said. "I had a sweet thing going. I don't care how it came to be, who did what. Any of it. As far as everyone was concerned, I won. That's all that mattered."

"The truth matters, Becky," Art said.

"No. It doesn't," she said. "It doesn't matter in Hollywood, it doesn't matter in Congress, it doesn't matter in the media, it doesn't matter in these stupid pageants. It. Doesn't. Matter."

"Well, it should."

Becky went full snark. "Says Mr. Honesty who didn't tell me he was a reporter *the first time we met*. But truth isn't important unless it's convenient, like when you can make a buck off it. Off *me*."

"It's bigger than you, Becky. It's bigger than me, and it's bigger than all your *adoring* fans."

"Don't be shitty," she said, hearing his snipe. "It doesn't suit you."

"Thanks," he said, not sounding wholly sincere. "But you know what I'm saying is true. If there's one thing I gleaned from our conversations, it's that you're the real thing. You come from a good place, literally and figuratively. You know what's right and what's wrong. And if you were back home reading my piece, not out on the road representing these users and leeches, you'd be nodding your head, saying 'Good job, Art. You outed the crooks.' But it hurt you personally, so you're mad. I get that. I don't blame you, but…"

After a moment of silence, during which Becky felt her ire roiling, with all of it aimed at Art Lane, she said, "But what?" She could hardly wait for *that* answer.

He surprised her. "But… I'm completely head-over-heels in love with you."

After letting that sink in a moment, Becky said, "Well, you picked a helluva way to show it," and hung up. Then she cried until Ben knocked on her door two hours later.

****

Seeing Becky's red eyes, Ben made her attest to her will to go on living. "I'm not going to do anything stupid," she promised him. "It's just…it's been a weird day."

"I can't even imagine," he said, and left for the airport.

Another hour later, he was back—without her bags.

"What happened? What do you mean they didn't have them?" she asked, horrified.

"Someone must've stolen them," Ben said. "They weren't in the missing baggage office or anywhere else."

Becky felt panic overcoming her. "But they have to be. Maybe they got on another plane and ended up in Lithuania."

"Lithuania?"

"I don't know," she said, fretting. "It just popped in. Shit!" She looked at poor Ben who appeared to feel worse about it than she did. "I don't have any money. My card. My wallet. My…"

Becky realized she had nothing of importance to her in those bags or anywhere else, other than her credit card. Her whole life had been reduced to someone else's fantasy. Her entire value as a human being had been reduced to nothing more than pushed-up cleavage and a fake smile. Tears returned.

Ben eased her onto the side of the bed and sat next to her, putting his arm around her shoulders but saying nothing, to show he was there for her until she could be on her own.

Five minutes later, that appeared to be the case when Becky said, "Okay."

Ben patted her shoulder and stood away. "Is there somewhere you can go?"

Becky had thought about that—a lot. "Home, I guess. I still have my house fortunately. I wasn't stupid enough to get rid of it. Just my pride and dignity and humanity and…"

Her tears started anew. "Shit," she said again. "I haven't cried this much since Bobby Horton dumped me because he said I had buck teeth."

"Did you?" Ben asked.

"Yes."

"You don't now."

"My parents got me braces."

"You have nice teeth."

"Thank you."

He nodded quietly then said, "I'd offer to buy you a plane ticket home but honestly, I don't have it. I made just enough on this job to pay my rent for last month and this month. If I don't pay it, my roommate will kick me out for some thirsty twink, and I'll be out on the street again."

"We don't want any of that," Becky said with a soft smile.

He said, "I don't think I can even cover your room here. I'm sorry."

"It's okay," she said. "It's not your responsibility. You're not my parent."

"What about your parents?"

"Long story, but no," she said.

"Okay."

"What about friends? Back home?" he said.

Becky looked up, *feeling* the dark circles under her eyes. He'd asked the question she had feared most.

Chapter Twenty-Seven

Becky and Ben decided the best thing, if not the most pleasant, would be to return her to the airport. With no money for the room, she had no other choice. The reporters were likely gone, so she shouldn't be harassed, and at least she could sleep on the floor until she found some money *somewhere* to get back home. And who knew? Maybe her bags would show up.

They trudged up to the motel office where Becky informed the same clerk who said his name was Arthur. "Arturo?" she asked, and he nodded.

Maybe it was a sign.

Ben had given her a five-dollar bill which she offered. "I took a shower. This is for the towels." Arturo chuckled, declined, and wished her good luck. She insisted he accept the fiver as a tip, which he did, and they drove away.

Ben dropped her at the Arrivals level so she could check on her missing luggage, gave her a hug in the car, wished her luck as well, then drove off. Becky had never felt so alone in her life—not even on those long shoots surrounded by sycophants and opportunists. Somehow, facing all that and whatever lay ahead felt worse.

She went straight to Baggage Claim, but they had not located her luggage. When pressed, they doubted it had gone to Lithuania. "Tracking labels show it arriving here in Miami." So, it looked like simple theft. "We can't watch every bag. If you weren't here to collect it, we can't be responsible."

It *sort* of made sense. "Okay." If Becky didn't blame herself, she certainly could blame the contest *frauds* or that *bastard* Art Lane.

"*Loves* me," she said to herself. "Right.'

But as Becky made her way up to the departure terminal in hopes of finding a charging station and a seat, she tried to identify her feelings for Art, which she decided were conflicted at best. She considered calling him for the money to fly home, but didn't feel right about it, not after she'd been so intentionally nasty to him over the phone.

After checking for follow-up articles about the fixing scandal—many popped up, mostly with more questions and no answers—and after calling everyone on her contacts list who had anything to do with the contest or the tours with not a single person picking up, Becky found a relatively quiet corner to ponder her options.

Her parents were out of the question. What she hadn't told Ben was that they hadn't approved of her actions after winning. They noticed the changes in her and pointed them out. When she got snippy with them as well, her dad said, "You're an adult. You'll figure it out."

She hadn't heard from them since, so she hadn't tried to call them, either. So, it seemed inappropriate to ask for money now—not to mention humiliating. She'd have to face them someday, but today was not that day.

Boy, could she use a drink.

After another few hours of worry and fighting more tears, bemoaning the entire sad endeavor, and feeling some regret over her behavior—though not enough to call anyone and apologize—Becky decided to buck up and make a call she had hoped to avoid.

****

"Darla, it's Becky."

Darla hung up.

Becky called again, several times, but Darla didn't answer. Becky left several plaintive messages, asking for understanding but not forgiveness and never money.

Darla didn't call back.

Becky then tried Myrna. No answer. Briana. No answer. She even tried a few friends of her friends, but no one answered. Had they *all* turned on her? Did they think she was so awful they could just ignore her? Had she personally insulted them?

Becky felt offended. Not that she didn't deserve *some* of it, but total snubbing? It seemed harsh. After all, she was still herself—somewhere inside. Even if she couldn't locate the exact spot at the moment. The "hicks back home" had clearly revolted and made their position known: Becky was on her own.

Despite all the disappointment and resentment, Becky went through every person she could think of with the same result. Apparently, she had become Pariah Numero Uno. She had only one person left to call—and dreaded it more than any other. The amount of crow she would have to eat…

****

"Floyd, it's Becky Darnell. You can hang up if you want, but I'm really in a jam and no one else will talk to me, and I don't have anyone else to call. I'm sorry."

She waited.

In the background, she could her Floyd's wife Nessie asking who it was. He told her, "Someone from work," and he'd be off in a minute. Nessie said something about a roast getting cold and he said, "Okay."

Becky said, "Thanks for not ratting me out."

He said, "Give me three reasons I shouldn't."

Becky said, "I don't think I can. I don't know if I can come up with *one*."

She explained her predicament, location and dollar specific, and he asked, "What do want from me?"

His tone didn't sound as churlish as his words, so Becky hazarded her request. "Can you front me enough to get home. I can pay you back as soon as I get back and get into my account at the credit union."

After a pause, he said, "How much do you need?"

"Enough for airfare and a cab or something home from the airport."

"Fort Wayne?"

"I imagine."

"Won't be cheap," he suggested.

"Well, I don't really have a choice," Becky conceded. She felt angry and humbled at the same time—angry that her pageant patrons had so easily turned on her and humble because she understood why. Her part in it as well as Art Lane's.

Floyd said, "I might need to think on it. Is this your number now?"

"Unless they cancel it too, like they did the credit card."

"You don't have another phone?"

"Not with me."

In truth, she wasn't sure if she still had another phone, and if she did that she'd been paying to keep it operational.

Floyd's longer-than-expected silence gave Becky

both hope and pause. Though she would never have imagined Floyd Bitterman would be her last hope for salvation, here she was. "Floyd?"

"I'm here," he said. "I gotta check somethin'."

"Okay."

After several minutes that lay quiet except for the clicking of a keyboard, Floyd finally said, "Okay." He told her he'd booked her a flight that would get into Fort Wayne the next afternoon at one-sixteen. "I'll be there to pick you up."

Becky wasn't sure she'd heard him correctly. "You're…coming, yourself?"

"It's Sunday."

"Oh, um…" Becky had no other words but, "Okay."

He said of the flight, "It's the long way around through Baltimore, back to Tampa, then up here, but it's what I can afford. Cash on hand, you understand."

"No, it's fine," Becky said. She was in no position to complain.

Floyd advised her to check with the carrier if her phone got cancelled. "If I can't get through to you, I'll leave a message there. In case anything was to happen."

That was so much like Floyd—always covering contingencies. "Okay, got it," she said. "I really don't know what to say. I've been so…I don't know…so fucking awful, I guess. That's what people seem to think."

"We all make mistakes," he said curtly. Then, "I better go. Nessie's got dinner out."

"Okay and…thanks, Floyd. Really. You're a life saver."

He said, "Well, I'm sure the worst of it ain't over yet. Have you got enough to get something to eat?"

"I'll be fine," she said. Ben had given her his last six dollars, and she could always ask for extra pretzels on the plane. It would represent more calories than the lingerie makers had allowed her on her last press junket.

****

As if Floyd had known what might happen, Becky's phone went dead somewhere between Tampa and Fort Wayne. When she landed in Fort Wayne at one-twenty-one, she checked with the counter to find a message from Floyd saying he'd had a problem and would be late. "Sometime around three," the note read. Becky used her last dollar to buy an apple slice. At two-forty-five, she moved outside the Arrivals level, found a bench, and sat to wait.

Floyd finally appeared a little past three thirty in his *classic* 1989 Olds Cutlass. As Becky climbed in, thanking him profusely, he apologized. "Had a flat. Went to change it but the spare was flat. Took me two hours on a Sunday and a ride from Pete Clemmons into the city to get 'em fixed and back on this old heap."

"Oh, Jesus. I'm so sorry," Becky said.

"That part ain't on you," he said, and they drove away.

After several quiet minutes, he said, "So, are you done with this sex thing?"

Becky chuckled. "It's not a 'sex' thing, Floyd. It's clothes and makeup. It's an *image*."

"TV said Sexiest Woman in the World every time I turned it on."

"That's what it said," Becky confirmed. "Not who I was…or am."

"So, you're back home now?"

"It looks that way."

"For good?"

Becky sighed. "Dear God, I hope so."

Floyd nodded. "I'm guessin' you'll be wantin' your old job back."

Becky realized she hadn't thought that far ahead. Probably because she hadn't wanted to. She said, "I'll have to check my finances, see what they left me I suppose, but it may come down to that."

Floyd cast a look.

She felt it. "I didn't mean it that way."

He looked away.

She realized, "Yeah. I guess I did mean it that way. I'm sorry."

"Ain't the most glamorous work on the planet. We all know it."

"But it's good, honest work," Becky said. "And I never had a problem with it."

"Until you got somethin' better," he pointed out.

"I guess, yeah," Becky admitted. "Though, I have to tell you, it wasn't all it's cracked up to be—what everyone said and reported. It was crazy, Floyd. You can't even imagine."

"But you stayed with it."

"I did, because…"

Becky had to think before finishing her thought. "Because…I'd never lived like that before. Never dreamed I would. Couldn't even imagine it. The clothes, the hotels, people waiting on me hand and foot, everyone saying how special I was and how sexy and wonderful."

"Could go to a fella's head."

"It did," Becky admitted. "Boy, did it ever."

"Must'a been fun while it lasted."

"It was at first. But…I don't know. The train ran

away without me on it. That's how it felt. Like I was left at the station watching everyone else barreling along with someone who looked like me strapped to the front of the engine. I thought I was in control of it but, as it turned out, I wasn't in control of anything. *They* were, and they're all crooks and greedy assholes who didn't give two shits about me."

"You didn't expect that?" What he meant lay under the surface.

"No. I should have, but I was naïve. Stupid. In so many ways." She would have cried again if she had any tears left. But Becky Darnell was drained dry—of emotion, of regret, of caring. She doubted she'd ever live any of it down.

After a silent mile or so, Floyd said, "Won't be easy comin' back. There's a few hard feelings floatin' around."

"I can imagine."

"Might be worse than you think," he counseled.

Becky looked over to see if he was being mean or sarcastic but saw only the usual stoic Floyd. So, she said, "I'll just have to deal with it. If you'll have me back."

"If that's what you want."

Becky wasn't wholly sure it's what she wanted, not after the last three-quarters of a crazy year, but at the moment, it seemed to be all she had left. And it might do her well to get knocked back down a few notches, even if the notion terrified her at least a little.

Floyd interrupted her ruminations. "Can't have your old job back, of course."

"I can't?" Becky hadn't even thought of that.

"Don't exist. Darla's got it."

"I thought Briana had it."

"Threatened to quit if I didn't put her back on the line, so I put Darla in. You're gonna be workin' for her, now. Under her. And I'll have to put you back out in the yard again. You'll have to work your way back up like anyone else. Otherwise, it's gonna look like favoritism."

"But I worked at the plant for fifteen years."

"Don't matter. You left. Stayed away more than six months. It's in the manual."

That damn manual.

Becky rode the rest of the way home in silence, vacillating between anger, acceptance, regret, and pity-brooding.

By the time Floyd pulled into her driveway, she'd worked through most of it, enough to be grateful again. "You're the only one who offered to help—the only one who even took my call," she said.

"Didn't recognize the number," he said.

Though she couldn't tell if he was kidding—Floyd never was one to get a twinkle in his eye to give anything away—Becky nodded. "Well, thank you for not hanging up when you heard it was me."

"Almost did," he admitted.

"Well, I'm glad you didn't."

"Nessie tore me a new one over it, but I reckon she'll let it go eventually."

"I'll call her."

"I wouldn't," he said.

"Okay," Becky said, feeling even lower. "And I'll get your money tomorrow."

Without looking at her, he said, "Bring it by the plant. You can fill out a new job app with Deena. I'll come down there to get it, the money, so you won't have to face anyone just yet."

"It might take a while to prove myself again."

"Likely," he said, still not looking at her.

"I can handle that." A surge of confidence filled Becky by being back home.

Floyd turned to face her. "You fucked up, Becky."

Her confidence evaporated. She blew out a resigned sigh and said, "I know."

"I know you know," he said. "But this is a small town and people don't forget so quick. Ain't got all that glamor and such to distract 'em. Might be pitchin' to go pretty hard on you, just because. It's most people's way."

"Jesus," Becky said, closing her eyes. She started to say *What was I thinking?* But she knew what she'd thought—winning was as great as it was unexpected.

"I understand," she said. "I'm sorry."

"Save that for when it might mean something," he said—and turned away.

It was as cold and hard a thing as Becky Darnell had ever heard in her life. But she knew exactly what he meant: *Buckle up Buttercup, it's gonna be a rough ride.*

Boy was he right.

Chapter Twenty-Eight

Back in her bed at home with all seventy tree paintings and one-eyed dolls close by, Becky slept hard for the first time in as long as she could remember. She hadn't been sure she'd even be able to drop off. But once she got past an initial bout of fear and regret, she slipped into a near coma and didn't awaken until nine the next morning.

Fortunately, her landline had been on autopay, so it worked. She called the lost baggage department in Miami first. No sign of her luggage. She then called the contest sponsor's office, and they answered. She said, "Hi, this is Becky Darnell and—"

They hung up.

"Fuckers."

She knew she needed to catch up to coming back home. "Gotta face the music, RJ." She knew it might not be easy or fun at all, but if Becky had learned anything in life, it was how putting off the inevitable never worked and tended to make things worse. It's what her father always told her, thereby why she called herself RJ that morning.

She took a shower, put on some old clothes—which felt remarkably wonderful—some light makeup because she couldn't not, bucked up in the mirror, gave herself a pep talk, then went into the garage to find out her car wouldn't start.

The battery was long-dead.

Back to the phone and AAA. But her membership had lapsed. "Can I renew it over the phone? Now?"

"Sure. You'll just need a credit card. But you won't be able to call for assistance for seventy-two hours."

Becky hung up and called her local mechanic at his garage. Some kid answered and said they couldn't get out for a few hours. "We're slammed right now. Sorry. Might be after lunch 'fore we can get there."

Back into the garage.

Becky found jumper cables left by husband number two and walked next door to ask her kindly retired neighbor Wally Simms for a jump. Wally's wife Zelda answered the door. When she saw who stood on her stoop, her face fell. Becky assessed she'd never seen a more dour, hateful look in her life.

"I'm sorry to bother you, Zelda. My battery's dead. I need a jump. Is Wally home?"

Zelda said, "I'll see," and turned away, but it sounded like she had no intention of finding him or even looking. She closed the door—and locked it.

"Shit."

Two minutes later, chubby and cherubic Walter Simms came around from the side. "Well, well. The prodigal child returns to the scene of the crime."

Though she worried about Wally's mixed metaphor greeting, she thought she saw a glimmer in his eye. "Hi, Wally."

"You really stepped in it, huh?" he said in his amiable way.

"I guess I did," she said.

"I reckon it'll all blow over in a year or two. Let's get you started. I'll back out."

A year or two. Jesus. But he was probably right, Becky figured.

She looked to see Zelda glaring out from behind a curtain. When Becky met her gaze, Zelda didn't turn away. She held. Never a good sign.

Fortunately, Wally remained pleasant as ever, even when Becky's cables weren't long enough to reach all the way into the garage to her battery and he had to go retrieve his jumper cables from his garage and "Jerry-rig" them in line to jump her battery.

After he got her going, he told her, "Keep it running for at least an hour. If you go anywhere, don't turn it off until your battery gauge says it's charged up." Then he reconsidered. "Your car has an amperage gauge, doesn't it? *Voltage* gauge."

"I don't know," Becky admitted. "What's the difference?"

"Same thing—six volt, twelve volt." He seemed to have flustered himself. "Just don't turn it off," he advised. "Maybe run by a parts store and have 'em check it before you go off and get stranded somewheres else. Might be hard to find help now." He raised his eyebrows.

"Right," Becky said, understanding well.

He smiled and drove the hundred feet back home then went inside. Zelda still peered out the curtains. The old Becky would have waved—a mix of genuineness and mild sarcasm—but given her current situation, she decided to get in her car and drive to the bank...where she turned the car off.

"Shit!"

She tried it immediately and, since it was still hot, it turned over and ran.

"Thank *God*!"

She then noticed she did in fact have a 'battery' gauge and the needle seemed to be dancing into the plus range. So, she left it running, locked the doors, and went inside.

The counter girl could have been a clone of Zelda minus forty years. "Oh. You look like…" She glanced down at Becky's handwritten withdrawal slip. "Oh."

She looked up with a barely-concealed scowl and opened her cash drawer. "How would like that, *ma'am*," she said as close to nasty as she probably thought she could get away with.

"Twenties are fine," Becky said.

No other unpleasantries were exchanged. Becky left the bank and drove to Littleman implements where she sat in her car with the engine on, staring at the employee entrance she had walked through thousands of times before. It felt even less welcoming than she had imagined—so much so she almost drove away.

She even came up with an excuse having to do with the battery dying again. But she was confident nearly every car in the lot had jumper cables—this was the Midwest—and if not, Ferdy Milton in the shop probably had a dozen in a cabinet somewhere. She switched off her sporty little compact and sat staring at the building.

It finally fell over her that Floyd had been right. This was going to be re-trial by the fires of hard judgement, far worse than her first days and weeks on the job so many years ago when at least some of the workers seemed to be pulling for her.

Today, there likely would be none.

Then, Becky had a revelation. Whatever might happen inside the spreader plant could not in any way be worse than what she had experienced when the organizers and sponsors realized their least favorite, least-likely-to-win contestant had in fact won. If she could survive that fiasco, she could survive this. She headed inside.

****

Deena Jacobs in HR took Becky's job application form without any visible emotion other than possibly detestation. "Floyd said you might come in."

Deena had never been a beacon of light and positivity—typical HR behavior—fake congeniality barely covering a satanic desire to find anything wrong with a performance review solely to gain points with Harold Harmon or his oft-dowdy secretary Charlene.

Deena slammed a time stamp onto Becky's app and said, "We'll let you know."

She sat staring.

"You'll…let me know?" Becky said, somewhat astonished.

"That's right. Do you have a working phone?"

"Deena," Becky said. "Of course I have a working phone."

"Mr. Bitterman indicated you might not."

"Mr.… *Floyd*?"

"Mr. Bitterman, yes. He will be your department manager."

"I know who Floyd is, Deena. You can stop the sour act."

"And you can stop being nasty if you'd like a position here at Littleman Implements. We only hire the best." She pointed at a wall plaque with those words for *proof*.

"Deena—"

"I prefer Ms. Jacobs in a professional setting."

Becky squinted. "How long have we known each other?"

"Not long enough, apparently," Deena said icily. "We'll let you know if something opens up." She put Becky's job app in her "Out" tray—at the bottom, covering it with a pile of other papers—then stared.

Becky said, "Wow. Okay." She stood. Though she felt about as angry as she ever had, she said, "I'll look forward to hearing from you, Ms. Jacobs."

Deena never cracked. Becky shook her head and walked out of HR.

She started to go to her car and drive home but decided, "Fuck it," and turned down the hallway for the main floor. After all, she had Floyd's money in her pocket and he no doubt could use it. So, dammit, she'd give it to him now.

Rough ride be damned.

Becky walked onto the main floor to find everyone staring in silence, apparently expecting her arrival. Deena must've seen her headed that way and called ahead. All eyes were on her. Not a word was said, not an expression other than blank hostility.

Hatred.

Becky met several gazes, including Myrna, Briana, and Darla. She had hoped to see some crack in their armor, some hint of old friendship, some understanding. But she got none. Just hard looks, cold eyes, tight mouths.

Becky nodded. Her way of acknowledging their anger and positions on it all as well as her culpability. After a moment, everyone turned away and went back to work. Becky felt as empty as she ever had, almost soulless. Ungrounded.

Unwelcome.

But she'd come down to repay Floyd for his kindness and his loan. So, she turned away from eyes she could feel on her back and walked to his office in the corner, from which he had a partial view of the floor.

She started to knock on his door frame then saw him leaned back in his seat, ready for her entrance. She said, "You were right, of course."

He nodded slightly without speaking.

"About what you expected?"

He barely nodded again.

"Anything I can do to undo it?"

He barely shook no.

"Right," she said. "Well, I brought your money." She reached into her pocket and pulled out four-hundred dollars. "There's a little extra for gas and having to get your tires fixed."

"Don't need it," he said. "Just the airfare."

"I insist," she said, and set the money on his desk.

He looked at it, then nodded slightly again.

"I had an interesting visit with Deena."

"Let you know how she felt, huh?"

"In spades," Becky said. "She stuck my app at the bottom of a pile and said she'd 'let me know if something opens up.' "

Floyd snorted a chuckle then shook his head and leaned up. "She's got an unusual notion of her purpose here, sometimes. But I guess you knew that."

"Honestly? I've never seen her like that," Becky said. "I'm assuming she won't be the only one."

"Likely not," Floyd agreed.

After a moment of silence, Becky said, "So…you'll call me if something 'opens up'?"

"Won't have to," he said.

Becky felt like she'd been punched in the gut. "You mean…she isn't going to call? You aren't going to hire me back?"

Floyd snorted another chuckle. "Boy, she really laid it to you, didn't she?"

Becky thinking, *At least* he *finds this amusing*.

Floyd stood. "I told her we'd be hiring you back. Must'a been trying to make an impression on you by expressing the general tone around here. Which, by the way, are you sure you can handle it?" He nodded out toward the floor. "Before we take you back."

Becky turned around for a glance. "Honest? I don't know, Floyd. This is…" She couldn't find the words. "Whatever. And it's not gonna go away."

"Oh, I reckon over time," he said. "Keep your nose down out there in the field. Not that you have any other options—smells as it does. But I'll get you back inside as soon as I can, according to the rules. And you'll have to behave."

"Behave?"

"Ps and Qs and all. Protocols. Do your work, do it well, like you used to," he said. "Maybe once they see you mean it, it'll go easier."

"Mean what?" she asked.

"Wantin' to come back," he said plainly. "Not just doing it 'cause y'ain't got no other options."

"I don't," she said.

"Sure you do," Floyd said. "We're not the only game in town, anymore. Money's flowin' again, and folks are hiring. You probably hadn't noticed with such a good job here."

"But I don't want to work anywhere else, Floyd,"

Becky said, almost realizing it for the first time. "I love it here. Always have. This is my home. My family. Where I belong."

He nodded again, the way he did when he had other thoughts, and said, "Well sir, all families have their problems, their black sheep. The wanderer. Comes back thinking nothing's changed." He cocked his head.

"You're saying things are different, now?"

"Depends on you, Becky," he said. "It all depends on you."

Becky knew he was probably right, but she had contradictory feelings.

Floyd must've sensed it. "I guess what I'm really saying is you're gonna need to give it time. Let it percolate and brew or whatever they say. Let everyone get used to having you around again. And right there's the best reason of all to start you outside. Give them and you a little time to adjust, to ease back into things. They'll come along, I think. But you're gonna have to show some patience. Can you do that for me?"

His direct plea hit Becky in her gut again, but this time in a gentler way. She heard it as kind and supportive, hopeful.

She finally smiled—barely. "I can, Floyd. I…well, I'll do my best. And you know what? There's no hurry. I'm not gonna rush it. I'm back home where I belong, and I'll remind myself of it if I get antsy or weird."

"Try not to get weird," he advised, which made her snort a chuckle this time.

"I will," Becky said. "And you know why?"

"Why?"

"Because you're giving me a chance you didn't have to. You went out on a limb for me."

"Not too long'a limb," he appraised.

"Long enough to earn you some pushback. Some nasty looks."

"Used to those," he said, lightly. "You gave me plenty in your time."

Becky groaned. "I'm sorry. I didn't mean any of it."

"They won't, either," he said, nodding out. "And besides, I'm the boss. I know when to say enough's enough. Tell someone to get back to work."

"You do," Becky said, remembering some of those times.

"See you Monday morning, early?"

Becky had hoped to start right away, but understood the wisdom of putting it off a week—give people a buffer to maybe get used to the idea.

One could hope.

Becky thanked Floyd again then stepped out of his office, expecting a sea of blank and angry faces, but most everyone had returned to concentrating on their work. Only Darla continued to stare. From what Becky could see and sense, a week wasn't going to put a dent in her resentment and sense of abandonment. Her anger.

Becky met her gaze without showing anything, she hoped, then turned away and headed for the employee door, thinking, *Dear God, please let my car start.*

Chapter Twenty-Nine

The sponsors wasted no time replacing Becky with Genie Vintier who appeared on every morning and entertainment show while Becky ignored endless phone calls from reporters and lawyers. Some wanted to sue her, some wanted to represent her. She returned none of the requests for interviews or representation.

The truth was Becky had done nothing wrong, at least as regarded the contest. She didn't know anything about the rigging, the lies, or the ulterior motives. Her aim had been true—enter it for a hoot. Nothing more. She ended up as surprised at winning as anyone else, just as she was when the truth came out later.

But it made perfect sense. She never thought she had a chance in Hell, not without help, and apparently she was right. Though the why of it confused her at first, after reading Art's piece a third time—then a fourth and a sixth and a tenth—it all fit. Greed had motivated everyone but her. Until the spotlight hit her full on.

"I was so stupid," she said, putting the article aside. It had never occurred to her that she might have won through trickery and dishonesty. She felt sick, knowing the whole con had revolved around her. "I should have known."

She said it aloud, but wasn't sure she believed herself. How *could* she have known? The whole thing was so multi-layered and devious. "Little Miss Becky

Darnell from Podunk, Indiana believed it as much as anyone else. More!"

On the other hand, Art's anonymous source "Bob" said his own research told him Becky would have won, anyway. However, with all the layers of deceit and trickery, she wasn't sure she believed even that.

Becky closed her eyes and sighed a thousand times before Friday came, but she finally stopped blaming herself for believing, for wanting—hell, for winning. It all happened so fast she had no clue. No *choice*.

As to what happened *after* winning, well, she couldn't blame that on anyone other than herself. Or could she?

The climbers and sycophants and opportunists ran with it the same as she had, if for different, darker reasons. She came to accept her title and all that came with it because, at least in the beginning, it was terrific fun. Exciting and luxurious!

So, why had it all deteriorated, spiraled down into a pit of obsequious dedication to fame and fortune? She said aloud, "Because fame and fortune *suck*!"

She meant as in *suck the life and integrity out of you.*

Who could have resisted? "Someone stronger," she bemoaned. "Someone with more integrity. *Some* integrity! Someone who'd seen the world and knew better."

Someone like Genie.

Becky watched Genie on TV every chance she got, marveling at her grace under pressure and avoidance of blame. She never once implicated Becky or anyone else. *It's a miracle*, Becky thought. *I couldn't have done it.* She figured she'd have been throwing blame around like mini candy packs on Halloween—keeping the full-size bars for herself.

But Genie deftly turned every negative question around to a positive, saying things like, "I don't think it's anyone's fault in particular. It's a new contest and things went a little haywire. Maybe some of those players behind the scenes did some things they shouldn't have, but I can tell you none of the girls or anyone else I dealt with directly was anything other than perfectly lovely and supportive. We'll get past this."

When pressed about Becky being in on the scheme, Genie shook her head. "I can assure you Becky Darnell is a stand-up gal and knew nothing about any of this."

A reporter asked, "What about these rumors of her swelled head and bad behavior?"

Genie said, "Rumors, right. But I can tell you from having done this a long time, it's not easy, even for someone with a ton of experience. The pressure is incredible. Sure, it looks like fun, sounds like fun—people swarming all over you every minute of every day with lip gloss and highlights and extra stays to make sure your tummy's tight."

Then she cocked her head. "You see what I'm saying."

"Not really," the reporter said. "It's all glamorous. The travel, the food, the—"

"The food?" Genie said, sarcastically. "You think they let us *eat*?"

She got laughs and Luke the interviewer tried to move on, but Genie held her track. "This thing will blow over and no one will remember it in a year. I can go on and do what they're paying me to do, which is to inspire women to accept who they are and find their own sexual IQ—like Becky Darnell encouraged them to do by being her authentic self. I think that's gotten lost in all this. She's a great gal and everyone thought so who knew her."

"But what about the rumors of drinking and drugs, of—"

"We covered that, Luke," Genie said. "Becky did her best. We're moving on, now." She said it so firmly that Luke shifted gears and never reversed.

Becky found herself grinning and leaking a few tears. "Thanks, Genie," she said to her TV. And for the first time all week, Becky saw a light at the end of the tunnel.

By Friday afternoon, the threatening phone calls had all but stopped and Becky felt encouraged to reclaim some of the joy of her former life. She put on her Bowling, Beer, and Burger T-shirt, grabbed her ball and shoes, and drove to the lanes to find the place empty.

Surprised, she walked to the counter where the alley owner Marcus Soffeler stood alone, stroking his very odd moustache.

"Hey, Marcus," she said. "Where is everyone? It's Friday."

He shrugged.

She said, "Well, um, I guess I'll take an alley and wait for everyone."

He shook his head.

"What do you mean?"

"All booked up."

Becky squinted, turned to look at all the open lanes, then turned back. "Marcus. There's no one in here."

"League," he said.

"What league?" she said.

"Friday league. Booked them all. They'll be in

directly, I suppose. Maybe after a while. Maybe not."

Becky grimaced. "Marcus. You're lying to me."

He shrugged.

Becky nodded. "I get it. Fine." She picked up her bowling bag. "But I didn't expect that from you, too."

He shrugged again.

****

Back home, Becky fought the urge to fall off her wagon. She was angry and hurt, but didn't cave in—to crying, either. She knew it was going to be a long, lonely weekend.

Her good feelings died.

She thought about calling Art Lane to bitch at him some more, but by then, she'd mostly decided he'd only done what he'd been paid to do. His job was to report. To go behind the scenes, find the truth, and tell it.

"Fucker."

Sure, he could have thought about how it might impact her, but that part wasn't his job. And he'd tried to warn her. She hadn't wanted to hear about it. She closed her eyes, let her head hang, said, "I was so awful," and climbed into bed with red eyes.

****

After enduring the longest, loneliest, horrible weekend of feeling sorry for herself since her eighth-grade body angrily welcomed her first period and voluminous acne, Becky bucked up yet again and headed for Littleman Implements. She parked in the lot, at the far end, walked in, found a pay card with her name on it, stamped in, and went to the locker room to change into what everyone called Shit Slingers—overalls and galoshes for "The Field of Lost Dreams." No one said a word or made eye contact.

She found the company ATV where it always sat, climbed on, started it up, and headed for the pasture where three of the newest spreaders stood next to small mountains of various manures—cow, horse, goat, and chicken. The smell took her back and she quickly remembered how to breathe through her mouth.

Then she saw the sign hanging on the new machine, shiny but for the shit all over it. The sign had a simple message:

Welcome back to Hicksville

Becky sighed—then chuckled. She'd done it to herself. Now, she had to atone. If that meant testing spreaders on piles of manure for the next month—the usual time required in the much-rued Research Area to sort out anyone not serious about working at Littleman Implements—she'd just have to do it. If it got her back in the plant, on the line doing *anything*, she'd pay her dues. Again.

Oddly, the thought didn't anger or bother her. She looked around, took a breath, and Home came back to her. All the jokes, the good times and bad, the two marriages and shitty divorces, all of it. This place was all she'd ever known, and she'd always been happy with it. It felt right to be standing right where she stood.

In the stink.

She didn't regret having seen the world, staying in five-star hotels, being flown on private jets, eating in Michelin-rated restaurants, throwing up after, wearing the nicest clothes, being waited on hand and foot. The works. It had all been great—until it wasn't.

Then it went to Hell faster than any other awful event in her life. Those had all taken years. Her descent under the title crown took nine months. Now, here she was, right back where she started—and it felt great.

She attached a small spreader to the hefty four-wheel ATV—she'd try the larger one on the big John Deere later—and started working the first pile of manure. She kept an eye on the machinery, looking for any problems, but it worked perfectly as designed.

Later, she'd make a note to that effect in the provided log and, when a farmer or big ag rep showed up for a demonstration, she'd give them a show, laughing and cajoling, giving the soft sell old Harold Harmon liked and required. She'd do it for the next month with no complaints, because anything was better than selling sex.

Chapter Thirty

On Day Three, with little to do but tool around on the big John Deere because all the machinery worked perfectly and really didn't need anyone out there field-testing anything—Littleman Implements had long ago perfected their products—Becky entertained herself spinning donuts to see how far she could sling manure.

She hadn't had so much fun in years.

At lunch hour, she turned back for the plant to park her tractor by its barn when she saw someone standing on the concrete pad—Darla.

Becky's stomach cinched up. Had Darla walked all the way out here to lay into her again? Maybe one last time? Maybe tell her they didn't want her back on the floor or anywhere else in the plant. In town? Maybe not in Indiana.

Becky parked the green beast and shut it down, bracing for the worst.

Darla hadn't moved.

Becky walked over and gave it her best nonplussed, "Hey. What's up."

Darla paused a moment, then said, "Floyd was gonna come out here himself, but I said I wanted to."

"Oh," Becky said, thinking she'd probably been fired since no one wanted her around anymore. Though she would have preferred Floyd pulled the trigger.

Darla said, "He wanted…we wanted to know if you

learned your lesson yet."

"My…" Becky stopped. "Is that what this was?"

Darla stared.

Becky blew out a heavy sigh. "D."

"Well?"

Becky let go a tiny second sigh. "I learned it before I ever came out here. This…" She pointed around and smiled. "This was my *reward*. It brought me back home where I belong."

Darla didn't flinch.

Becky took it as confirmation of her demise and said, "I'll find another job. I hear a lot of people are hiring. There's got to be someone out there who doesn't hate me."

Darla said, "We don't hate you, Becky. We hate what you did. Who you became."

"And that's fair," Becky said. "You're right. I was wrong. I don't know how many times I have to say it, but I know it, and I'd say it a hundred thousand times if I had to to make you and the girls believe me."

Darla nodded again, eyes a bit red. Then she said, "You can have your old job back. I fucking hate it." She turned around to walk back.

Becky said, "Will you ever forgive me?"

Darla stopped, then said, "I already have. It's…" She didn't say more.

Becky picked up. "Gonna take a while."

Darla stood there a moment, back to Becky, then turned back, face red. "What the fuck, Beck!"

Becky knew what she meant. "I lost my mind, D. I'm sorry. I let everyone down. And after you all believed in me even when I didn't."

Darla nodded and looked off. Wiped a tear. "It was

289

fucked up, what you did. What you said. Really, really fucked up."

"I know."

After a moment, Darla walked closer. Becky thought she was probably about to get slapped—or punched. That would be pure Darla—and she braced again.

Darla got close and looked Becky in the eye. "It hurt, Beck. It hurt bad."

"I know. I'm sorry I said what I said. It was uncalled for."

"It's more than that," Darla said, steely. "It was betrayal."

"I know. I'm sorry."

"You can't just keep saying that!" Darla barked.

"Well, what am I supposed to say? I hate it! I hate what happened. I hate what I did. I hate how I behaved. I hate having *won*. I didn't know how to handle it. I had no…experience in those areas. It was harder than you think."

"That's no excuse."

"It is!" Becky bleated, then backed off. "And it's not. I get it. But I don't think you…or anyone knows what it was like."

"It's not. An. *Excuse!*" Darla shouted.

"It's not supposed to be!" Becky shouted back. "It's the truth! It's what happened. It sucks. I hate it. I'll never live it down. I'll never forget it. I'll never feel good about it. But it happened. I can't pretend it didn't. And I won't. You don't have to worry about *that*."

Becky turned away then back, her own tears coming again. "D, it was awful, and it was wonderful, and it was weird, and it was…like a…runaway train, loaded up and barreling down a hill and I couldn't stop it. I didn't know how. And the worse it got, the worse I got, and...*fuuuuuuuck!*" Becky screamed to the heavens then lowered her voice. "I wanted to come home so many times, to stop the craziness, but they wouldn't let me. I had a contract. They'd sue me to Hell and back if I quit. So I drank and I took pills and I said shit I shouldn't have said. And I was horrible to the people I worked with, and I was horrible to you and everyone back here and they hated me, and I hated me but it was...new! It was...exciting! It wasn't like anything any one of us ever imagined. It was..."

Becky stared a moment then blew out her heaviest heaving sigh yet. "Fuck it. I give up. I fucked that up, and I fucked this up, and I guess I'll probably fuck up whatever I try to do next. I guess that's who I am, now. A big, lousy fuckup spinning donuts in giant piles of shit!"

After a moment, Darla said, "Yeah. And you got some on ya." She nodded down.

Becky looked down to see that she had in fact managed to fling manure from the tires all over her boots and pantlegs. "Great."

Darla said, "Did you really want to come home—and give up all the glamor and glitz? The *fabulous perks*."

Becky started to state yes unequivocally, but she opted for the greater truth. "Not at first. It was fun. But then it got...complicated. And I freaked out and...the pills and booze and...I didn't even know where I was half the time. *Who* I was."

She looked away then back. "And yes, like a bad Lifetime movie, at one point, I woke up in some strange bed somewhere, in a hotel I didn't know where I was, and all I wanted was to be back here with you and Myra and Brie, and Floyd. He was the only one who came to my rescue, you know."

"We heard," Darla said. After another pause, she said, "Are you here to stay this time? No more running off to be a big shot model?"

Becky chuckled. "Are you kidding me?"

Darla said directly, "No. I'm not."

Becky saw Darla's angst, concern, and maybe even fear at reaching out, unsure of what she'd get back. So, she reached out, touched her oldest friend's arm, and said, "D, I missed you the whole time. I missed you all. I missed Bowling and Burgers. I missed driving around the county with you and going into Auburn and Fort Wayne. I missed work and being on the floor with you guys, making fun of Floyd and Charlene and Deena. Marcus and his ridiculous moustache. The Hot Dog Shak and Monte's Bone House. All the dumb stuff we did to entertain ourselves. Throwing firecrackers over Jed Culley's fence to make his stupid geese go crazy. All of it. All we said and did, because it was never mean. It was all fun, and…"

Becky shook her head. "There wasn't any real fun out there. Just…lots of shiny stuff that looked great until you realized it meant nothing. And that all those people meant nothing, because I meant nothing to them. But you guys… We're family, man. Dysfunctional as all fuck, but real and honest and…"

Becky held open her arms. "May I?"

Darla said, "If you promise—"

"Darla! Jesus! I'm pouring my heart out here!"

"Do you mean it?"

"Of course I fucking mean it! Bitch!"

Darla snorted a laugh. "All right. One hug. But that's it."

Becky laughed that time—and hugged her old best friend like she hadn't seen her in a decade, because that's what it felt like.

Darla returned it. And when they finally pulled apart, she said, "Let's go eat lunch. I'll drive."

She climbed in the beefy ATV. Becky hopped in the passenger seat, and they rode off. Becky said, "Do you really hate being floor manager?"

"I don't know how you stood it," Darla said. "A few more months and I swear I was gonna end up hating everyone. I don't know how you did it."

"Because I love everyone," Becky said, only half-kidding.

"Well, you're a better bitch than me," Darla said. And that was that.

Becky's wilted Hot Dog Shak foot-long tasted better than any filet mignon or lobster bisque she'd had in the last nine months—better than any food ever.

Epilogue

As predicted, the whole Sexiest thing played itself out and blew over. A bunch of executives lost their jobs and were replaced by new executives who were probably no better than the last bunch even if they pledged to do better.

Six months later, several of them were out, replaced by new promisers.

Genie served out her three months as official Sexiest Woman in the World to great acclaim, which resulted in a board position on the pageant—which she turned down in order to compete in other contests. She wouldn't win another for two years at which time she decided to retire from pageant life. She married an accountant and settled down.

Two months after returning home, Becky answered her doorbell to find her luggage sitting on the front porch. When she stepped outside to see who'd left them, she found Art Lane off to one side. He said, "I have a friend who tracked them down in Alaska. I had them send them to me, so I could…you know. Bring them."

Becky said, "Thanks. I'd given up hope."

A raft of emotions ran through her, from happiness at having her things returned to mild queasiness at seeing Art in her front yard. No words came.

He said, "May I come in? Would that be okay?"

Becky thought a moment then said, "Okay," and

moved aside, even if she wasn't sure—about anything.

Art carried her bags in and set them on the living room rug while she closed the door. Then she came over to face him—to eye him and see what she might glean.

"I really did fall in love with you."

"I'm not moving to LA."

"I didn't think you would—or would even want to."

"I don't."

"Did you see my latest piece in *Rolling Stone*?"

"No," she said honestly. "What's it about?"

"Do you really want to know?"

"Probably not."

"Then I won't say," he said. "But you're not in it."

"Thank the Lord for small blessings."

Becky moved for the couch. "You want to have a seat?"

"Sure, but I can't stay long." Art took a seat on her antique couch. "I'm on my way to Terre Haute. There's some issue with—"

"I read about it in the local paper—on their website," Becky said, cutting him off. "So, they're bringing in the big guns."

"I'm not that big," Art said. "Working on it."

He smiled in a way that reminded Becky of how she'd felt some affection for him as well—if not love. She said, "Best we can do," and wondered if he heard the double meaning.

After an awkward moment, he said, "Anyway, since I was in the area…"

"The same state."

"Closer than LA."

Becky nodded, giving him that.

"And," he said, "if you're ever out that way…"

Becky gave him a soft smile. "I doubt it, but you never know. One thing I learned from all this is—"

"You never know," they said together, then chuckled with a tinge of darkness, and Art asked, "So…your life has gotten back to normal?"

"More or less. It took some work—some grinding humility. But I deserved every bit of righteous scorn I had thrown at me."

"Maybe not," he said.

"You didn't see me at my worst."

"I heard you," he said, referring to their phone calls.

"I was pretty angry," she said.

"Rightfully so," Art said. "I ruined it for you."

"You did," she said. "But I deserved it—and I didn't deserve the title."

"There I disagree," Art said. "My source said you would've won anyway."

"That's the irony, isn't it?" Becky said. "Small town girl who shouldn't win does win and it almost ruins her life only to have a truth-seeking investigative journalist swoop in to out the liars and thieves, and the ego-whore crashes and burns along with everyone else."

"I'm not proud of that."

"It had to be done. Might as well have been you. You…you did the right thing."

"I suppose so," he said. After another pause, he stood, "Anyway, I wanted you to know—"

"I know, Art," Becky cut in. "And…thanks, I guess."

"Yeah," Art said, nodding at the floor.

Becky waited for him to look up then held her arms open. "One hug?"

"Sure."

After a warm hug that felt real to Becky, he pulled back and said, "If you ever want to tell the whole story, I'm here. I think it would make a great book."

Becky soured. "Is that why you came? Really?" She pushed away.

"No," Art said. "I came to see you and apologize and wish you the best in whatever you do the rest of your life, and maybe…try to get you to come out to LA."

"Ain't gonna happen, Arturo."

"I know that now."

"But you write your book. I'll download it and not read it like the rest of my e-reads. Not because it won't be great, I'm sure." She heard some sarcasm in her voice but didn't feel like softening her edge.

"Thanks for the support," Art said as if responding seriously. "But I wouldn't write it without your input and approval."

"That boat sailed two months ago," Becky told him, making her position clear. "Never to return."

"I understand," he said, but apparently couldn't resist adding, "But if you ever change your mind…"

"Goodbye, Art. Thanks for finding my suitcase."

He chuckled. "I get it."

"Good."

****

Becky never heard from Art Lane again, but two years later, his book came out, titled *How the Sexiest Woman in the World Fooled Everyone—When Beauty Fails Us All*. Becky didn't read it.

A word about the author...

Glenn A. Bruce, MFA, is the author of over thirty-five traditionally-published novels, including thrillers, horror, westerns, and literary fiction. He began his career in Hollywood where he wrote the hit movie Kickboxer, plus Victor One: The George Aguliar Story, and Cyborg Cop, with episodes of Walker: Texas Ranger, Baywatch, and the original G.L.O.W. Show, plus sketches for Cinemax's Assaulted Nuts. He taught screenwriting at Appalachian State University for over a dozen years and currently lives in Florida where he continues to write in a variety of genres. www.glennabruce.com

Thank you for purchasing
this publication of The Wild Rose Press, Inc.

For questions or more information
contact us at
info@thewildrosepress.com.

The Wild Rose Press, Inc.
www.thewildrosepress.com